Dolly

G·K
Hall
&Cº

Also published in Large Print from
G.K. Hall by Anita Brookner:

Family and Friends
A Friend from England
Latecomers
Lewis Percy
A Closed Eye

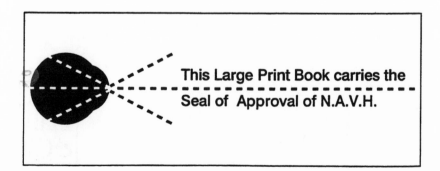

This Large Print Book carries the
Seal of Approval of N.A.V.H.

Anita Brookner

G.K. Hall & Co.
Thorndike, Maine

Published in 1994 by arrangement with Random House, Inc.

G.K. Hall Large Print Core Collection.

The text of this Large Print edition is unabridged.
Other aspects of the book may vary from the original edition.

Set in 16 pt. News Plantin.

Printed in the United States on acid-free, high opacity paper. ∞

Library of Congress Cataloging in Publication Data

Brookner, Anita.
    Dolly / Anita Brookner.
      p.   cm.
    ISBN 0-8161-7445-8 (alk. paper : lg. print)
    1. Women — Fiction. 2. Family — Fiction. 3. Large type
books. I. Title.
    [PR6052.R5816D65 1994b]
    823'.914—dc20   94-10925

Dolly

1

I thought of her as the aunt rather than as my aunt, for anything more intimate would have implied appropriation, or attachment. Attachment came later, in a form that was wistful, almost painful. At the same time it is only fair to say that I never felt for her that simple affection which is unreflecting, almost a background to one's emotional existence, something one takes for granted, as if it had been born with one, or rather as if it had come complete at one's birth, part of the panoply of family life. I liked to read about this sort of thing, even as a child, as if I were missing it, longing for it, when all the time I was perfectly happy, at home and at peace with my mother and father.

In these contexts, both real and imaginary, Dolly — the aunt — was a misfit. It was without surprise that I learned that Dolly was not her real name, though I doubt whether in the long run this has much significance. She was a presence, or rather an absence, which seemed to give rise to a certain anxiety, at least on the part of my mother, who was her sister-in-law, and whose beloved brother Hugo Dolly had married, in circumstances of great romance, or so they seemed to me when I first came to know their story. It was a favourite story, recounted when I was very young, again by my mother, who was present at their first meeting. Dolly's absence I took for granted, for in the manner of fairy stories I assumed that after the apotheosis it was natural for people to vanish. In fact Dolly lived abroad, in Brussels, with my uncle Hugo, whom I thought of as my uncle, and was encouraged to do so by my mother who loved him dearly. He was a hero in her eyes, although even at a young age I sensed that my father felt less warmly towards him. Given their remote degree of affiliation this was allowed, and consequently did not seem to matter.

Dolly was the wife my uncle had acquired before my birth: I knew neither of them. A brief family visit to Brussels, when I was four or five, did not bring us any closer. My mother was concerned about her brother's health, and I was aware of anxious discussions behind closed doors. For that reason I was taken out on long walks by my father, and of that visit I remember Dolly as part of the general discomfort, no more important than the wearisome length of the Rue de la Loi, where their flat was situated, and the, to me, menacing arch of the Cinquantenaire, which I thought marked the limit of the known world.

Images of discomfort abound from that brief visit. My uncle was in bed, and every now and then I heard the tinkling of a bell which signified that he was awake or that he was hungry. He seemed lively enough for an invalid, was certainly exigent, ringing the bell at half-hourly intervals.

The bell was answered by the maid, Annie Verkade, a grim silent woman of whom I was vaguely
frightened, although she paid no attention to me.
I thought that Dolly and Hugo must be very poor,
for there was no carpet on their shiny creaking
wooden floors, and the bed I was put into was
in a room so bare that the only distraction was
to watch the squares of light from the windows
of the houses opposite, and to calculate who lived
there and what they were doing. I liked to make
up stories in which children featured, and as far
as I could see there was not another child in the
whole of Brussels. I was clearly an embarrassment on that visit, when urgent family matters
were being discussed. Because I had no idea what
these could be I was fretful, aware only of dis-
quiet, of long anxious colloquies between Dolly
and my mother. I sensed that my mother was
upset and that Dolly was the cause of her un-
happiness. I know now that Dolly had to bear the
brunt of these discussions because my uncle had
removed himself from them, but at the time I registered Dolly as an active agitated presence who
abruptly stopped talking when I entered the room
and aimed a dazzling artificial smile in my direction, as if expecting me to be impressed by her
gallantry.

I was not impressed: I was if anything insulted,
for I knew that there were secrets, and that these
were secrets in which I could have no part. I resented Dolly even then for invading my parents'
peaceful world, and for removing me from Prince

of Wales Drive to this unfriendly town. I was parcelled out between my father and Annie Verkade, who was no more fond of me than I was of her. In the event the visit was hasty, rushed, confined to a mere long weekend, for my father had to get back to his office, to which he was exceedingly loyal. My impression of Dolly, on that occasion, was of a stranger in a black and white dress, which I thought was too tight. She did not fondle me or take me on her lap, as I smugly expected her to do, but simply smiled those vivid and meaningless smiles at me, and adjured me, in a heightened voice, to be a good girl and not to upset my mother. I had an impression of blackness and of whiteness: black eyes and white teeth, and the white handkerchief which dashed away her tears. The tears were followed by a particularly public smile. 'I keep going,' she said, to my troubled mother. 'I don't let him see how worried I am. I carry on; I hide my misgivings. That's what one has to do in this world, Jane.' (This last was for my benefit.) 'Let them think of you as always singing and dancing.' At four, or possibly five, I thought this advice negligeable.

After our return to London, myself tired and disturbed, a strange conversation took place between my mother and father.

'He has always been delicate,' my mother said.

'But you can't look after him,' my father replied. 'That's her business now. She seems to manage well enough.'

'I don't understand why she feels so poor. After

all, Hugo has his job, and it seems to be rather important.'

'I dare say she exaggerates.'

'Of course they go out a great deal, or seem to.'

'There you are then. He can't be so delicate. Or so badly off, for that matter.'

'I hate to think of him so far away. I keep hearing the sound of that bell from the bedroom.'

'It was only the flu. They take it so much more seriously on the Continent. In France, for example. In Belgium too, I expect.'

'They said something about coming over next year. To see Mother. And us, of course. Perhaps we should do something to entertain them.'

'They won't stay here,' said my father calmly. It was not a question, merely a statement.

'Oh no,' said my innocent mother. 'They will want to stay in Maresfield Gardens.' This was the home of my grandmother, my mother's mother, to whom, now that I come to think of it, Dolly bore a distinct resemblance. They were both Europeans, vain. My mother had escaped the influence entirely.

After I had been put to bed in my own room I forgot Dolly completely, and was glad to do so. I had identified her with that creaking flat in the Rue de la Loi and its various discomforts, with Annie and the Cinquantenaire and with the ball-point pen which my father had bought for me in a curiously shaped department store which he said was almost a historical monument. The pen splut-

11

tered and leaked when it was suggested that I write a postcard to my grandmother. Both pen and postcard were abandoned.

'That's right,' said Dolly, passing through. 'Keep busy. I always keep busy. Annie will give you your *goûter*.'

This foreign word was another sign that I was far from home, a feeling I attached to Dolly herself. To be with Dolly was to feel far from home. This was the interesting and valuable insight which I brought back with me from that visit. It is not true that children do not understand adult feelings. They understand them all too well, but they are powerless to deal with them. I knew then, as I was to relearn later, that Dolly signified a sad estrangement from everything which I assumed to be rightfully mine: my family, my friends, my school, my peaceful English life. My father, I think, felt the same, and for this reason was anxious to distance my mother from her brother and sister-in-law. And in this, for as long as he could keep my mother under his benevolent and somewhat hypnotic gaze, he was successful. He worried over her, thinking her as frail as the bedridden Hugo, who only had the flu. She had had a heart murmur as a child, although this had disappeared. To me they were both invincible. The look of care on my mother's face I attributed to Dolly, the aunt. It must have been at that time that I cast her as the aunt, a generic form of life, rather than as my aunt, a member of my family.

At the end of the year — it must have been

at Christmas — they came to England. My mother, who had been quite peaceful, was jolted once again into anxiety. This time the anxiety was caused by her desire to entertain them, in a suitably attractive manner, 'for we must seem very dull to them,' she explained to me. 'They go out such a lot.'

'Why are there no children?' I asked.

'Oh, poor Dolly,' said my mother.

'Why?'

'Well,' she said carefully. 'There is no room for them in the flat. You saw that.'

I accepted this explanation. I had to: my mother was already making plans.

'Perhaps we should have them for Christmas,' she mused. 'But then Mother would be upset. No, we shall have to go there. We must think of something else.'

The matter concerned her for several days.

'We must take them out to dinner,' she announced to my father.

'Very good,' he said, courteously laying aside his evening paper. 'I'll book a table at Francesco's.'

Francesco's was our local Italian restaurant: we always went there on birthdays.

My mother looked shocked.

'Oh, no, darling, that would be far too dull. They are used to a very active social life, you know.'

'But we are not.'

'All the more reason to make an effort.'

'What were you thinking of?' he enquired, even more courteously. 'The Ritz?'

Her face lit up. 'Of course! How clever of you!

We must take them to dinner at the Ritz.'

My father was an honourable man. He did not point out that this would be excessive, that we were not the sort of people who dined at the Ritz. Already he foresaw the agonies of indecision into which the prospect of enjoying herself, and of ensuring that her brother enjoyed himself, would plunge my mother.

'They don't dress these days,' he said kindly. 'Your blue silk suit will do very well. I had better book the table tomorrow. If you're sure,' he added.

'Oh, quite sure,' she said, her face a vivid pattern of fear and determination.

'Will I be there?' I enquired.

'No, darling. You wouldn't enjoy it. Miss Lawlor will be here to give you your supper and stay with you while you are in bed.'

Miss Lawlor was our daily housekeeper and by way of being a family friend. She had been passed down the line from my father's mother, with whom her own mother had been in service until she retired, when Miss Lawlor took over. My Manning grandmother had sent Miss Lawlor to the marriage of my parents as a sort of wedding present or dowry, evidently doubting my mother's ability to keep her husband clean and fed. This state of doubt, or more properly speaking incredulity, was inspired by her violent antagonism to my other grandmother, Antonia (Toni) Ferber, whom she considered to be a frivolous and unworthy woman, incapable of instructing a daughter in her marital duties. Her antagonism was warmly returned, to the apparent satisfaction of both parties, who thus had a perfect excuse not to meet. In this, as in everything else, my mother was entirely innocent. It was understood that my father would visit his mother on his own, and that he would accompany my mother to Maresfield Gardens when the occasion could not decently be avoided. In this complicated situation Miss Lawlor was the equivalent of oil poured on troubled waters. She was a tall wistful silent woman, rather like my mother, in fact, and her social life revolved around the Women's Fellowship at her local church. She lived in Parkgate Road, so that it was quite convenient for her to come in every day to give my mother a hand. I believe that she was unhappy on her own with nothing to do, and looked forward to the company. She seemed to melt into the shadows of our rather dark flat, whose windows looked out onto the bushes and trees of Battersea Park. Sometimes she sang a hymn in a tentative girlish voice, as, rubber gloved, she passed a yellow duster over the cumbrous sideboard (also a Manning inheritance) in my parents' dining-room. At half-past midday my mother and Miss Lawlor sat down to a light lunch, which my mother prepared. My mother called her Violet: she was Miss Lawlor to my father and myself. She had been a feature of our household for as long as I could remember.

I did not mind staying at home, although I wanted to see my mother in her ball gown.

'Oh, no, darling,' she explained. 'Nobody

dresses these days. It is just dinner, you know. Just to mark the occasion.'

I thought she looked very nice in her blue silk suit. In fact I thought she looked incredibly beautiful, but then I always did. My father wore his mild expression, which, I was later to realise, denoted forbearance. His face softened when he looked at my mother, as it never failed to do.

'I shall have to wear my old coat,' she said apologetically.

'You can leave it in the cloakroom,' he told her. 'Nobody is going to examine your coat.'

'Goodnight, darling,' she said, embracing me. She smelt, uncharacteristically, of some pungent scent, a gift, no doubt, from my Ferber grandmother, who was always trying to liven her up. There was a contest of wills there too, although my mother never consciously entered into it. Smiling negativity was her tactic with her mother, who recognised it for what it was, and more or less accepted it, perhaps as a just punishment. All in all my parents were a haven to each other, finding in Prince of Wales Drive, and in the largely wordless company of Miss Lawlor, a peace that neither of them had ever found at home with their contentious parents.

The following day my mother looked preoccupied. Nothing was said to me: no relic of the fabulous meal was smuggled home, as I had hoped it would be, in my mother's handbag. That evening my father took refuge behind his newspaper, as usual. He was not a man who could stand a great deal of conversation. My mother stared unseeingly at her book, which she eventually laid aside.

'Well, I think they enjoyed it,' she said.

'They should have done. It was not exactly an inexpensive evening.'

'I'm sure we did the right thing. Of course, they are used to going out.'

'I gathered that. The champagne alone . . .'

'But that was quite appropriate. I think they enjoyed it,' she repeated, this time a little more doubtfully. 'Although Dolly was disappointed that there was no dancing.'

'Thank God.'

'She looked lovely, didn't she?'

'No better than you, my love.'

'And Hugo is happy when she is happy.'

'Oh, there was no trouble with Hugo.'

'Did you notice Dolly's coat?' said my mother. 'That was mink, you know.'

'Yes, I noticed it,' said my father reflectively.

'They are a handsome couple, aren't they?'

'They have been, no doubt. A little past their best now, perhaps.'

'Yes, Hugo looked much older, I thought.'

'Shall I put the kettle on?' he enquired. They usually drank a cup of tea in the evenings, a habit which I have inherited.

'Tea!' said my mother. 'I will invite them to tea! At the weekend, before they go back. I should like them to see the flat. You will be here, won't you, darling?'

My father, who usually went for a very long

17

walk on a Sunday afternoon, winter or summer, a walk which he would be obliged to forego, merely said, 'Of course.' I repeat, he was an honourable man, although my mother knew that he thought her brother a lightweight, married to another and lighter weight. I think he merely considered them no business of his. He had not inherited much in the way of family affections, and regarded my mother, whom he loved, as supplying all his emotional needs. 'They may not come,' he warned her. 'We are quite a long way from Maresfield Gardens. Quite a step to take on a Sunday afternoon, when public transport is not exactly at its best.'

'Oh, I'm sure they'll come,' said my mother.

The next day I got a sandwich and milk for my lunch, as Miss Lawlor and my mother made small delicate butterfly-shaped cakes and pastry tartlets ready to be filled with fruit. These were covered with clean tea towels and stored in the larder.

'Toasted teacakes, I thought,' said my mother. 'And cucumber sandwiches.'

'I'll come in after church and give you a hand,' said Miss Lawlor.

'That is so kind of you, Violet.'

'Will you want me to hand round?'

'I shouldn't dream of spoiling your Sunday afternoon. Jane will help me, won't you, darling?'

Silver teapots and cream jugs were polished; more clean tea towels laid over more plates. There was enough food for at least ten people.

My main interest in all this was not in the handing round, which I had done on numerous occasions and which I thought I did rather well: my expertise was beginning to bore me. I did not particularly look forward to seeing Dolly again, since, like my father, I thought she had nothing to do with me. But I did look forward to seeing my uncle Hugo, since I thought he might turn out to be a friend. My mother had told me that he was very fond of me, yet how could that be when he hardly knew me, and I knew him not at all?

'He sent you that lovely coral bracelet when you were born,' said my mother. 'You cut your teeth on it. He saw you when you were a baby, you know. He said he thought you were beautiful.'

We are always kindly disposed towards those who have the good taste to think that we are beautiful. Yet Hugo's actual presence filled me with a vague disappointment. He had perfected the same meaningless smile as Dolly, to whom he delegated the business of greetings and compliments.

'So this is Jane,' he said, in a deep, beautiful yet actorish voice. Having said that he showed no further interest, but subsided into my father's armchair, joined his hands at the fingertips and smiled beatifically into the distance. I examined him carefully, and was not predisposed in his favour. He seemed to me to be rather fat, or perhaps merely shapeless round the waist. Both my parents were thin and I was used to their more modest proportions. Hugo, leaning back in my father's chair and gazing at the ceiling, did not show to his best advantage. In addition his hair had receded, and he wore thick, slightly tinted glasses. When he took these off his eyes looked alarmingly naked. He glanced frequently at his wife, who was tremendously dressed up, as if for a wedding. A fragrant mink coat had been deposited on my parents' bed; what was revealed was an artfully draped silk dress, at which my mother exclaimed in admiration.

'That is Belgian work, my dear. *C'est fait à la main, tout ça.*'

Again the foreign words, which distanced her from me and from my mother.

'Not too much trouble getting here, then?' asked my father genially. He was already bored.

'Oh, we hired a car,' said Dolly. 'The chauffeur will call for us in about an hour.'

'Oh, but that is far too soon,' protested my mother.

'But darling Etty, we are expected out for drinks in Highgate. And how else should we have got here? You live in the middle of nowhere, you know.' She gave a small annoyed laugh. She seemed as bored as my father, but less able to hide it. She regarded the afternoon as a chore, as it no doubt was, and had no reason to impress my mother with her stoicism now that Hugo was apparently restored to health. She had highly polished social manners which nevertheless released something of her original intentions, so that my mother felt it her duty to express gratitude that Dolly had bothered to visit her at all. One felt dissatisfaction in the air, and also tiredness, frustration, all covered up by a tremendous show of goodwill, of resolute generosity.

'Then we'd better have tea straight away,' said my mother humbly. 'It's all ready. Jane will hand round.'

When we returned from the kitchen, having removed the shrouds from the plates of cakes and sandwiches, Hugo was shaking his head ruefully over the disastrous bridge hands he had held on the previous evening.

'Couldn't do a thing with them,' he went on, although my father, who did not play bridge, could not have been interested. That was their way, I was to learn, to trail one entertainment on to the next, so that one always heard a great deal about what had happened on the previous occasion.

'No thank you, dear,' said Dolly, as I relentlessly proffered plate after plate of food. 'I never eat in the afternoon. And you shouldn't either,' she warned my uncle, as he took two sandwiches and laid them in his saucer, where they absorbed a little tea.

'You see what a terror I married,' he said to my father, who was not used to such playfulness from men. He leaned over perilously, dislodging a little more tea, and pinched Dolly's cheek. She smiled a small taut smile.

'At least you can make up for it this evening,' she said. 'We'll be going on later for bridge,' she explained, in the face of my mother's constraint. My father turned away and busied himself with his cup. When he turned back towards us

21

his face was entirely serious.

I examined Dolly, leaning against her chair for a better view.

'Don't do that, dear,' she said. I registered the fact that she did not like children.

I could see that she was in the grip of some tremendous impatience, although the journey to Prince of Wales Drive, in a hired car, could not have been very arduous. With the percipience of childhood I sensed that she was struggling against increasing weight or some such bodily discomfort. Women were not yet quite as at ease with themselves as they are today. In 1969 or 1970, when this tea-party must have taken place, they had heard the calls of liberation but had not yet developed into those speedy slimmed-down versions of themselves that they were to become in the 1980s. And then I think that work had a great deal to do with this transformation. Women who did not work, like my mother, or, more conspicuously, Dolly, aged more quickly and along more traditional lines. Dolly must have been in her middle forties at this time and was aware that the age of fading attractions had arrived. More specifically, she was aware of such fading in her husband, who, after youthful good looks, had developed a complacent personality and a saurian aspect, the smile still on his face, his eyes frequently closing behind his glasses. His evident comfort in my father's armchair, and his absent-minded but constant ingestion of my mother's food, as if his restoration to the bosom of his family had temporarily effaced his social pretensions, had bred an indignation in Dolly, whether she was aware of it or not. Like an automaton he continued to deal out largely meaningless social noises, none of which was of relevance to my mother or my father, but a loosening of the usual performance had taken place, and he seemed both older and younger because of it, younger because he looked to my mother with a sort of trust, which might have been quite foreign to him in his usual everyday incarnation, and older because he no longer had the means to charm and to please, as had formerly been his habit, and his right.

Dolly, despite her constrictions, was still a handsome woman. I was aware of this, as I was simultaneously aware of a sense of strain and frustration, for children are alive to these conditions in the adults who are supposed to be superior to them. Dolly made the same impression of blackness and of whiteness as she had made in the course of that visit to Brussels, although the dress she was wearing was of royal blue silk with a pattern of tiny white diamonds. Out of its draped neckline rose a throat that was full at the base and slightly suffused with colour: this must have conveyed to me the impression of frustration which was so at odds with her otherwise impeccable appearance. She was a vivid woman, with a questing ardent expression, as if she could not bear to be wasting time, as she evidently thought she was doing on this occasion. This sharpness of gaze gave her an air of vanity, which I dare say was justified. Her hair and eyes were dark, her skin a beautiful clear olive and flushed over the prominent cheekbones, but her most characteristic feature was her mouth which was long and thin, the lips as smooth as grape skins, the lipstick worn away into an outline by her eager tongue. When the lips were drawn back, into one of her exclamatory laughs, the laughs she lavished on more brilliant assemblies, the teeth appeared, flawless and carnivorous.

As a child I was aware of her bulk, which I thought a trifle unseemly, or at any rate uncomfortable. She had a squat European figure, with shortish legs and a full bosom, the whole thing reined in and made impregnable by some kind of hidden structure. I was aware too of a sense of heat which came less from her actual body than from the ardour of her desire. Why this should be I had no idea: I simply assumed that she wanted to be elsewhere, as of course she did. With hindsight I now see that she was seriously put out by Hugo's losses at cards on the previous evening and was impatient to get on with the next game, in which it was to be hoped that he would have better luck. They continued to discuss their temporary condition with my parents who grew bewildered at their insistence on the importance of the game, almost as if it were a profession, as indeed it might have been. When pressed to take it up — and as astonishment was expressed that they did not already play — my mother explained, blushing slightly, that she and my father preferred to read.

'Oh, read,' said Dolly. 'Well, of course, I am

a great reader myself, but in our circle one has to mix, otherwise one would know no one.'

'I suppose you have a great many friends,' said my mother.

'Yes, I can certainly say that we are well liked. Not that we mix too much with the expatriate community, except for bridge, of course. Our dear friend Adèle Rougier is the one we see most constantly. Her husband was our ambassador to Zaire, you know. She has a most beautiful house in the Avenue des Arts. *Very* well off, my dear. Now that she's a widow she seems to lean on me, and of course I do my best to help her. And she adores Hugo.'

'How did you find Mother?' This question was asked, in a lowered tone, of Hugo.

'Grumbling, as usual. I managed to cheer her up, but she really is an old misery. I wonder you don't go over there more often, Etty, though I can hardly blame you for staying away.'

'The sad fact is that Mother and I don't get on. She is too tough for me. She never forgave me for being born just when she thought that part of her life was over. Anyway, she always preferred you, Hugo. She doted on you, still does.'

Hugo laughed complacently. I later read Freud's remark that the man who has been his mother's favourite will feel a hero all his life, and although I had known him so little I applied the verdict to Hugo straight away.

'Oh, Hugo goes down very well with the ladies,' said Dolly. This was evidently true: he had an easy way with compliments, was adept at putting a woman at her ease with the sort of flattering badinage which means very little. It was as much his stock-in-trade as the bridge games, on which they seemed to have a considerable dependence. If I could see him now, and if he had lived, I would have pictured him at the bridge table, a cigarette smouldering in a glass ashtray at his left hand, his eyes watering with the smoke and the lateness of the hour, the amiable smile still on his lips. I can see him quite clearly, but I cannot see Dolly at his side. I was aware, even at that time, that of the two of them Dolly was the more viable. There was something collapsed and self-indulgent about Hugo, whereas Dolly was made of stronger, more durable material. When she said that Hugo went down very well with the ladies it seemed to me that she detached herself from this remark, as if she registered its applicability but no longer believed in it herself.

'The time, Hugo,' she reminded him. 'Don't forget the time.' And turning to me. 'I expect you want to go off and play, don't you, Jane?'

I recognised this as a ploy to get rid of me but failed to take the hint. At that age I thought myself indispensable to any gathering. In any case I was fascinated by Dolly and her many contradictions. It no longer seemed strange to me that she had no children, for I thought she might have been angry with them, as she was certainly ready to be angry with me. The slightly swollen throat alerted me to hidden reserves of bad temper.

Whether my presence inhibited the conversation or not was a matter of indifference to me. I was beguiled by the fat necklace of artificial pearls which clasped that swollen throat. She saw me looking at them, and said, with a glint of humour, 'They're not real, Jane. The real ones went a long time ago. Maybe you'll do better than I have. But they're pretty, aren't they?'

That was the only time I saw her face soften. Quite soon after that, and for no reason I could make out, it resumed its mask of irritability. As the afternoon wore on her impatience grew, until finally she heaved herself to the edge of her chair and announced that it was getting late, that the car would soon be returning, that they must not keep their friends waiting, that it would take an age to get to Highgate.

'Why don't you move, Etty? North London would be far more suitable. You would be nearer Mother, for a start. And it would be better for Jane later on.'

'Why would it?' I asked.

She ignored me.

'Well, goodbye Etty, Paul. Come and see us again soon, when I have more time to show you round.'

'Will you ever come home?' asked my mother.

'You never know,' said Hugo. 'For the time being I can see no change. The job is there, and I seem to be well liked. And of course Dolly is a great success with everyone.'

'Don't forget us,' said my mother, who was

aware that the afternoon had been a failure of sorts, although everything had been done correctly. I sensed that she was blaming herself; my father, who was always quick to defend her, sensed this as well and moved to her side. Together they looked less vulnerable. I knew that they were measuring themselves ruefully against the expectations of Dolly and Hugo, that Dolly and Hugo had reminded them uncomfortably of family ties which they had long ago sought to sever, so as to be all in all to each other, that they felt suddenly at a loss, as if they had not done as well as they had thought or anticipated, and that I was there to be brought up by the two of them alone, without the support of brothers or sisters, or, it was clear, uncles or aunts. My uncle had withdrawn from responsibility, while Dolly was already thrusting her hands into her gloves. If anything were to go wrong with our little family there would be no help from that quarter. At this point my father put his arm round my mother's waist, as if he too shared this realisation. There was nothing to signal hard times to come, but a moment of apprehension had been shared. He was anxious to see the back of Hugo, of whose luxurious and childish nature he could not but disapprove. As far as Dolly was concerned he withheld all comment, both then and later. I believe he felt for her a certain ironic admiration, while disliking her intensely. Finally he was as eager to see them go as they were to leave. Air was kissed on both sides of my mother's face; hands were shaken.

'Give me a kiss, Paul,' said Dolly. 'Not frightened of me, are you?'

He laughed, and kissed her.

'And we thought you'd never get yourself married,' she said to my mother. 'But you did rather well for yourself in the end, didn't you? Clever girl. Goodbye, Jane,' she added sharply. 'Don't forget. Always make a good impression.' I thought this another indication of her failure to understand children, but by this time I was tired and bored, but not too bored to notice how her spirits rose as she was delivered of this family chore and could look forward to the evening's entertainment. By the time she reached the front door she had been transformed into a glamorous and pretty woman. And I noticed something more: an excitement, a girlishness, unexpected in that almost matronly figure, as if in the course of that evening, or of the next, or of the one after that, some event might occur, some meeting, some transforming circumstance, that might just change her life for ever.

The next thing we heard was that Hugo had died, suddenly and unexpectedly.

There must have been an influenza epidemic at that time for both my parents were ill and Miss Lawlor moved in to look after us all. It was nearly spring, but it felt like bitter winter: the light was white, hard and unfriendly, the ground like iron. My parents moved round the flat cautiously, as if not too sure of their ability to do so. My father was the more affected and had to take several days off from the bank, where he worked as an investment analyst; he found being at home in the daytime mildly disturbing, evidence of an unsuspected change in his normally robust health. My mother spent her days on the sofa in our drawing-room, too tired to read.

It was in this melancholy atmosphere that the telephone call came from Brussels, to say that Hugo had died after a bout of flu which had turned to pneumonia of a particularly virulent kind. The call was from a strange woman who spoke English with a pronounced accent and who said that she was looking after Dolly. Dolly, apparently, was too stricken to speak to anyone. All arrangements had been made, said the voice, and abruptly ceased. Attempts to get back to Dolly's number were unsuccessful: either there was no answer, or the call was answered by strangers. Finally my father got through to Annie, who seemed both alarmed and annoyed.

'Elle n'est pas là,' she said. 'Elle est chez Mme Rougier.'

'Et les funérailles?' asked my father.

'Vous voulez dire l'enterrement? Ah, pour ça, Monsieur, je ne suis pas au courant. Il faudrait demander à Mme Rougier. C'est Mme Rougier qui s'en occupe.'

He replaced the receiver and looked at my mother, who had her hand to her mouth. She was pale with shock.

'I shall have to go over there,' she said.

'There is no question of that. If anyone goes it should be me.'

'I can't let you go, Paul. You are still quite ill.

30

Besides, you haven't been out of the house for days.'

'Perhaps we had better wait until we hear from Dolly,' he said. He was anxious to do the right thing, but secretly grateful for the delay. It was manifestly clear that they were both too weakened to travel, or even to get as far as the airport. For the duration of one long silent day they both sat, unspeaking, in the drawing-room, waiting for Dolly's call. Then, as the light gradually faded, it became clear that they would have to wait another day. Yet those long hours of silence, which would otherwise have been hours of recuperation, accomplished something, some ritual of mourning, so that at the end of that long day they both arose quietly, handkerchiefs put away, as if a natural conclusion had been reached, as if vain agitation would henceforth be irrelevant, as if further speech or action must come from Dolly, who now assumed a tragic and central importance.

'We must defer to Dolly,' said my father. 'If she wants us there she will let us know.'

The following day was equally silent. With the continued silence tension renewed itself. A further telephone call to Brussels failed to elicit any response. The flat seemed to be empty. It was now several days, perhaps as much as a week, since Hugo had died, and there was still no word from Dolly. Two more days were spent in the same entranced silence. Finally, on the morning of the third day, a telegram arrived. 'Coming home. Going straight to Mother's. Dolly.'

'How will she live?' asked my mother mournfully. 'I expect she'll go back to Brussels. After all, her friends are there. But I dare say she will want to stay with Mother for a bit.'

'It might not be a bad idea if she moved in with your mother permanently. As far as I can see it would suit them both.'

My mother brightened. 'I'll suggest it,' she said. 'As soon as she gets in touch.'

'She seems to have worked it out for herself. Why don't you wait to hear what she has to say?'

My father was careful with my mother, who had been unnaturally calm: he knew that at some point her grief must surface. It surfaced, abruptly and violently, a couple of days later, when Dolly came to see us: the two women fell into each other's arms, uttering the raucous sobs of uncensored grief, harsh ugly sounds which made my father go pale and pat his mouth with his handkerchief. Although I had been removed by Miss Lawlor I found my way back to my mother's side and took her hand. It seemed to me essential to protect her.

'It's all right, darling,' she said finally. 'Only Dolly is rather sad. You see, Hugo is dead.' She faltered, but recovered herself, perhaps impressed, despite herself, by Dolly's renewed composure. Dolly, phoenix-like, had pulled herself together and put away her handkerchief.

'He went just like that,' she said, snapping her fingers. 'Annie had just taken in his tisane: he looked at her, closed his eyes, and died. I wasn't even with him. Of course, I collapsed when I was

32

told. If it hadn't been for dear Adéle Rougier, who took me home with her, I don't know what I would have done.'

'We were expecting to be told about the funeral,' said my father.

'Adéle Rougier saw to everything. It was beautifully done. We had a Mass at S. Joseph . . .'

'A Mass?' said my mother, bewildered. 'But Hugo wasn't a Catholic.'

'Well, I'm sure he would have wanted it. In any case, it was more or less expected. Everyone was there.'

She looked slightly cheered at this evidence of social success.

'What will you do now, Dolly?' asked my father. 'Will you stay in Brussels?'

'How can I, my dear? There is only a very small pension, nothing like enough to live on. No, I shall come back here. I'm sure Mother will tide me over.'

Whatever Dolly hoped for, from a circumstance in which there was practically no hope, was unclear. Yet although the eyes were sad and lost the thin lips were resolute.

'Don't worry about me,' she said, heaving herself forward in her chair with the movement I recognised from her previous visit. 'I'm a survivor. I'm not one to feel sorry for myself. If I have to put on an act I'll put on an act. Singing and dancing: that's what it's all about.'

This seemed to be her motto, translating a profound belief. It seemed to her essential to cultivate popularity, and she believed, perhaps shrewdly, that she would be socially unacceptable if she appeared to be unfortunate. At this distance I can only admire her for it. She was a chameleon, as I came to learn, changing one country for another, one language for another, without any of the panic or strangeness which affects even the seasoned traveller. Dolly's curious career, the details of which I learned only later, had left her unmarked, as if all her experiences were instantly absorbed, leaving no shadow or taint in her mind. She lived in the present, which is actually quite a difficult thing to do. Even now her face brightened as Miss Lawlor brought in tea. It was only years later that I could appreciate Dolly's courage. Yet she herself did not register her peculiar quality as courage. To her it was merely common sense, allied with a certain basic shrewdness. Singing and dancing, as she said.

'We are here if you need us,' said my father, taking both her hands in his.

'If you could just get me a taxi, Paul,' she said. It was clear that she found my father attractive. My mother had settled back on the sofa, her face drawn with grief and illness. She was silent and thoughtful for the rest of the evening. My father, who was by now largely recovered, decreed an early night for them both. By half-past nine the flat was silent.

Dolly turned up again the following week. I was out with Miss Lawlor; when I got back Dolly was having tea with my mother. Neither appeared to want to talk to me, for which I was grateful. Dolly seemed to me as she had always seemed: fierce. When she left our house reverted to its normal calm.

That evening my mother recounted the day's events to my father.

'Dolly was here,' she said.

'How was she?'

'Not too happy. It seems she has fallen out with Mother.'

'Entirely foreseeable. Any particular reason?'

'It seems that Mother was furious about the Catholic funeral.'

'Your mother has never seemed to me a woman of profound religious conviction.'

'Yes, darling, but she is Jewish. One tends to forget it: she is so untypical.'

'I doubt if I should want to go that far.'

'Well, anyway, she and Dolly had a falling out. Dolly told her that Adéle Rougier had taken charge, and that annoyed her even more. She said she thought it better if Dolly had a place of her own: she would help towards it, and give her a small allowance, but not to rely on her. She said she could see they were both too independent-minded to get along.'

He smiled. He seemed tremendously interested in what had taken place.

'And how did Dolly take all this?'

'She is quite remarkable. She said it was up to her to make a new life for herself. She was almost cheerful.'

'Shall we have a cup of tea?' he asked. 'Now that we are back on an even keel I don't think it will keep us awake.'

They drank in companionable silence. Finally my father laid aside his cup and turned to face my mother.

'How much?' he enquired.

My mother hesitated. 'Five,' she said. There was a pause. 'He was my brother, after all.'

'You have a child, remember.'

That was his only reproach, and yet it was not so much a reproach as a statement of the facts in the case. These facts were not revealed to me until much later. Many of them I had to supply myself. It seemed to me important to reconstruct the story, even to the point of doing a certain amount of research. I did this for my own satisfaction, to re-establish those elusive facts. In this I revealed myself to be my father's daughter, the daughter of both my parents, those innocents abroad in a world which they persisted in believing to be both orderly and benign.

2

My mother's name was Henrietta. My father called her Henry, which I thought was rude of him, until I was old enough to recognise it for what it was: a term of endearment. He would look up from his book with a gleam of pleasure and raise himself fractionally from his chair when she came into the room. They were a placid reticent couple, and as time went by they spoke less and less, conferring with each other almost by osmosis, a process which was successful, since they rarely disagreed.

They met at a recital of French songs at the Wigmore Hall. They sat in adjoining seats, and when my mother dropped her programme he picked it up and handed it to her.

'What do you think?' he asked her in the interval. This was her first taste of his elliptical mode of speech, and she responded to it without hesitation.

'She seemed to me to be under the note in those last three,' she said.

'Perhaps she has a cold,' he observed, and, gazing sternly ahead, remained silent for the rest of the interval. At the end of the concert they applauded moderately, while the rest of the audience expressed fervent appreciation and demanded encores.

'Would you like coffee?' he asked, as they left their seats.

'I should, but my mother will be expecting me home.'

'Then I will find you a taxi.'

They met in the same place in the following week, although no arrangements had been made. After this second meeting he persuaded her to drink a cup of coffee with him in a café in Wigmore Street. She looked excited and apprehensive, as if such a thing had never happened to her before, although it must have done, since she had been an undergraduate, had left university (Bedford College) the previous June, and was now filling in time until she decided whether or not to do a teacher training course, a prospect which her mother found displeasing since she thought it guaranteed lifelong spinsterhood.

'I like children,' confided my mother. 'But I doubt if I could keep them in order. I like a very quiet kind of life.'

It may have been at that point that he decided to marry her.

They proceeded cautiously. Concerts at the Wigmore Hall were eventually interspersed with visits to exhibitions at the Royal Academy and the Tate Gallery. The conversation became more profuse, but was never in any sense unedited or unguarded. Each retained a certain dignity, and it was the recognition of this quality in the other that bred a particular kind of respect, a respect, moreover, of which, for varying reasons, they had

had little experience in their past lives. During an unusually effusive walk in Kensington Gardens one evening in late summer, each made a moderate confession of attachment to the other. After this, it seemed as if marriage was inevitable.

'I'm glad this happened in the park,' said my mother.

'Yes,' he replied. 'The Wigmore Hall would not have been suitable. And the intervals are so inconclusive.'

None of this was necessary as an explanation, for no more than a few sentences had been exchanged, but a rite of passage had been successfully negotiated. Linking arms, they strolled on, emerging into Exhibition Road, where he stopped a taxi for her and stood on the pavement waving goodbye until she vanished in the direction of Maresfield Gardens. Then he turned on his heel and walked back to Prince of Wales Drive, where he occupied a large bachelor flat. With a little adjustment he thought it would do very well for the two of them.

That was the easy part. The difficult part was to introduce each other to their respective families, or in this case mothers, for one was divorced and the other widowed. Both were problematic. Of the two of them Antonia (Toni) Ferber had the edge on Eileen Manning, whose only crime was wrongheadedness. Mrs Ferber, however, had a more awesome repertory of grievances, trailed clouds of distant glory, and was more likely to confound expectations and to raise difficulties. The fact that she was not fond of her daughter did nothing to guarantee her eventual acceptance of the marriage.

Toni Ferber, whom I later came to regard with a high degree of sympathy, was still, at the time of her daughter's putative engagement, embroiled in the mythology of her early youth, and regretting that she had not misspent it while she had had the chance. She was marked by her girlhood, as some women are, but in an almost fatal sense, as if all the events that had occurred in later life were a disappointment, a tragic disillusionment. This realisation or understanding gave her handsome face a disdainful look, as if multiple miseries had been undergone. By a supreme irony nothing remained of her earlier prettiness, the prettiness that had made her her father's darling. Now she looked agelessly adult, as if she had never had a girlhood at all, let alone a legendary one. What grief there was behind that almost Roman façade was all for herself. My mother sensed it, and at the same time knew that nothing she could ever do would make those grim features relax into a fond smile. She resigned herself, therefore, to the task of giving no further offence. Nor did she think that she would be much missed, although it meant that her mother would be left alone. The hardness of Toni's heart acted as a kind of preservative: my mother was confident that no harm would come to her, alone in the house in Maresfield Gardens, with only a daily help for company. In a confused and genuinely helpless sense my mother recognised that she would leave no gap in her mother's life, once she had left home.

They were no doubt too fundamentally different ever fully to understand one another. Toni Ferber had been born Toni Meyer, the daughter of an ophthalmologist, in Vienna. She had been given the names Antonia Sara, this last in deference to not too distant Galician forbears, but was always known as Toni. Her father was moderately successful in his profession, which was something of an irony, as his own eyes were weak and occasionally watery, which gave him a melancholy appearance. This ocular melancholy might even have masked something more profound, as if a genuine grief were manifesting itself in this singularly appropriate symbol. Vienna was alive with metaphors: no explanation was too far-fetched.

Dr Meyer was a widower, his wife having died in childbirth. His household was supervised by a certain Frau Zimmermann, whom he took care never to address as Gusti, although his daughter did. But this was done to annoy, since the infant Toni could not bear her father's attention to be diverted by any female presence other than her own. She worshipped her father: every morning, before Dr Meyer left the apartment in the Berggasse to cross the landing to his consulting room she performed for him various little songs and dances which she had learned at school or with her music teacher on the previous day. He was uneasy about this, for he could sense the disapproval of Frau Zimmermann, who had strict notions of discipline and to whom Toni was a constant source of aggravation. Sometimes he could sense this disapproval very strongly indeed, for Frau Zimmermann stood rigidly in a corner of the breakfast room while Toni, as she evidently thought, made a fool of herself, and would not leave until the doctor had issued out of the front door to begin his day's work. Only then would Frau Zimmermann unbend and go about her duties.

The beautiful child — and she was beautiful, for I have seen photographs — experienced both grief and frustration throughout her early years, for with her father's absence in the daytime she was left to the mercies of Frau Zimmermann, and even during her years at school she felt a certain anguish when she returned home to the apartment in the afternoon, to find a glass of milk and the sort of pastry that is wrongly called Danish on the table of the breakfast room, and the sort of silence that made her long for the presence of even Frau Zimmermann, whom she hated. Therefore, when her father came home in the evening, she was almost hysterical with relief and gaiety, and set about entertaining him to the best of her ability. He was touched, but he was also embarrassed: she was too fervent, too ardent, and he knew that her affections were too febrile to secure her the serious love of a serious man. There were such men in Vienna, but he knew them too well, men who would delight in a pretty virgin, but only for a few months. For his daughter, of whose eventual marriage he was now beginning to think, he wanted someone simple, someone reliable, someone stalwart. Unfortunately, most of the men he knew were diabolically clever, and although he realised that his daughter possessed both shrewdness and cunning, there was about her a helplessness that made him suffer.

She became twelve, she became fourteen, and then sixteen, and although she was popular with her friends, all of whom he found too spoilt and too shrill, she had not succeeded in securing the attention of any of her friends' brothers. And still she flirted with him, not recognising the impropriety of her gestures as she perched on his knee or laid her head on his shoulder. At eighteen, when he decided to consider her an adult, whether she liked it or not, he took her with him on a visit to London, where he wished to consult a colleague. The colleague, who was an old acquaintance from medical school, invited him to dinner, to meet his wife.

'Bring your daughter, of course,' he added.

Toni's poise deserted her as her father's attention was devoted entirely to his conversation with Dr Fischer, as if for once in his life he could behave as an adult, without caution, without emollient words, the words he was habitually forced to use in order to keep the peace between his daughter and his housekeeper. His unusual vivacity may also have been inspired by the fact that he was momentarily away from Vienna and its complications, principally his relationship with Frau Zimmermann, which had recently come to the notice of his daughter. Toni, of course, had suspected this all along, but suspected as a child suspects, with fear and indignation. As he laughed and joked with Fischer he glanced across the table at Toni and intercepted a look of anguish. In a second his pleasure turned to dust.

'Mrs Fischer,' he said later, stirring his coffee in the drawing-room, his eyes watering more than usual. 'Can you do something for my daughter?'

Mrs Fischer enlivened an entirely respectable existence with a little matchmaking, a fact of which Dr Meyer was unaware. He simply considered it a duty for mature women, who would of course be married, to look after young girls. Mrs Fischer's outlook was slightly different. She considered that young girls had a right to be looked after by mature men. The ideal match, according to Mrs Fischer, was between a very young girl and a man considerably older than herself, whose money could then be spent in any way deemed appropriate by the virgin bride. Marriages, as far as she was concerned, were largely financial contracts: compensation was to be made by the husband for removing his wife's inexperience and inducting her into matronhood, a process also supervised by Mrs Fischer.

'I will give a dinner party,' she said.

She already had someone in mind, Arthur Ferber, an Englishman with a German name. This, she thought, could be brought into use as a conversational ploy if they were in want of something to say to each other. He was thirty-eight, and reasonably wealthy. He had inherited a wholesale stationery business and went off to a suburb every morning, Hayes, she thought, or Keston, where he sat in an office and directed operations in the warehouse, which was substantial. This Mrs Fischer considered entirely appropriate: she did not approve of men who stayed around the house all day. She thought Ferber a dry stick, unemotional, but doubted whether Toni Meyer could be trusted with more combustible material. She saw tears there, hysteria certainly a possibility.

'There is someone I want you to meet,' she said.

Arthur Ferber, whom I never knew, seems to me far more foreign than my grandmother ever did, for after twenty-five years of marriage he left her, and they were divorced while my mother was still very young. This event gave Toni a certain tragic grandeur, although the fault was all her own. She had taken quite kindly to Ferber and to his house in Maresfield Gardens, although she was never to love him. Nor did he seem to love her beyond the initial pleasures, which he appreciated more than she ever did. His nature was resigned, and he put up with her increasingly bad temper for the sake of a well-run household. She accused him of being secretive, which he was: he preferred to keep all his thoughts and feelings to himself. Perhaps he might have been encouraged to be more expansive had Toni not turned all her attention away from him and focused it adoringly on her son, Hugo. Here was a golden child made in her own image. With the same astonishing lack of understanding which had led her to perch on her father's knee and lay her head on his shoulder she trained the boy to be her consort, which effectively removed him from any care or guidance which might have been provided by Arthur Ferber. Ferber, an engima by all accounts, or rather by Toni's account, augmented in due course by Hugo's, was if anything grateful for this additional show of indifference. His plans, it may be assumed, were already laid.

At fourteen Hugo was his mother's dancing partner at the largely Jewish weddings she attended, or at the lavish seaside hotels which she liked to frequent. Her husband never accompanied her on these occasions, which he thought of with contempt. Marriage to Toni had bred in him a mild strain of anti-Semitism, but the more he disapproved of her the more perversely attractive he found her to be. She had been a ravishing girl when he married her; she had become an impressively handsome woman. Had it not been for the uncertainty of her temper he thought they might have got along quite well. But he could not stand the sight of his son being fondled, could not stand his son's attentive response, could not stand the symbiosis between the two of them. Basically, I think, he could not stand his son, whom he thought of as spoilt and unmanly, Viennese, in fact. Hugo was certainly unmanly, or perhaps he was simply un-English. His father was too disgusted by the son's charming and insinuating manners to supply any manliness that might have been lacking.

Hugo, whom I knew so briefly, grew up into a passive and agreeable youth, although by the age of twenty he appeared curiously inert, as if worn out by his attentions to his mother. He was always to remain gratified by a show of feminine interest in his welfare, of concern for his wellbeing. It was a sign of Dolly's acumen that she recognised this at once, for her experience of men was far greater than Hugo's experience of women. But Hugo had no thought of marriage, although his mother's tireless companionship was beginning to irk him. Perhaps for this reason he quite enjoyed being in the army, where he was a singularly inept soldier. Sent to camp at Catterick, he was endlessly referred for further training. A mild degree of popularity was ensured by the lavish parcels sent to him by his mother. He never enquired where the chocolate and the biscuits came from; it was entirely natural to him that his mother continued to spoil him, as she always had. He did not enquire how so many sweet things came his way: he assumed that his mother had sources of nourishment denied to the rest of the population, as indeed she had. When he was demobbed he wore the same amiable smile as he had worn when first introduced to what was in fact a relatively harsh life: he had, after all, been used to having his bed turned down, his curtains drawn, his fire turned on, his meals delicately, anxiously prepared. He returned home to his mother, who clasped him in her arms, her heart throbbing with emotion.

'You have been so brave,' she murmured.

He had done nothing more arduous than sign requisition forms, at which he was rather good, but he accepted the tribute with a modest smile. He too was glad to be home.

He returned to university, but not to Cambridge: his mother could not bear another absence. He went to King's College, in the Strand, and took his law exams, after which he joined the Westminster Bank. He continued to live at home with his mother, for his father, who had been a far more important serving officer, was still overseas, and had volunteered to remain there after the war. Thus Arthur Ferber spent many agreeable and instructive months in Vienna, where his wife had been a girl. It served to reunite them for a spell: nevertheless, after spending his leave in London, he signed on for a further term of duty. This suited them all very well. There was in any case an acute shortage of paper, so he was not needed either at the office or in the warehouse, to which he appointed a manager and a supervisor. Hugo and his mother spent evenings at home, where she taught him to play bridge. Occasionally, bravely, she urged him to go out and enjoy himself. Occasionally he did. But he found he cut a poor figure among the returning officers, and the girls were not as nice to him as his mother was.

The epochal moment of his marriage must be left until later in this narrative. What concerns me now is the birth of my mother. It has been necessary to dwell on Toni's history and comportment in order to explain my mother's apologetic personality. My mother was born when Toni was forty-three: her stupefaction at finding herself pregnant again had turned her against her daughter for life. Incredible though this may sound, my mother was kept in another part of the house under the supervision of a nanny who stayed until my mother was twenty years old. Thus two ménages coexisted under one roof: different meals were eaten in different rooms. While Hugo was in the drawing-room playing bridge with Toni, my mother and Nanny Sweetman were keeping each other company in what had been designated as a servant's quarters. Occasionally she joined them in the evenings. Hugo was very kind to her. In return she adored him almost as much as his mother did.

Toni's attitude to her daughter was also dictated by her daughter's looks. My mother was thin, pale, shy, self-effacing, not by any stretch of the imagination a beauty, towards whom Toni might have relented. Toni's response to my mother's timid overtures was one of annoyance, almost of contempt. This was compounded by the fact that Arthur Ferber had by this stage asked for a divorce. He disliked his son, might have loved his daughter, if distance had not worked its enchantment on him. On his final return from Vienna he sold the business, and settled money on his daughter, enough to provide her with an income for life. This final injustice did nothing to soften Toni's feelings towards my mother. Her son, she thought, had been slighted, although she herself had done very well out of the divorce settlement. Arthur Ferber retired to Collioure, where he painted landscapes, badly, in the manner of the Fauves, and eventually married a Frenchwoman, Clothilde Lemaire. For a time he sent postcards to his daughter: then the postcards became more widely spaced and finally stopped.

'Do you think he is dead?' Henrietta asked her mother.

'Never,' was the reply. 'He is too careful for that. And too devious.'

In any event, as far as Toni and her daughter were concerned, he had ceased to exist. He survived in my mother's memory only as a tall vague figure, glimpsed only occasionally, and regretted only in so far as it became a daughter to regret a lost father. Even this regret was limited, since he was presented to her as something of a wastrel (Collioure, the landscapes). If she ever pictured him in later life it was with a puzzled but by no means frustrated curiosity. She imagined him to be like Gauguin, a renouncer of families. This latter trait she respected. The last communication she had had from him was a photograph of one of his landscapes. Even she could see that this was extremely poor. After a while she accepted her mother's verdict, and Arthur Ferber was effectively discarded.

To say that Toni neglected my mother is not quite accurate: she also exacted a sort of revenge. When she went out my mother had to accompany her, as if she were a lady companion. If Toni were reconciled to Hugo's eventual marriage — for she was not a complete fantasist and considered it her duty to guarantee his survival — she had no such plans for my mother. My mother was to assure Toni's comfort as she grew older, until such time as she might require assistance. At those hotels where Toni liked to spend Christmas, my mother would sit resignedly on the edge of some ballroom while Hugo whirled his mother round the floor. No one was likely to ask her to dance: at fifteen she looked no older than eleven, and in any event her mother did not like her to talk to strange men. It was at one of these hotels that Hugo met Dolly, while my mother loitered palely on the sidelines. The brief courtship that followed was watched with agonised approval by Hugo's mother. She consented to the marriage, half hoping that Dolly could be installed in the house in Maresfield Gardens. The one event for which she was not prepared was his request for a transfer to the Brussels branch of the bank. She suspected, rightly, that this was inspired by Dolly, who nevertheless addressed her as *'Maman chérie'*. In due course this was changed to *'Chère Mère'*, but by that stage Toni had found fault with Dolly as well.

My mother grew up in her separate quarters in Maresfield Gardens, and grew up entirely without rancour, humbly accepting her indifferent status and the petty duties that were demanded of her. In time Toni's dislike turned to indifference, although she never valued my mother as my mother deserved to be valued. She continued to regret her appearance, so that my mother grew up believing herself to be ugly. Her mirror told her that she was in fact far from ugly, but she believed her mother rather than the mirror. At the age of twenty she announced that she had decided to go to college. Nanny Sweetman had by this stage retired. My mother must have sensed that she must not settle for what had been devised for her, and put her case quite strongly.

'Very well,' said Toni, who by this time had various cronies in Maresfield Gardens, strong-willed women like herself with pliant sons or daughters. 'But you must live at home. I can't be left alone. You must see that.'

She agreed, of course. But she had learned that escape was easier than she had suspected. She took to going out by herself in the evenings, when Toni was entertaining her iron-jawed friends. That was how she found herself in the Wigmore Hall, where she met my father.

He was, I think, the first person to love my mother, for Arthur Ferber hardly counted, and he loved her to the end of his life, as she loved him. By contemporary standards their courtship was slow, archaic: for five years they went to concerts, took their walks. I think well of this, although my generation is more cynical, less hopeful of a good outcome, and tends to be derisive of such obvious chastity. Toni's attitude was cautious. She knew that something was afoot, but chose not to know. For that reason my mother introduced Paul Manning to Maresfield Gardens on an evening when Toni was giving one of her weekly bridge parties. At these affairs lavish refreshments were served. As they entered the room seven heads were lifted from their coffee cups. Toni, in the face of such public witness, was gracious. 'So nice to meet you,' she said. 'You will have coffee, won't you? Etta, find Paul a chair. Next to me, dear. That's right.' When she found out that he worked in a bank she became more gracious. 'My son is in our Brussels branch,' she said. The Westminster Bank had become 'our' bank. And in the presence of her friends it suddenly became her to have a marriageable daughter. At the end of the evening she clasped Paul's hand and said that he must come again soon. Her friends exchanged significant glances. For a brief moment Toni enjoyed her status as mother of the bride.

This harmonious state of affairs was not to continue for very long. I am sure that Toni hoped to draft her future son-in-law into residence in Maresfield Gardens, but my mother and my father were to be adamant on this point. 'Very well,' she said finally, when this matter was settled. 'But don't expect me to visit you. Where did you say? Prince of Wales Drive? Somewhere in south London, isn't it? Too far for me. But if you have decided . . .' She heaved a pathetic sigh. I imagine that at this point she had begun to feel her age. My mother was thirty when she married, which makes Toni seventy-three at the time. She was in good health but moved around very little. My father's attitude was simple. He saw that no real affection bound Toni to her daughter, and therefore he felt only a very slight affection for Toni. He recognised her for what she was, a selfish and resilient woman. He had disliked the atmosphere at Maresfield Gardens, the hawklike profiles raised enquiringly from the coffee cups. He thought the ambience perfervid, haunted by the ghost of Freud and other Viennese associations. Even the conjunction of the Berggasse and Maresfield Gardens was, he thought, too apt, too prompt, too symbolic to be a mere accident: no good could come of it. He regarded my mother's innocence as all but miraculous. By comparison Prince of Wales Drive seemed sane, rational, uneventful. They could walk in Battersea Park, which they could see from their windows. And so it was to be. Toni kept her word: she rarely visited them. They, for their part, were enjoined to visit her in Maresfield Gardens. This arrangement continued, at increasingly lengthy intervals, until her death, by which time her legendary indifference to her daughter had reasserted itself.

One visit to us I do remember. I must have been small, watching from a window. I was drawn to the window by the ticking of the cab, a sound which still draws me to the window today. My grandmother stepped heavily from the taxi, planting one foot in front of her and slowly disengaging the other. She was wearing a bright blue suit which fitted her rather too closely: she had put on weight and was very conscious of it, although she remained an impressive looking woman. She was carrying a cake from some Swiss Cottage bakery, the reason, no doubt, for her increasing girth: she was never to lose her sweet tooth. She raised her head and saw me at the window. Her brief wintry smile hardly disturbed her morose features which were tremendously bedizened with make-up: lipstick, blusher, eye-shadow, all chosen to bring out the blue of her still startling eyes. Her hair was dyed a defiant apricot. She looked as if she owed her appearance to an entire morning spent in front of her dressing-table mirror, and all to see my mother, of whom she was not particularly fond, and the grandchild whom she watched carefully but did not fondle. Whether she had hopes for me or not I never knew, but I think she pitied my mother for her tepid existence, for never having known the hothouse love she had known as a girl in Vienna. At that stage, in her old age, she had come to realise that that love had held an element of parody, even of tragedy; her failure to captivate her father stayed with her, as did the image of Frau Zimmermann, watchful in the background. In the recesses of her infant mind she had always known of their liaison, known it imperfectly, but known nevertheless. Her ultimate lack of fulfilment she attributed rightly to this period in her life.

We visited her, in Maresfield Gardens, after Hugo's death. She sat in a chair, apparently turned to stone. Her face was thickly powdered, but her lips and eyes were pale: tears, which we were not to witness, had obliterated all the colours. There was something reproachful in her attitude which I only later came to understand. Hugo's death had made her not only sad but bitter, as if it were inevitable that the men in her life should let her down. In her heart I think she knew that my mother was the better of her two children, but by then her disappointment was so comprehensive that she expected nothing further in the way of joy or gratification, knowing that in her life she had received only the barest minimum, and regretting the days of her youth and the ways in which she had spent them, or misspent them, hanging hysterically on to her father's arm, while he made plans to dispose of her. She was a widow who had never enjoyed being a wife, a mother whose favourite child had predeceased her. Slowly her expression changed to one of outrage as she contemplated her fate. I remember that adamantine face, menacing and pale. Although I had very little to do with her, and indeed hardly knew her, although it was not possible to feel for her the glimmerings of something so intimate as affection, I retained a sort of admiration for that hieratic face, that four-square position in the wing chair, that formal, distant, almost cold insistence that we taste the various cakes she had provided for our teatime coffee. I find the idea of her making her lonely way to Swiss Cottage, on what must have been one of the worst days of her life, immensely impressive. And I have no doubt that she dressed carefully for that short journey, and bid acquaintances good morning, and returned their condolences in as steady a voice as usual. The follies of her youth were long gone, its excesses banished for ever. Of her solitude I can hardly bear to think, although I understand it very well. My own ability to tolerate a solitary life is, I am sure, an hereditary factor: it is the way my grandmother, whose influence on my mother was notable for its absence, lives on in me.

My other grandmother I knew even less, a fact which I did not regret since she seemed, from what I heard of her, to be slightly mad, and may even have been so, for all I know. She was a widow living in South Kensington with two small wire-haired terriers to whom she devoted all her leisure hours. She really should have been a dog breeder rather than a mother, for she felt for her son a mild affection only one degree warmer than indifference, whereas she would actually play games with the dogs, for whom she also bought expensive rubber toys. The dogs were taken out morning and afternoon for an extensive run in Hyde Park, where my tireless grandmother, dressed winter and summer in trousers, a short-sleeved blouse, and an old tweed jacket belonging to her dead husband, threw balls and sticks, shouted instructions and encouragements, and scarcely noticed the seasons changing all around her. The only thing my father seemed to have inherited from her was her love of exercise: he too was impatient unless he had the prospect of a long walk before him.

My Manning grandmother wore an eager religious expression which it was possible to mistake for friendliness. In fact she was meditating on the universal Oneness of things and attended some institution devoted to psychic research and spiritual growth conveniently near her in Queensberry Place. Her religious exercises, which she was fortunately able to pursue while romping with the dogs, consisted of exerting the power of love, a gospel which she never ceased to proclaim. To love everyone is a noble enterprise; unfortunately it denies one a certain faculty of discrimination. My grandmother loved everyone, whether they liked it or not. In fact very few people were aware of this love since she had very little time for friendship, and in due course knew only the people at the psychic research place, all of them as eager as herself on the occasions on which they were gathered together, and all of them putting in claims for the distinction of total transforming conviction. Very few people visited her, although she was invited out to tea by the more sociable of the believers. On such afternoons she dressed in an archaic navy blue suit, with hard shoulders and box-pleated skirt, which transformed her appearance but did not flatter it. This was a pity for she was quite an attractive woman, with a fluff of gingery hair above a small sharp-featured face. She was the natural version of which my grandmother Toni was the work of art: the same reddish hair, the same blue eyes, the same fine skin which she had allowed to fall into a dozen tiny cracks, like an apple which has been stored too long. The daunting fervour of her expression, allied to her

almost total absentmindedness, made her a somewhat enigmatic parent, and indeed she seems to
have expected my father to fend for himself from
a very young age. There was no other parent in
the house; my father liked to say that his father
had died in childbirth. In fact Richard Manning
had been run over by a car outside South Kensington tube station. My father suffered no damage
from this dereliction, and was philosophical about
his mother's shortcomings. Her indifference may
even have served him rather well. She provided
him with a satchel when he went to school, with
a briefcase when he went to university, and with
several items of unwanted furniture when he left
home. These pieces of furniture, of uncanny size,
were a feature of our life in Prince of Wales Drive,
since there was no prospect of anyone paying good
money to take them away. One could see why she
had found them to be superfluous.

When my mother went to meet her for the first
time she was nervous and suffering from a cold.
To Eileen Manning, who never suffered from anything, this was a sinister affliction. She surveyed
my mother with narrowed eyes.

'You don't look very strong,' she said. 'You look
chesty. Are you chesty?'

'I'm very fit,' said my mother, coughing slightly.
She had taken a mouthful of scalding tea in her
eagerness to please and had swallowed it too
quickly.

Eileen Manning's suspicious look was replaced
by her habitual expression of enthusiasm as she

tried to expound her psychic gospel. My mother, I am sure, listened politely, her eyes occasionally straying to the man she was to marry as if to reassure herself as to his sanity. Later, when he had taken my mother home, he returned to South Kensington and announced his intention to become engaged.

'Oh, I don't think that's wise, Paul. Not if there's lung trouble in the family.'

'Henrietta is perfectly well, Mother.'

'I doubt that, dear. But you must please yourself, of course.'

She was in absent-minded attendance at the small reception Toni gave after the wedding, no doubt in her box-pleated suit, but after that was content to receive a weekly telephone call, in the course of which she would enquire, 'And how's that poor girl of yours?'

Once a month my father would undertake to visit his mother, combining the visit with one of the long walks he so loved. He would go round Battersea Park, along Cheyne Walk to Pimlico Road, across to Sloane Square, along Sloane Street and into Hyde Park, where he might linger to watch the dogs, and, in winter, the red globe of the setting sun. Then he would leave the park, perhaps regretfully, and present himself at his mother's flat in Ennismore Gardens for a cup of tea. He doubted whether his mother got much pleasure from these visits, but she received him placidly and reached up to kiss him when he left. I think she was an entirely contented woman, but

I have to admit that I never consciously knew her. I think she broke the habit of a lifetime and visited us when I was a baby, but if I registered her presence at all it was only as another face bending over to examine me. These, with an infant's privilege, I ignored.

By mutual consent she and my mother rarely met; had they done so my mother would have been interrogated on what Eileen Manning was convinced was her progressive deterioration. When Violet Lawlor — part old acquaintance, part domestic relic of her early married life — sent her usual Christmas card in the winter of my parents' marriage, Eileen Manning, as usual, sent back a card with a postal order tucked inside it. She then performed the one good deed for which my mother knew her, and despatched Violet to Prince of Wales Drive 'to look after poor Henrietta'. Having thus disposed of nearly everyone she knew she then took the dogs out for a run. Yet at a mere sixty-five, after a lifetime of healthy exercise, she suffered a fatal heart attack, appropriately enough in the park. It was the barking of the dogs which alerted passers-by, rare at that hour, for it was getting dark. My father was very subdued for a while, yet when my mother pointed out how fitting this death was, how painless the manner of her leaving this life, he cheered up. Death is arbitrary, after all. No one is safe.

Against these fairly unusual backgrounds my parents stand out emblematically, like pale creatures newly liberated from engulfing darkness,

61

slender pillars of English virtue advancing, hand in hand, towards the light of common day. Having effectively divorced themselves from home and family, they felt free to invent their lives, as if they were characters in Dickens. This meant doing the opposite of what they had been brought up to do, living lives of the utmost orderliness and decorum. I felt a painful love for these mild and conscientious parents, whose moderate voices unfitted me for the realities of the world I was to inhabit.

'The snail's on the thorn,' my father would announce, his signal that he was about to go for a walk. And then, politely, 'Would Jane like to come, do you think?'

I was too young or too small to accompany him, but the formalities had to be observed.

'I'm afraid I shall need Jane to help me make pastry,' my mother would inevitably reply.

'Very well. Then I shall look forward to eating it.'

I never felt excluded from their lives, never witnessed any primal scene, was not encouraged to formulate any family romance, although I was to do this later in the books I wrote for children and for which I became quite well known. As far as I was concerned my parents were two grown-up children, rather like myself. I longed to preserve their innocence, while my own innocence was as yet unformulated. I resented on their behalf any gross intrusion, any shadow of *louche* adult concerns. Into this category I put both debt and sexuality. I reckoned myself the ideal company for my mother, with the possible addition of my friend Marigold Chance: anything more worldly, I suspected, might damage her. In this conviction I was remarkably prescient. As I say, and try to explain in my stories, children are alive to adult feelings. I mounted guard on my mother, keen to protect her, for no one knew her vulnerability better than I did. My grandmother Ferber I could just allow, for she seemed to keep a respectful, even a mournful, distance. My first misgivings about the impermeability of our world came during that first visit of Dolly and Hugo to our flat. Since Hugo was to die shortly afterwards my feelings of caution, of anxiety, of guardedness, became focused upon Dolly. Yet at that stage Dolly too was innocent, or as innocent as she ever managed to be. I rather think that innocence was not in her nature, yet that this was not entirely her fault. Or maybe it was. I had reason, in later life, to be impressed by the simplicity of her motives, and at the end, of course, she was as disarmed as the rest of us.

At that stage, however, at the moment of our first meeting, I merely registered her as an unusually taut presence, conveniently symbolised for me by the tautness of her silk dress, which, as she took care to point out, had been made by hand. Her enthusiasm, which was her normal mode on social occasions, nevertheless had something fitful about it, as if she longed to be somewhere else, as of course she did. Yet I could not quite forgive her impatience, since it seemed to make my mother anxious, while my father's politeness became even more pronounced. I lingered in the room long after the time at which I was expected to leave it, for Dolly had the gift of arresting and detaining one's attention, a gift which she was never to lose.

I have mentioned the primal scene, that imaginary sexual encounter which children reconstruct for their parents and which some believe that they have actually witnessed. This primal scene I unhesitatingly ascribe to Dolly and Hugo. Her angry smiles, her sidelong glances at her husband, her brightening of expression as the day drew towards evening, all put one in mind of a sexual life lived not too far out of sight. At the time of our first meeting Dolly was in her middle forties: was it the anguish of ageing that had brought these matters to the surface? Yet I do not believe that she thought of her substantial attractions as waning, rather the opposite. Her impatience, as I now see, had to do with frustration, as if the amiable Hugo had failed to come up to the mark. In this respect, as in so many others, she might have been the natural daughter of my grandmother Toni. Toni too had been embroiled in a primal scene, although of a more authentically Viennese stamp. Toni too had had expectations of men and had been disappointed. Both Toni and Dolly had the same restless imperious turn of the head, the same beautiful predatory hands. I see those hands now, stretched out to take the cards, beringed, vainly admired. Their initial ardour, which was succeeded by the most virulent antagonism, also indicates a closeness of relationship which was always denied to my mother. For this reason my mother became involved as a witness to their drama, from which she always considered herself to be slightly removed. In this, as in most other matters, she felt apologetic. I upheld her, of course, as I always did, even when such feelings were still a mystery to me. But then, for as long as I can remember, our particular closeness had no need of explanations.

3

Marie-Jeanne Schiff, who was always to be known as Dolly, was born in Paris, in the rue Saint-Denis, in March 1922. Her parents, Jacob and Fanny Schiff, had arrived in Paris from Frankfurt two years earlier, a surprising move given the anti-German feeling of the time, but they were politically ignorant, as they were in most worldly matters. They migrated partly in order to better their prospects: they were poor at home, they would be rich abroad. They were naïve, hopeful, and a little unrealistic, as if one place were as good as another, so long as it held the possibility of wealth. Jacob Schiff was congenitally restless and was always ready to try a new town or city where he could exercise his not very advanced skills as a watchmaker. It was probably his wife who chose Paris: she was a dressmaker, in an extremely small way of business, but already more determined than her husband was ever to be. She knew him to be indecisive, unstable, and unreliable as a breadwinner. He had already left her and returned to her three or four times, not for another woman but from a simple desire to be elsewhere. On his return he was eager for her welcome, as if nothing were amiss, but was unapologetic, wide-eyed, smiling, and indefinably dilapidated. A *Luft-*

mensch: the type is less common today, or if it exists is to be found among the young, a left-over from the hippie years and therefore slightly different in character.

They settled in the rue Saint-Denis, fifth floor, no lift. The flat was tolerable and more than they could afford: there were two main rooms opening out of one another, a bedroom, a kitchen, and a *cabinet de toilette*. When their child Marie-Jeanne was born, Fanny Schiff slept with her in the bedroom, while her husband lay on a couch in the living-room under a mock tigerskin rug. Shortly afterwards he decamped, this time for good. Fanny received a postcard from Colmar, but otherwise never saw or heard from him again. She moved herself into the living-room, together with the dressmaker's dummy she had bought: the child, whom she called Dolly, had the bedroom to herself. Soup simmered all day in the kitchen. Dolly was always to remember this as the smell of childhood. The memory was alternately resented and cherished.

In the street Fanny Schiff greeted the ladies who walked up and down with a timid *'Bonjour, Madame'*. I think she hardly knew that they were prostitutes: she thought of them as young girls in search of a husband, as she had once been. Now all that was over: she only wanted the child to grow up beautiful and healthy. She also wanted her business to prosper, as it had begun to do. Her sore eyes, her few hours of sleep on the couch in the workroom, and the eternal smell of soup

67

were a small price to pay for solvency, a solvency she had never previously known.

She soon had a clientele among the girls, cheerful, stoical, good-natured creatures who petted the baby and took to spending their off-duty moments in the workroom with Fanny. There was nothing downtrodden about these girls; they regarded ordinary married women with scorn and pity. All were actively saving up for their retirement. Those who had a man were planning to open a bar or a small restaurant, somewhere in the south. Nice, they said, Saint-Raphaël, Fréjus. Fanny listened as she stitched away. The child Dolly, of whom they made a great fuss, also listened. Another life! A better life! She loved her mother, could see her tired eyes at the end of the day. As soon as she was old enough she was sent downstairs to buy *mille-feuilles* and éclairs: one of the girls, Lucette or Michèle, always brought a present of good coffee. They were kind and generous, felt sorry for Fanny and Dolly, knew that there would be no time for them to have more than soup for their supper, as the machine whirred on late into the night. Their diet was irregular: a great deal of coffee, cakes when the girls came, on Sunday a couple of slices of ham with potatoes in oil, sometimes a cutlet followed by a spoonful of preserves. Nevertheless Dolly grew up beautiful.

She was dark haired, with a taut faintly gleaming French complexion. She held her head high, even as a child: her dark eyes, her direct gaze challenged all who came within her field of vision. She went to school, where she made no friends; in any case she preferred the company of Lucette and Michèle and others like them. Sometimes she dropped into a church on her way home but left again discontented; there was nothing there to feed her solitude and her longings. Moreover she resented the atmosphere of self-denial she encountered among the shabby women in the pews, and took her resentment to the highest authority. Who was Jesus to say that she must not lay up treasures on earth? Where else could she enjoy them? Even at a young age she had strong desires, impulses, movements; she had nothing in common with those women in headscarves, their knotted hands patiently joined. She felt murderously towards them, as if they were undermining her own existence. Jesus she held directly responsible for her mother's uncomplaining nature and also for her hard life, the one being a consequence of the other. She resolved to be different, not knowing, or if suspecting not believing, that her slender resources might not take her as far as she wished to go.

She had more ambition than her mother, but less application, knew only that she did not want to work as her mother continued to work, did not as yet connect her idea of a better life with a man. The men she saw passing up and down the street she considered far less important than the women. When she was sixteen, seventeen, she began to attract attention, but the word went out that she was not to be touched. She already considered her future to lie elsewhere, away from the rue Saint-

Denis. She was determined, but dreamy: she wanted to live in a better house, with better food, and for her mother not to work so hard. Her heart was rudimentary. She was only prepared to love one or two people, one of whom would almost certainly be her mother, and the other probably herself.

Her mother kept her at home, for her business had picked up and she was busy. Lucette and Michèle had brought other girls, for whom she made short swinging skirts and beautiful crêpe de Chine blouses. Dolly was sent out to buy buttons, *passementerie,* perhaps a length of fabric. The rest of the time she sat brooding in the workroom. With the rumours of war one or two of the girls spoke of leaving Paris, but most of them stayed. If France were invaded business was bound to be good. It might not be what they were used to, but there was an officer class in every army, and after the war, which would surely end quickly one way or another, there was that bar in Saint-Raphaël to be thought of, that bright reward for their many days and nights of hard work. If they worried about anything they worried about the fate of Fanny and Dolly Schiff, for 'Schiff' denoted a suspect foreignness. Fanny, who had learned a certain amount of worldly wisdom, gave it out that she came from Alsace, although Schiff is not the most common of Alsatian names. Remembering her husband, of whom she never thought, she said that she was from Colmar. The disappearing husband had also been Jewish, but that was easy to overlook. These days she sometimes went to church if she were not too tired, but, like her daughter, in matters of faith she was entirely uninvolved. She did not need to learn patience, judged her fortitude to be equal to the task, and felt only discomfort when asked to contemplate Christ's wounds.

After the Occupation, it did not occur to her to pray for her own safety. She was too simple to believe herself in danger: in any event she had the protection of a street network of girls, many of whom had joined up with German officers. In due course Lucette and Michèle, Simone, Sylvie and the others had gone up in the world, had been elevated to the status of regular mistress, were being shown the sights of Paris as they had never seen them before. Their wardrobes increased exponentially: Fanny was busier than ever. She was paid in comestibles as well as in money, so that they never went hungry like the majority of Parisians. In this way they did quite well under the Occupation.

Dolly brooded throughout the long dark evenings, when there was nothing to do and nowhere to go. Her impatience was growing, the impatience which was to be so marked a feature of her later life. At twenty she was still a virgin, and her expression was becoming a little fretful. When the Americans liberated Paris she was in the crowd in the place de la Concorde: within minutes she was being picked up, kissed, whirled around by the tallest man she had ever seen. Because she was so darkly pretty, because she was so beautifully and simply dressed, she was appropriated by her tall American and given what he called a raincheck for later in the evening. He told her to meet him in the bar of the Crillon, a hotel she had hardly ever walked past. But there was no point in going home, and she was not frightened. She squared her shoulders, and marched into the Crillon, her own proud looks and her mother's exquisite dressmaking guaranteeing her a respectful welcome.

Her American, Charlie, was with several of his friends; all seemed eager to know a French girl. She taught them a few words of French, for which they seemed exaggeratedly grateful, and in return she learned her first few phrases of English, which she was to perfect rapidly in their company. The genius of Dolly was her adaptability. No sooner was she in the company of strangers than she learned their language, studied their habits, noted their susceptibilities. With Charlie and his friends, all handsome in their olive drab uniforms, with that crew cut cleanliness she found so refreshingly different, she went through several stages of a belated girlhood: she danced, flirted, and above all seduced men, one or two of whom were genuinely in love with her. She also ate the enormous meals to which the conquerors were entitled, smuggling home chocolate and American cigarettes in her handbag. Fanny Schiff was delighted with these midnight feasts. When Dolly sat on her bed, on the rug of mock tigerskin, and fed her mother a *petit four,* Fanny smiled and laughed as she saw her daughter's glowing cheeks. She slept at last with a taste of sugar in her mouth. She may even, in her simple way, have thought that marriage was in the air. More probably she wanted her daughter to enjoy a freedom which she herself had never enjoyed. She had little time for men, but resigned herself to envisaging a man as part of her daughter's future.

But Dolly could not settle for one man; she was having too good a time. She quickly learned that these Americans were relatively chaste, that they did not want to sleep with her but only to flirt with her, to practise their French, and to teach her the new dances. How they danced! Whirled around, thrown around, Dolly was in her element. Fanny had made her a short skirt cut on the bias which flared out as she moved; it was her favourite garment, and she could not wait to get dressed for the evening's entertainment. But as these evenings wore on the Americans became solemn and homesick; they could not drink like Frenchmen, and tended to become tearful, passing round photographs of the girls back home, some of whom they had married hastily before embarkation. None of this interested Dolly, but her adaptability stood her in good stead, and she feigned a sympathy which she did not feel, yawning a little in the ladies' room and noting at the same time that her face did not reflect the lateness of the hour. She knew that all this would soon vanish, that she would be reduced once again to ordinary life. She liked the Americans well enough, loved their extravagance, their kindness, their well-groomed good looks, but she was a realist, far more of a realist than her mother had ever been. She sometimes reflected desperately that when they left, as they were bound to do sooner or later, life would be very hard, harder than ever now that two sources of protection had disappeared. The prostitutes who had consorted with German officers had gone underground, obtained false papers, turned up with a clean record in a different city. Fanny missed them. Dolly sometimes calculated their chances and was not optimistic.

But she was young: if necessary she would sell herself. She had nothing against this as an idea, but it seemed that surprisingly few men wanted to acquire her on a permanent basis. Perhaps they regretted the simplicity of dancing all evening with an attractive partner. In this way she retained as much of her virginity as would be useful to her when she was in a more serious marriage market, although for two years she had been subject to such kissings and rubbings and explorations as necessitated a new make-up before she went home to her mother. She became aware that some men were clumsy when they made love, and she made a vow to seek refinement. In this way she knew she would respect her mother as well as herself. The time had come for her to take on the burden of their mutual existence.

When the Americans left their difficulties increased. The presumed Alsatian origins of their surname did them no good at all. Despised as Germans, hated as collaborators and dealers on the black market, they began to consider the possibility of leaving France. But where to go? Suddenly they had no friends. It was Dolly, with her new-found fluency in English, who suggested London. What could they lose? Fanny could make clothes for the English as well as for the French. Besides, they were very cold, and they knew that the English had coal fires. Once again their ignorance protected them. They shut up the flat and slipped away in the darkness of a winter evening. Three days later they were in the Grosvenor Hotel, Victoria.

They were immediately homesick. This took them by surprise. They had thought to find a flat and settle in, but most of the buildings were bomb-damaged and those that were not were requisitioned. Wandering around the rubble-strewn streets they knew an awful fear, as if the streets were to remain for ever desolate. The people looked so cold and so poor that Fanny realised that her career was over, for who would want fine clothes when it had become a matter of pride, of patriotism, to look shabby? She was, to all intents and purposes, redundant, had brought about her own retirement. She was not altogether sorry. Her eyes troubled her far more than she let her daughter know. But Dolly was aware of her mother's drooping spirits, and made a decision to spend some of the money they had saved on a holiday for them both. In the foyer of the gloomy hotel she found a brochure advertising Christmas breaks at another hotel, newly re-opened, on the south coast. In this manner Dolly and Fanny Schiff found themselves under the same roof as Toni, Hugo, and the young Henrietta Ferber for three days which were to change Dolly's life.

On their arrival they were immediately homesick once more. The desolate empty coastline, populated by stoical walkers, was minimally more discouraging than the other guests, large women with accommodating husbands who seemed content to doze in armchairs and let their wives conduct their social lives without their active assistance. Out of fear they stayed in their room until the evening, thus missing the afternoon tea hour at which Toni made a ceremonious entrance, flanked by her son and her teenage daughter. She knew the hotel well, had stayed there before the war, assumed that a certain deference was due to her, as indeed she did in most situations, and nodded graciously at one or two old acquaintances, women like herself who intended to keep a strict watch on their offspring. In consequence of this there were few young people about. Hugo, whose excuse for accompanying his mother was that he would have otherwise been alone in London, and hungry, since Nanny Sweetman was on holiday, was already bored stiff. But at the age of twenty-six he had inherited that agreeable pliancy, that almost meaningless acquiescence in a woman's whims that must have marked certain of his Viennese ancestors. Certainly he managed to keep a smile on his face in most circumstances. Few people managed to know what he was thinking, or indeed if he were thinking at all.

Fanny and Dolly dressed determinedly for dinner. Knowing that they had to stay, that there was no home awaiting their return, gave them a last spark of courage. In the restaurant they were circumspect, picking daintily at the terrible food. Dolly was wearing one of her mother's most beautiful creations, a sea-green faille with a shawl collar and the new very full skirt. Fanny, discreet in black, looked like every respectable continental mother. They could scarcely bring themselves to glance at their fellow guests, but caught glimpses, out of the corner of their eyes, of maroon crêpe and cross-over bodices; they permitted themselves a desolate smile of recognition, as if to register the failure of what must have seemed their last, their final enterprise. But from the adjoining ballroom came the sounds of a band tuning up. That saved them. Dolly breathed more freely, and when they stood up to leave their table they seemed more erect, more confident. A few iron-grey heads were turned; one or two mute interrogations were exchanged. The first chord of the evening was struck, and the band broke into a fervent rendition of 'Everything's in Rhythm with my Heart'. This was judged suitable for an ageing clientele which might take a turn round the floor and would certainly reminisce about pre-war musicals.

Dolly installed her mother in a chair and waited in an agony of impatience on the edge of the floor. She wanted to dance; she would even dance with the fogies who waddled behind their wives and beat time complacently to the music. As she was the only young woman in the room and Hugo was the only young man it was inevitable that sooner or later they would dance with each other, but first they had to do their duty, Hugo to his mother, Dolly to various roguish oldsters on whom she bestowed her prettiest smile. My mother, who was present on this occasion in an entirely subordinate capacity, told me that at this stage in her life Dolly was ravishing. When I knew her she was stocky and highly coloured: she had a middle-aged hairstyle and carried a handbag like the Queen's which swung vigorously as she walked. But when she was twenty-six (except that she gave it out that she was twenty-three) she was dark and slim, with big rueful eyes and an ardent expression. It was this expression, in which could be discerned a rapturous pleading for pleasure, which so appealed to men. It was more virginal than they knew; it was the expression of a girl at her first dance, a turning up of the face, a smile of anticipation, a readiness for, and an expectation of, enjoyment, and more than enjoyment; it was a plea for every kind of fulfillment. Dolly turned up her face as others might make a wish, with a longing for happiness, a trust that if certain words were imparted, certain promises made, all her dreams would come true. Many years later I was to see that expression again, whenever the afternoon faded into evening, whenever an engagement, however apparently dull or worthy, was announced. When the lights were switched on and the stage was set Dolly would brighten, sit up straight, metaphorically square her shoulders, and ready herself for pleasure.

By the time I knew her that expectation of pleasure was more limited. She was no longer a girl with a painful need for validation, for status, for security, but a respectable and slightly disenchanted matron. Yet still she brightened at the thought of diversion, and if her diversions were now notional, almost meaningless, she retained the hope that somehow, against the odds, one such diversion might change her for the better, might propel her into a more satisfying life, among happier, more beautiful people. The smile that came unbidden to her face and transformed her rather hard features into something ardent and melancholy gave her a look of distinction that was almost troubling, putting one under an obligation not to disappoint, to be generous, lavish, indulgent towards the person whose smile expressed such yearning. To her great credit Dolly was ignorant of this. She believed that any good fortune that came her way was richly deserved, but remained unaware that another face had peered through the resolute social face she presented to the world, and thus quite misjudged the effect she produced, congratulating herself on her good sense, and not knowing that for a moment she had shown herself to be the most passionate and most languishing of maidens.

'You could ask her to dance,' Toni instructed her son. She had remarked upon the beautiful dress, the respectable mother in discreet black; she had noted the expression, and some impulse from her distant girlhood prompted a faint smile. Hugo, who obeyed his mother unhesitatingly when it cost him nothing to do so, advanced obediently. When the girl was in his arms his own expression changed to one of surprise, admiration. They were marvellous dancers. Hugo had been trained by his mother, Dolly by the Americans. He was naturally inclined to the Viennese waltz, but she soon indicated a few new steps and he followed her at once. If she wanted to be thrown about and flung over his shoulder she managed to conceal the fact. This no doubt set the pattern for their life to come. On that evening there was no hint of discord, nor, to Dolly's credit, was there ever to be any open disagreement: one simply knew her to be bored. Gradually the jolting middle-aged couples left the floor. Dolly and Hugo danced on and in the end were rapturously applauded. Hugo led Dolly over to his mother.

'You dance very well, my dear.'

'Thank you,' said Dolly in her pretty accent, which she was to lose so quickly.

She introduced her mother, who nodded and smiled. As Fanny spoke no English many an awkwardness was evaded.

'Such a beautiful dress your daughter is wearing,' said Toni loudly, with exaggerated intonation, as if speaking to a native from the other side of the world.

'My mother is a well-known dressmaker in Paris,' said Dolly.

'Ah, yes,' replied Toni. 'You have so many clever dressmakers. Chanel. Patou.'

'*C'est Monsieur Dior maintenant,*' offered Fanny shyly. In her tentative smile could be seen the ghost of her daughter's desire. But where Fanny's smile merely offered friendliness Dolly's offered ardour. By the end of the evening some sort of accord had been reached, although it was still unformulated. Toni saw in the girl a prospective daughter-in-law whom she could almost take to as a daughter, that is to say as a replica of herself: that hint of appetite, that imperious raising of the head she recognised as if they had come from her own background, whereas my fifteen-year-old mother, looking shy and pallid in an awkward dress made out of parachute silk, would obviously, so she thought, never do her credit and could be left in the care of Nanny Sweetman. And the name, Schiff, like a taste of home . . . He might marry her, she thought. She saw no difficulty in persuading him to do so, she who had held his hand until he was eleven years of age.

On the floor again Dolly and Hugo were striking up an even more rapid acquaintance. Dolly, flushed with pleasure, pressed Hugo's hand: his own hand returned the pressure on the small of her back.

'Tomorrow?' he enquired. 'Or, better still, to-night?'

'I am here with my mother,' she explained.

He made a face. 'So am I.'

She liked him: he was kind. He would do her

no harm. He was a good son and could therefore be counted on to behave decently to her mother. She saw, with her expert eye, which had been trained on several previous men, that he would be a complaisant husband. She determined to marry him. She would not necessarily love him, but he was the equivalent of the bar in Fréjus, the restaurant in Saint-Raphaël, coveted in a fantasy by Lucette and Michèle, those girls for whom she retained a feeling of the utmost friendliness. She would put up with the old lady and the little girl: she would have to. What else could she do? She did not have the courage to return to Paris, even if that were a serious option, as it no longer seemed to be. Her mother's eyesight was now too bad to permit of further work and therefore of further income: Dolly, in the room they shared, had come upon her trying to read the printed sheet giving the times of the evening's festivities on the dressing-table, her head bent fatally close to the paper, her face, when she raised it, distant, puzzled. Her mother's eyesight was the deciding factor. I have no doubt, even at this distance, that Dolly was an honest woman. I simply believe that her scruples derived from a different set of circumstances. As far as I know she was never unfaithful to my uncle after their marriage. But he failed to banish that look of expectation which she habitually wore, as if it were time to get dressed and to make her way back to the Place de la Concorde and the Crillon and the evening's pleasure. In time, of course, that look of expectation had acquired a patina of trust that was almost childlike in its simplicity.

In the course of conversation — again, on Toni's part, articulated very clearly — Dolly pulled matters together by saying that they were staying in an hotel in London while looking for a flat. Did Mrs Ferber perhaps know of anything? Toni did. She was the owner of the house in Maresfield Gardens in which she occupied the ground-floor flat. A military man and his wife had the first floor, but the second floor was momentarily free. There was now no need for her to advertise, or rather to take in someone on the recommendation of her friends: she mentioned the empty flat to Dolly who clasped her hands with joy and embraced her mother. Toni liked that; she liked to see that closeness, which she had never felt for her own daughter, but which she was suddenly prepared to feel for Dolly. In fact, of the two of them, Toni and Hugo, Toni was the more infatuated. She had been bored for years, with a deadly boredom, of which her son's boredom was a mere shadow; even the war had bored her. She wanted a lively pretty companion, a vivid presence about the place. She had no doubt that if Dolly married Hugo they could all live together in her flat, with the mother conveniently put away upstairs; in that way there would be someone to look after her when she became ill, although at the age she was then she regarded that eventuality as remote. In the meantime she and her daughter-in-law could spend days in town, looking through the stores, taking coffee in the new cafés that were beginning to open; they could have delicious feminine discussions, while Hugo went to work and returned faithfully each evening. Eventually, when petrol came off the ration, she would buy Dolly a car, so that Dolly could drive her out into the countryside, in which, it might be noted, she had never taken the slightest interest. In this love affair between Toni and her prospective daughter-in-law Hugo was slightly overlooked. Fortunately he was acquiescent. Nothing could please him more than to have his mother's approval for something so attractive and so simple: a very pretty girl who liked him, and who apparently liked his mother. Sexually Hugo was not enterprising, nor had he been given much chance to experiment. He was to remain in awe of the fate which had presented him with Dolly, and consequently never to understand her. She in turn kept her thoughts to herself.

Early negotiations went forward with consummate ease. The four of them returned to London together, stopping on the way to pick up four suitcases from the Grosvenor Hotel. Dolly and Hugo were permitted, even encouraged, to consider themselves a couple. In Maresfield Gardens a more reflective mood took over. The top flat was empty and entirely denuded of furniture. Dolly had to beg a bed, a table and chairs from Hugo.

'Can't they bring their things over from Paris?' enquired Toni, rather annoyed.

'You forget, Mother. The Germans took everything.'

'But surely they got it all back? One hears that the Germans behaved rather well in Paris. Apparently Hitler told them to.'

'If you say so, Mother. In the meantime they need somewhere to sleep. And a table. Chairs,' he added guiltily.

'Oh, very well. That spare bed in the dressing-room will have to go.' That spare bed was the one formerly slept in by Arthur Ferber, now no more than a memory, and sometimes considerably less. 'And ask Nanny to let you have that table in the nursery. And ask Dolly to come down here when she has a moment. If she is not too busy.' This was said ironically. 'I haven't seen her for a day or two.'

Harmony was maintained, by means of considerable sacrifices on Dolly's part. She was aware that she would have to serve an apprenticeship before Toni would give her son in marriage. Every afternoon she left her own mother, sitting forlornly in their empty living-room, and went down the stairs to the ground floor flat to keep Toni company. She remained there until Hugo came home for dinner, when she was allowed to greet him, after he had greeted his mother. If she stayed for the evening she was given a lesson in bridge, at which she made disconcertingly rapid progress, as she had done in English, which she now spoke with the merest trace of an accent. Her speech was always more rapid than that of a native Englishwoman, more emphatic; by comparison my mother, and ultimately myself, seemed slow, reflective. At eleven o'clock she kissed them both, went upstairs, and climbed into bed with her mother, hugging her for warmth and for comfort. She knew that the last stage of her apprenticeship was adumbrated: her mother would have to go. Fanny's eyes were now so bad that she occasionally bumped into their table or knocked over one of the two chairs. Besides, she was lonely (they were both lonely); this was no life for her. By great good fortune Dolly, before leaving Paris, had obtained the name of *Les Hibiscus*, a select retirement home on the outskirts of Nice; by even greater good fortune she had heard, in a letter forwarded from the rue Saint-Denis, from Lucette, now installed in a *maison de tolérance* in Nice itself. On the management side, as she made clear. Dolly wrote back to her, outlining her plans. The reply was immediate; a room had been reserved for Madame Fanny at *Les Hibiscus*. Lucette would be delighted to see her old friend again. Dolly could get married, get on with her own life, and *bonne chance*.

It was a brave decision, and it turned out to have been the right one. Fanny Schiff lived happily in the sun until the age of eighty-eight, her days enlivened by the company of Lucette and her new colleagues. The pain of her daughter's absence was severe, but she had seen how that daughter's future was to take shape, and had acquiesced in the arrangement. As for Dolly, she was never to forget her mother, who remained the greatest love of her life. This I understand. Fanny's departure signified the onset of an era of greater coldness, the onset of a belated adulthood. Subconsciously she blamed Toni for her mother's removal, whereas in fact it had been entirely her own idea. But the arrangements, which had seemed so hopeful, had begun to stagnate, and something had to start them up again. Hugo, she realised, was not particularly anxious to get married now that he had both Dolly and his mother at his beck and call, vying with each other to satisfy his every whim. Dolly, of course, saw this, and began to feel for him that faint contempt that she was careful never to show. Every evening one of Toni's unattached male friends came in to make up a fourth for bridge. Every evening Dolly was obliged to go upstairs to bed. This she did not mind, for Hugo did not attract her sexually, but she felt slighted. Finally, after a year of filial obedience, she managed to activate Hugo into making a proposal. Her face radiant, but this time her expression determined, she announced the news to Toni and her bridge partner, an elderly Austrian dentist. This time, in front of a witness, there was no going back.

They were married quietly. Why quietly, I asked my mother, when both Toni and Dolly were so fond of display? Apparently Toni had insisted on a quiet wedding, which she now saw as an occasion for less than rapturous self-congratulation. An antagonism had grown up between Dolly and herself. Dolly continued to address her as '*Maman chérie*', although it cost her a great deal to do so, while Toni, for her part, tended to give orders, now

that she could no longer dismiss Dolly to the upstairs flat. There were house rules, and the rules
remained those of Toni Ferber. Another six
months of filial obedience followed. Finally, now
that she had traditional means of persuasion at her
disposal, Dolly prevailed upon Hugo to apply for
the Brussels post which he had described to her
in all innocence. Hugo was undoubtedly less adept
than his wife. However, he too was sick of
Maresfield Gardens and the company of so many
women, that of his sister and Nanny Sweetman
as well as his mother and Dolly. They left with
enormous pantomimes of regret. Toni watched
them from the window, her face set in that stony
expression which I remember from the time when
I so briefly knew her.

We seek to form attachments where no attachments properly exist. Toni accepted her disappointment, which mirrored exactly her disappointment
in both her father and her husband. Unlike most
people she had learned something from this. When
Hugo, her last love, left, she concentrated her considerable resources on living alone, although my
mother and Nanny Sweetman remained a guarantee against total solitude. She dressed carefully
every day, was in regular attendance at the hairdresser, and played cards with her friends in the
evenings. Gradually she went out less and less,
and preferred her own neighbourhood, where the
shopkeepers knew her, to any other. She knew
now that she could expect little from Dolly; the
removal to Brussels had told her that. She grad-

ually came to see that Dolly had never liked her, but had used her, as she in fact had hoped to use Dolly. She was a lonely woman, but too dignified ever to admit to this loneliness. Hugo telephoned from time to time, but never often enough. Dolly wrote, in a wild scrawling hand, giving details of their life, which seemed to be exciting, and ending with protestations of affection. When they came back to Maresfield Gardens for Christmas she felt she hardly knew them. Their conversation was full of names unfamiliar to her. 'Whom did you say?' she would ask. And Dolly would later remark to Hugo, 'I'm afraid *Maman* has aged a great deal. Don't you agree?' He saw no difference in his mother, who had always seemed to him to be the same age, but by that date he accepted his wife's views on everything, from force of habit, as he had once agreed, half listening only, to his mother.

Nevertheless Toni's first visit to Brussels was a moderate success. Her heart beat like a girl's as the taxi drew up in the Rue de la Loi: it had come to seem like a great adventure. She was congratulated enthuiastically on having made the journey, as if she were a hundred years old; several times she caught Dolly, her head on one side, with a fixed sentimental smile on her face. Clearly she was to be regarded as no more than an elderly relative, someone venerable but not quite up to the mark. Hugo, when he returned from the bank in the evening, joined his wife in profuse expressions of delight. Apart from this there seemed to be very little to talk about, although the litany of unfamiliar names, now longer, formed the burden of the conversation. Dolly seemed older, more settled. She was beautifully turned out, beautifully coiffed and manicured, but she seemed to Toni to have lost some of her zest, to have become glossier but more watchful. Once more showing her genius for adaptability, she even managed to look Belgian: there was a higher colour in her cheeks, and she carried herself with a kind of added consequence which was not entirely characteristic.

Toni felt a pang of genuine regret when she remembered Dolly's younger self. She felt an even keener regret when she contemplated her son, whose once golden curls had become sparse and were grey above the ears, and whose once lithe figure had thickened disadvantageously, so that he now had a little round stomach, of which he seemed rather fond, for he tended to give it free rein, sitting slumped in his chair, his chest caved in, his stomach well to the fore. Toni sighed and realised that she must now be considered old herself, although until now she had not been conscious of age. When she thought about it at all she congratulated herself on putting up a good fight. She was forced to admit that Hugo was not putting up half so good a fight, but when he looked up from his soup, which he had been drinking rather greedily, and smiled at her, as he had smiled at her when he was a young boy, her heart smote her and she made a pretext of tiredness after the journey in order to weep a few tears in the privacy of their spare room. She spent a sleepless night watching a square of moonlight reflected in the tall mirror hanging on the dark blue patterned wall to the left of her bed and imagining that she was a girl in Vienna once again, sleeping in a similar bedroom, with a similar polished wood floor, and the same smell of beeswax fustiness that now came back to her with hallucinatory reality.

This bad night weakened her a little, so that she faced the following day with diminished enthusiasm. The maid, Annie Verkade, brought her coffee at eight o'clock, after which she trailed timidly into the dining-room in search of something more substantial. There she found Hugo, surrounded by the crumbs of several croissants, being berated by his wife. Conversation was abruptly halted when she entered the room, to be replaced once more by profuse expressions of welcome. She was given more coffee, and was invited to help herself to the one remaining croissant. She was then told that she would be left to her own devices that morning ('Remember, *Maman,* you are on holiday!') but that the afternoon was to be kept free, for a treat was to be provided: the person invariably referred to as dear Adèle Rougier was coming to tea. Annie would be rather busy all morning preparing for this event, and so Toni would quite understand if she, Dolly, were to make herself scarce as well. Dear Adèle had such a sweet tooth, and various items must be bought with which to tempt her always fickle fancy. In the end Toni opted to walk to the bank with Hugo; it was the only time she managed to get him to herself. Then she wandered around, gaining confidence, found a café, ordered and drank more coffee, and with a revival of her hopes and expectations made her way back to the Rue de la Loi in time for lunch.

The afternoon was not so successful. At five o'clock the living-room, where she had shyly joined Dolly after the rest she had been persuaded to take, was ready to receive Adèle Rougier, who seemed to have assumed a phenomenal importance in Dolly's life. Toni detested her on sight. Adèle Rougier was a tall vague elderly woman, brilliantly dressed, perfumed, coiffed and generally ministered to in a concerted effort on the part of her friends, minions, and hangers-on to conceal her very real ineffectuality and incompetence. Toni saw at a glance that whereas she herself was comfortably off this woman was massively, helplessly rich. The Congolese mines which had provided her family's fortune had no doubt also yielded the diamond and sapphire brooch pinned to her left shoulder, the diamond and sapphire earrings that peeped from below the dry bronze waves of her hair, and the triple row of faultless pearls which adorned her long thin neck. Immediately a discussion took place as to whether Adèle Rougier should retain or discard her almost ankle-length mink coat; her hesitations and misgivings were met by endless praise and reassurance. Toni saw at once that she had been surpassed, utterly downgraded in importance by Adèle Rougier, to whom Dolly now addressed her energies as if she were that devoted daughter she had once been in reality. For Adèle Rougier needed an intercessor between herself and the menacing outer world: when she left the comfort of her home she needed to know that there was someone at the end of the journey — always made in her chauffeur-driven car — to whom she could recount her various tales of woe: her favourite scarf mislaid, no doubt stolen, a disturbing dream which she would insist on recounting in muddled detail, as she did now, her fork playing with the fragmented macaroon on the plate which Dolly had reverently placed before her, her fur coat laid on the back of her chair in case she suddenly decided to put it on again. Toni remembered her dream of the night before and smiled to herself ironically. To whom could she now recount such dreams? To whom could she confide that the presence of Annie in her bedroom that morning had for a moment confused her into remembering the silent watchful figure of Frau Zimmermann, whom her father had finally married, and who had persuaded him to retire to Lausanne, where they had both ended their days?

'And how long are you staying?' asked Adèle Rougier at last, making a heroic and visible effort at interesting herself in something other than her own concerns.

Toni watched Dolly take a tiny embroidered napkin and carefully adjust Adèle Rougier's gleaming lipstick which had leaked from the corners of her discontented and childish mouth. She made a rapid decision.

'Three days,' she said.

'But *Maman*,' Dolly protested. 'You promised us a week.'

'I'm rather tired, my dear,' said Toni, playing the old lady card. Suddenly she could not wait to get home.

'Then we must take you out tomorrow,' said Dolly.

Toni noticed how she was now the guest not of Hugo and Dolly but of Dolly and Adèle Rougier, a woman who could not even tidy up her own lipstick. Had she been less phlegmatic she would have been violently angry. But by now she was a cold woman, cold in her disappointment, and her doctor had warned her that she had a tendency to high blood pressure. Therefore she merely smiled enigmatically, held out her hand to Adèle Rougier, and went to her room.

The next day was spent in Adèle Rougier's car, or rather in the back of it, crushed between Dolly and the woman who was now apparently her hostess, and suffocated by that same woman's asphyxiating scent. Any scenery she managed to see was glimpsed through misted windows, for the car was heated, even uncomfortably so. Nevertheless Adèle Rougier wore her mink coat. Toni wore her travelling coat of grey lamb, which she thought much more suitable.

'Poor me,' said Dolly, 'in my old cloth coat.'

It was to Adèle Rougier's meagre credit that she

took no notice of this remark.

On the evening of the second day Adèle Rougier came for bridge. She was an inveterate gambler and a bad player; nevertheless Hugo continued to lose to her. She gathered up her winnings in a dry red-nailed hand and put them in a small purse of gold mesh. She then turned jerkily to Toni and proffered the same hand.

'So nice to have met you,' she said, in the English her governess had taught her. After which Toni had felt herself dismissed.

She loved and mourned her son, who had seemed to her to be as good-humoured and as distracted as he had always been but simultaneously spoilt and diminished. He had accepted her presence as inevitable, but had not seemed particularly pleased to see her. In this she was mistaken. Hugo loved his mother, but was under the influence of his wife. Used to being dominated by a woman, he accepted, perhaps ruefully, that he had made a choice (or that it had been made for him) and that he now took his lead from Dolly, whom he sometimes took to be his parent, a replacement for that original parent who was now so far away. Whatever frustration this state of affairs occasioned Dolly was only visible in her quick bright angry smiles, her fidgeting impatience, and her increased social ambition. The beseeching look of anticipation — 'Love me! Save me!' — was no longer to be seen.

It was consciousness of this last fact that sent Toni off once again to Brussels, two years after her original visit. She was not entirely heartless, and she thought her son might need advice. But once again she was subjected to the company of Adèle Rougier, and a day in the back of the car, this time filled with three fur coats. It was understood that an excursion of this nature was something of a privilege: another was decreed for the following day. This she could hardly bear to contemplate, but the alternative was to be left in the flat with Annie, who this time struck her as laconic to the point of insolence and somewhat dirty in the mornings. She longed for the peace of Maresfield Gardens, for the discreet company of her daughter, now a quiet and agreeable young woman, whose wedding she must organise. (My parents relieved her of this duty by walking to the Registry Office one sunny Friday morning.) When she got home, after that second disappointing visit, she sank gratefully back onto her own feather pillows and vowed never to travel again. And I know she never did. That was the beginning of Toni's reclusion; her mind remained active but she aged in body. Perhaps she mourned her son prematurely; perhaps she always had. At any event when he died she was dry-eyed and stoical. She realised, after that disastrous visit to Brussels — belated in every sense — that Dolly had removed Hugo from her, but that Dolly was not perhaps as pleased as she might have been with the exchange. Yet the marriage had lasted; it had even lasted for a respectable number of years, a fact more to Dolly's credit than to Hugo's. When he died there was nothing more for Toni to feel. She endured, she continued, but she had become silent, strict; she did not welcome interruptions. She was not pleased when Dolly turned up after the funeral, accompanied by Annie, her fur coat, and several pieces of luggage. It seemed that she was prepared to stay, but where? The top flat which she had once occupied with her mother was no longer empty.

'There is very little room,' said Toni moderately, although she was appalled.

'Annie can sleep in Etty's room,' replied Dolly, in a manner that was almost cheerful.

Indeed Dolly was cheerful, a fact which finally antagonised her mother-in-law. From time to time she gave way to explosions of grief which nevertheless had something enthusiastic about them. She was older, of course, more stolid, harsher: she had had to come to terms with change as well as with age. The pallid sister-in-law, of whom she had taken no notice, was now a married woman and a mother. Her mother-in-law was now a grim but not enfeebled old lady, whose censoriousness could be taken for granted. When she died — and that day could not be far distant — Dolly would make over the flat, she decided, brighten it up, maybe sell it and move nearer to town.

But Toni had her own views on the matter. She felt no animus against Dolly: she simply wanted her to disappear. What animus she felt was for Adèle Rougier and the fiasco of the Catholic funeral which she had so insistently arranged and for which she had no doubt paid. Dolly referred to this several times, hoping either to impart comfort or to impress, possibly both. Toni's response was not what she expected.

'Let us come to an understanding, Dolly,' she said. 'There is no room for you here. In any case I am used to being alone. You had better find somewhere else.'

'But *Maman chérie,* my resources won't stretch to it. You know how extravagant Hugo was.'

Toni had not known this, had seen no signs of it when Hugo had lived at home.

'You can rent a small flat,' she said. 'I will help you out initially. In fact I will make you a small allowance. But it will be small, Dolly. You will have to get rid of your maid.'

'Annie stays with me,' said Dolly flatly.

She found a flat off the Edgware Road, in one of those streets which lead into St John's Wood. Toni never saw it, which was just as well, as the flat was rather spacious, with separate servants' quarters and a drawing-room large enough to accommodate four tables of bridge. She settled in quite well, but never forgave Toni for what she considered her insolence. She had not been snubbed in so decisive a fashion since she was a girl at school, jeered at because her mother consorted with prostitutes. Ancient social resentments were stirred in her, just as ancient snobberies had been revived in Toni, on whom she was now dependent for her allowance. By mutual agreement they never met, but chose to communicate through my mother, whom Dolly took to visiting quite frequently.

'*Chere Mère,*' said Dolly, screwing up her mouth into a humorous grimace. 'I'm afraid she's getting old and intolerant. *Very* difficult. I don't envy you, Etty.'

Old and intolerant Toni was, but she was still capable of settling her own affairs. Shortly before her death she sold the house in Maresfield Gardens and moved into a small suite in a private hotel. She died quietly in her sleep one night, without giving any trouble. She left her money to my mother, with a sum in trust for myself. Dolly's allowance was to be paid by the bank on the first Monday of every month.

'Dear Etty, you deserve every penny of it,' said Dolly, with a caressing glance at my mother. 'So devoted. And Jane too.' This surprised me: my mother had been dutiful but not devoted, whereas I had hardly known my grandmother.

'As for me,' said Dolly, 'I shall just have to be brave, shan't I?' She gave a brave laugh. 'It won't be easy, but I've never been one for indulging in self-pity. Remember what I told you, Jane?'

'Yes.'

'And what was that?'

'Something about singing and dancing.'

'That's right. You won't see me with a frown on my face, despite my difficulties. And I must go to Nice soon, to visit Mother. So many expenses.' She sighed. 'Well, this won't do. Such an out of the way place you live in, Etty. I wonder you don't move. Jane, are you clever enough to ring for a taxi?'

I considered myself grown-up at the time — I must have been nine or ten — and was therefore discomposed at the suggestion that I might not be up to the task of making a telephone call, I who talked to my friend Marigold Chance for hours.

When I returned to the drawing-room I saw Dolly clasp my mother in a lavish embrace.

'Dear Etty,' she said, holding her at arm's length and contemplating her, head on one side. 'Funny girl,' she added. She then took and held her hands for a long and musing moment. There was the merest whisper of paper, so faint as to be barely noticeable, as the cheque was handed over.

4

I grew up English and unafraid. My parents' world was my world: I inherited the long walks, the afternoons of reading, the almost silent company of Miss Lawlor, without surprise, without rebellion, peaceably and comfortably, with a sense of order which I have never recovered. I was happy with my lot, with our modest existence, which I now realise was far from modest by contemporary standards: my father's work at the bank was secure, while my mother had her own income. Modesty, to me, signified a certain unostentatious prosperity, never indulged, never advertised, and never, ever, mentioned in conversation. I was not aware of money, or of the need to make money. As far as I was concerned I would go to Cambridge, as my father had done, and then something interesting would come along, some job in publishing, which would surely be suitable for someone with my love of books: I thought I had only to advertise this love for the publishers to come running towards me from all sides, with offers of appreciable salaries and agreeable conditions of work. It will be seen that I had confidence in a world of full employment, one which no longer existed. We were on the threshold of the 1980s and although we knew nothing of what was in store for us, the best years of our lives were over. But at the time we could detect no change; our world, or rather my world, was fixed, ineluctable, of the same order as the rising and the setting of the sun.

Some of this confidence came from the sun itself. We had had two radiant and prolonged summers, so extravagant, so unexpected, so altogether exceptional that they had done something to alter our perceptions of ourselves, as if we had been granted a more favourable situation on the planet. Suddenly people had sought shade, coolness; expeditions to shops were undertaken in the very early morning, while the afternoons were given over to drawn curtains and an uncharacteristic siesta. In Battersea Park, where I walked in the blissful glory of the sun, bodies lay under trees in violent outflung attitudes, like the peasants in Brueghel's *Land of Cockaigne*. 'Don't go too far,' my mother would warn me, as I set off on one of my walks. 'Keep in the shade.' But I loved that efflorescence and thought the effort of walking negligeable. Sometimes I walked into town, which was not a great distance. I wanted to look at pictures, either in the National Gallery or in the Wallace Collection. This last was a haven of coolness, even of gloom, yet it was deserted, except for discreet knots of American ladies looking at snuff boxes in glass cases. To this day I can retrieve the sensation of walking over the hot gravel of the courtyard, my head hammering from the unforgiving glare, and the sensation of dignity which descended on me as I made my way up the stairs.

Ahead of me were the great Bouchers, master-pieces neglected by most visitors but to me of the same order as the astonishing weather, which, if I turned my head, I could see through the dusty windows. In comparison with the pictures the sun suddenly looked tawdry, exhausted. I remembered the bodies of the young men lying under the trees, dreaming like children in their brief half-hour of liberty, and I turned back to the pictures, to the effortless immaculate soaring of the figures in their spectacular universe. The throbbing in my head died away, as did all bodily sensations, as I stood at the top of the stairs, drowning in blueness.

That is my memory of those summers: the glory of the weather and the refreshment of art. It seemed to me that most of life was mirrored in art, or perhaps that it was the great distinction of art to hold a mirror up to nature, to be an interpreter of phenomena, of situations. It will be seen that my understanding was fairly primitive. But it has remained a resource for me, to search for an analogue in painting for some emotion which I could either not conquer or bear to examine. Later on, of course, I was to find these analogues in music. I never, or rarely, appropriated them from literature, which I was able to study more objectively. Literature for me was a magnificent destiny for which I was not yet fully prepared. Like my parents I read a great deal, sinking into my bed at night with one of the books my father chose for me, but too often distracted by the flushed sky or the solemnity of the advancing night. The nights were short; the mornings dawned brilliant and very early. And then there was another marvellous day to fill.

Like everyone I remember only the summers. I know that in 1976 the autumn was abrupt and wet, but was somehow of lesser importance than the summer it had succeeded. This propensity to remember the summers of our youth has begun to interest me. I think it is inspired by regret for something which has been lost along the way, since it seems to be a universal feeling. Elderly people remember golden days long past with identical expressions of joy and tenderness, or, more properly speaking, longing. As life proceeds, and the long journey is recognised for what it is, the look that is cast back unconsciously falsifies. That there were winters is a fact which is discarded, seemingly forgotten. And the longing for more summer, more life, intensifies as the dark days wear on, as if light and life have become interchangeable, as perhaps they are.

But the summers of which I speak were real enough, as were my long walks, which my mother accepted, as she had accepted the walks she used to take with my father. She no longer took those walks, preferring to move dreamily but contentedly round the flat and to wait for my father to come home and join her. The heart murmur which had been diagnosed when she was a child had resurfaced after years of giving no sign. She was not ill — in fact she had never seemed better — but she obeyed her doctor, rested, and saved her energies for our various homecomings, when she would greet us with joy and satisfaction. Occasionally she would stand still, as if listening to music, and then we knew that her heart had missed a beat, but she was so used to this that it did not seem to alarm her. If my father were present he would unconsciously hold his breath until she began to move freely again. Yet within seconds they would smile at each other and go about their business, as if disorder had no place in their universe, and as if they therefore had no cause to fear.

When I got home from one of my walks my mother would express gratification at my audacity and would hasten to pour out the tea, summoning Miss Lawlor to witness my prowess. I remember Miss Lawlor standing at the door of the drawing-room, her straw hat already in place (she usually went home in the early afternoon, but occasionally liked to linger) and miming admiration in her typically muted fashion. We were all affected by the weather in one way or another.

'Sit down, Violet,' said my mother. 'You're not going out in this heat without a cup of tea. It's supposed to cool one down, although I can't see how it can. It is simply the best drink of all; ours not to reason why. And help yourself to cake. Jane? Eat something, darling.'

But there was no need to encourage me. I ate and drank substantially, as did my parents. Miss Lawlor, as I have said, shared my mother's lunch, and mine too if I were at home, and helped to prepare our dinner. Gradually she fell into the habit of joining my mother at teatime, which pleased my mother, as they were very fond of each other. Of the two of them Miss Lawlor was the more discreet, if that is possible. Her conversation consisted largely of gentle murmurings of agreement. She was a timid woman who had long sought a shelter from the world's harshness, and had found this in the church. My mother tried to make her feel at ease in our home and I think succeeded. Although she had come to us from my father's side of the family she loved both my parents equally well, and was content to share their lives rather than seek one of her own. I never knew her age, although she must have been a good fifteen years older than my father. But age had not attacked her as it attacks more robust women; she simply became a little more tentative every year, while from her faded face her large brown eyes shone forth with undimmed faith in the world beyond this world, which my parents, free-thinkers, took care never to disparage in her presence. Even when we were alone together no aspersions were allowed: the world to come was left intact for those who believed in it. This was considered part of a general courtesy, all the more impressive in that it was completely undemonstrative. Such a training is difficult to lose, even in situations which call for something more decisive. I never lost my temper, even as a child, and have remained incapable of doing so to this day.

After tea my friend Marigold Chance might receive a visit. She lived in Bramerton Street, a short walk over the bridge. She had been my friend since we had started school together at the age of four, and now that our schooldays were approaching their end we had become aware that life might separate us: I would go to Cambridge and Marigold would begin her nurse's training. I loved her, as I loved everyone; I was not jealous of her beauty, which was considerable and was to remain so until after the birth of her third child. If I envied her at all it was for her relations, who were numerous. I particularly envied her for her two great-aunts, Catherine and Eleanor — Kate and Nell — two vigorous and heroically built women who travelled down from Glasgow every summer with a cargo of shortbread, whisky, Shetland pullovers for Marigold's father and brother, and kilts for her mother and for Marigold herself. Kate and Nell, who lived together in harmonious spinsterhood, or single blessedness, as they put it, felt vaguely sorry for the perfectly capable girl their nephew had married, simply because they felt sorry for any woman held in bondage to a man. Paradoxically, they doted on Marigold's father and brother, and were always trying to devise treats for them. From the double bed in which they had spent their chaste night they would rise and make the early morning tea, anxious to get everyone out of the house so that they could get on with some serious baking. 'Sit down, dear,' they would say to Marigold's mother. 'Let me do that. Or let Nell. That's what we're here for, to give you a rest.'

The idea that aunts could be benevolent was new to me. The only aunt I knew was Dolly, who was selfish, capricious and shrewd, but who could not be imagined in the act of doing anyone a good turn. Therefore it was particularly disagreeable to me to get home and find Dolly installed in either my father's or my mother's chair. Her visits were now less frequent than they had been after my grandmother's death, for she seemed to have a mysteriously flourishing social life. She had inherited from my grandmother, or rather she had appropriated from her in lieu of anything more marketable, my grandmother's entire circle of friends, 'the refugees', as she laughingly called them. The old ladies who were my grandmother's contemporaries still loved their game of cards and were intrigued by Dolly, who seemed anxious to carry on her mother-in-law's traditions. And these old ladies had married sons and daughters, all of them substantial people, who were not averse to going to St John's Wood for tea on a Sunday and staying on for bridge and Annie's canapés. These soirées were remarkably successful. Curiously enough Dolly got on very well with the women, all of whom became her dearest friends until she fell out with one or other of them. These *déboires* would be reported to my mother with full accompaniment of heaving bosom and flashing eyes. 'That woman,' she would say. 'Don't even mention the name to me! When I think of all I've done for her!' My mother knew better than to enquire on this point; she knew that her role was

108

essentially a humble one. 'I've introduced her to various people, influential people,' Dolly would continue. 'And then she has the effrontery to tell me not to rely on her making up a four in future. She's going to be busy, she says.' This was uttered with a fine show of scorn. Neither of us said anything. We knew that Dolly and her ungrateful friend or enemy — it was often difficult to know which — would be on the telephone to each other as usual the following morning. I did not understand such behaviour then, but I do now. It is the behaviour of the true primitive.

Dolly would come to see my mother in the spirit of a benefactor visiting her indulgence on the unfortunate. No doubt she came for another, simpler reason as well, but my mother was so discreet that we never knew whether this was or was not the case. My father never asked her again, aware that to do so would cause her embarrassment.

'Dolly was here today,' she might say apologetically. Later that evening she might sigh, 'Poor Dolly.' For whatever pity Dolly felt for my mother was as nothing beside the genuine pity my mother felt for Dolly.

One particular day I got home to find Dolly drinking tea with my mother. It was a chill rainy autumn day, but Dolly was in one of her beautiful silk dresses: she seemed to generate her own microclimate, another characteristic of the primitive disposition. It seemed that she was about to go to Brussels to see Adèle Rougier. She was always about to leave for either Brussels or Nice, although

I doubt whether she left London as frequently as she said she did: we had no real notion of her movements since she disregarded matters of fact like dates and times. Her conversation was, as always, filled with the names of people entirely unknown to us but known to Dolly through her bridge-playing afternoons. Sometimes she did go to Nice, to see her mother, but had nothing to say when she returned. Indeed we did not quite know when she had returned, since she was uncharacteristically reticent about her mother, on whom she continued to lavish her entire store of tenderness. The tenderness, I suspect, undermined her: she preferred a more embattled attitude to life, which she was able to exercise more satisfactorily in London or Brussels. Visits to Brussels seemed to yield more in the way of argument and patronage, two of her more preferred modes, as if she were eternally pitted against adversaries, on whom she might decide to confer friendship. My mother, who was treated to a full account of Dolly's recent triumphs, had nothing against these visits; in fact she encouraged them, no doubt in more ways than one. She regarded Dolly's life as flighty, even tragic; she wished to get her away from the card table and put her life on an even keel. She saw attendance on an elderly acquaintance as a more serious undertaking than the endless telephone conversations of which her mornings seemed to consist.

'Poor Adèle,' Dolly said on this occasion, screwing up her face in that well-known grimace. 'Poor old thing. I'm afraid she's not what she was. Not that she was ever very bright, but with her money she didn't need to be. *De gros sous,*' she added. 'I go over to give her a hand, really. I do little things for her, post her letters, remind her to take her pills. She's always been so fond of me that I can't really do anything less.'

During the absence of response that this tender eulogy called forth the thought came to both of us, no doubt simultaneously, that the exchange must have been mutually beneficial.

'Not that it's very entertaining for me,' Dolly went on. 'There are so many people I'd rather look up. But I'm very loyal. And I don't let her see . . . I suppose I'll go on looking after her for as long as she needs me. Poor old girl,' she added pensively. Her face was a beautiful study in compassion.

'You stay with her, I suppose?' said my mother.

'Well, of course, Etty. Where else would I stay? Her house is all the home I have now.' Now that your mother has sold Maresfield Gardens was what she meant. This left my mother feeling properly reproached. Dolly, magnanimous in victory, then turned her attention to myself.

'And what about you, Jane? What are you going to do with your life?'

'Well, I'm going to Cambridge next year . . .'

'Are you indeed? Well, you know best. But I always think that charm is more important to a woman than a lot of degrees. Don't underestimate charm,' she said, peering at me to see if she could detect any.

I was lacking in charm, of course, a tall thin girl with no visible assets and no figure to speak of. For many years I looked younger than I was, which encouraged people to be quite outspoken in my presence, as if I were too obtuse or too juvenile to understand them. Dolly, in particular, was given to dropping huge hints to my mother over my head. If she caught me looking at her she assumed that I was so dim that I would be grateful for any show of interest.

'When I was your age, Jane, I was thinking of other things, I can assure you.' She sighed. 'What wouldn't I give to have those days again! But times were hard, harder than they've ever been for you, Jane. But still I'm sure you'll want to get married one day.' She looked dubious, as if such an eventuality were barely credible.

'Jane has plenty of time,' said my mother gently.

I think she sensed, instinctively, as I did, that Dolly would examine any romance I might have had for possible worldly advantages, and was as determined as I was to keep this area of my life unexamined. Dolly may have intuited this, and have felt some of her usual contempt for our decorum. But the matter was dropped, except for the fact that she could not resist a final sally. She kissed my mother fondly, patted her cheek, and said that her car must not be kept waiting. She had taken to using the services of a car-hire firm in the Edgware Road, which she said was cheaper than taking taxis. At the door she turned to me and lifted a warning finger.

'Don't forget, Jane. Charm!'

She was back some ten days later. As she had not been expected I was not there. I heard my mother describing this second visit, so close to the previous one, to my father.

'It seems she had a misunderstanding with this friend of hers, this Adèle Rougier,' she said. 'Quite a serious one, I believe. She says she would have stormed out of the house, but she had nowhere to go.'

'Couldn't she have gone to an hotel?' asked my father.

'Oh, no, darling.' She sounded genuinely shocked. 'As she said, what would that have looked like? So they stayed in their separate quarters and the maid brought them their meals on trays. It must have been very uncomfortable.'

She left it at that. No doubt she felt genuinely sad that the trips to Brussels were to be discontinued. At the same time she took on the burden of tiding Dolly over without a moment's hesitation.

My father merely said, 'Shall we have some music?' I think he considered Dolly to be something of a joke. Any regrets he might have had that my mother was so vulnerable he kept to himself. But I think her vulnerability was on his mind, and he determined to protect her as best he could.

'I've asked John Pickering to dinner,' he said.

John Pickering was a slightly younger colleague of my father's at the bank, a correct and apparently ageless creature whose almost heroic reticence con-

cealed a certain emotivity. My father had befriended Pickering after the latter had been involved in a painful divorce suit: his wife of only
five years had announced that she was leaving him
for another man, with whom she had been having
an affair, and that she was divorcing him for mental
cruelty. Mental cruelty was what she called his
apparent impassivity, which was in fact an extreme
form of discretion, and a desire not to burden her
with his preoccupations. He was a grave man, and
perhaps not easy to live with, but his wife was
cruel to denounce him. 'You never make me
laugh,' she is supposed to have accused him, but
her bags were already packed. Pickering, as well
as losing his wife, lost face, for the case was made
public. My father offered friendship at a difficult
time in Pickering's life; he appreciated and trusted
the younger man, and this appreciation and trust
were returned. They never confided in each other,
for that would have involved additional loss of face,
but walks were taken together, and at one point
powers of attorney were exchanged.

'If anything happens to me John will look after
your affairs,' he told my mother.

'But nothing is going to happen to you,' she
said lovingly.

'No, of course not,' he replied.

Perhaps because she sensed disapproval of
Dolly's visits (and the reason for those visits) she
took to sending me over to Dolly's flat, with a
discreet envelope and some of Miss Lawlor's biscuits.

'You needn't stay,' she said. 'Just ask her how she is. You can walk there,' she added encouragingly. 'You know you love your walk.'

The Edgware Road was not as attractive to me as the Wallace Collection, but in the winter the Wallace Collection had lost some of its charm. The blue of the Bouchers had faded into the surrounding darkness and I began to dislike the silence. I was quite glad to exchange the museum for the animation of the streets. Nevertheless I timed my visits to Dolly at unusual hours so that she would not detain me. I was due to leave school the following June; my penultimate Christmas holiday seemed then a harbinger of better holidays to come, of vacations, in fact, when I could devote myself to the business of reading. Dolly seemed to me of minor importance, indeed of no importance at all.

'She might ask you to lunch,' said my mother. 'You know how busy she is in the afternoons.'

Indeed, Dolly was invariably busy. I thought the late morning the best time to catch her: certainly it would leave me free for the more important business of the day. So I turned up at about eleven, only to be informed by Annie, *'Madame fait sa toilette.'*

Annie's attitude towards me was one of uncompromising intransigence, as if I were an importunate creditor, or an employee from the Gas Board come to read the meter. I have reason to believe that she behaved like this all the time, although as she was generally silent she was thought to be a good and loyal servant: certainly she officiated at the afternoon bridge parties graciously enough and was appreciated by the guests; Dolly was envied for having a live-in maid, rare at that date, and certainly in those circumstances, although nobody was quite sure of the exact nature of those circumstances. Annie's taciturnity was otherwise charmless and her physique was unpleasing: she had a grim unadorned face framed in dry faded brown hair, a short stocky body, and the powerful forearms of a much larger woman. The surprising thing about Annie, which I was to learn much later, at a time when Dolly released more of the truth about their lives, was that she was a married woman, or rather a widow, like Dolly herself; she had been abandoned by her husband, from whom she had never heard again, just as Fanny Schiff had lost sight of her own husband after his departure for Colmar. But unlike Dolly, Annie had had a child, a daughter, now living on the outskirts of Ostend with a husband and children of her own. At moments of high mutual antagonism Annie would declare her intention of abandoning Dolly and going back to Belgium. These disagreements were uninhibited, and were pursued with liberal amounts of criticism on both sides. Both had the gift of losing their tempers without actually inconveniencing themselves, so that having any kind of argument was something of a recreation for them, a therapeutic airing of views, rather like a party political broadcast, which is meant to be taken seriously but so rarely is. Annie's attitude to Dolly was tight-lipped; she both approved and disapproved, admired and grudged. Too genuinely shy and misanthropic to have friends of her own, she enjoyed the bridge parties, where some small tribute generally came her way ('Your lovely sandwiches — you spoil us, Annie'), but deplored the fact that life behind the scenes was frankly unimpressive, in a rented flat, with saucepans and linen of a left-over nature, with a Hoover that failed to work, and no decent shops near at hand.

Dolly appreciated her for her solidarity, for the reliability of her general duties — the bath run, the morning coffee brought to her in bed, the generally excellent service in the drawing-room — but also because Annie was in a way her only intimate friend. In this she was quite different from Dolly's other friends, who were also her enemies, and whose misdeeds and treacheries she complacently recounted to my mother, without ever explaining how their perpetrators had ever come back again into favour. Or if she did explain it was with a large-hearted gesture of emotional superiority: 'But I'm like that, Etty, I can't stand pettiness. I could have taken offence but life's too short. Besides, I hope I'm big enough to forgive and forget. As to my real opinion of her, well, that's my business. I'm sure I don't have to explain myself to all and sundry. If I feel a little hurt I just rise above it.' Singing and dancing again, I said to myself, for I was present at this explanation, which was one of many: Dolly fell out with her friends on a regular basis. I had the choice between two admonitions, if my expression, over which I usually had excellent control, veered towards hilarity. If she caught the tail-end of an agonised twitch of the muscle she chose to believe that it expressed concern of a more general nature. But though obtuse where I was concerned, as she was with anyone young, she was quick to sense criticism. So it was either her recommendation of singing and dancing that was on offer, or, more usually, 'Charm, Jane, charm!'

I also believe that Dolly appreciated Annie because with her she managed to reconstruct the atmosphere of her mother's workroom, and with it the unthinking acceptance of female company. Dolly, whose relations with the world were of a confrontational nature, whose plans were devised in secret, whose strategies were masked by a smile of affability, needed comfort, although she seemed to need it rather less than anyone else, certainly less than any of her acquaintances, for I do not think she looked on them as friends. Dolly and Annie did not keep one another company except for one brief moment in the middle of the day, nor would either of them ever dream of confiding in the other. But they shared the same opinions, and that may be a more significant similarity. They held exactly the same views on the people who came to the house, so that Annie always knew and accepted Dolly's passing antagonisms, and more often than not expressed her own, however briefly. 'Celle-là!' she would say, with a dismissive pursing of the lips. None of this prevented her from being utterly impassive while she was on duty. Like a butler in a grander establishment she took a pride in her most expressionless efficiency. Serving the coffee, returning each fur coat correctly to its owner, bidding each guest a muted farewell, she was the epitome of dutiful discretion.

I found her arguably more human than Dolly, who always impressed me as a sort of mutant, not quite a real person. In this I did her an injustice, but I had been brought up in an atmosphere of simplicity and found it hard to credit the deviousness of Dolly's behaviour, if indeed it was devious: with the benefit of hindsight I now see that it was remarkably, even transparently straightforward. But one has to grow into an understanding of such matters, and at the time of those visits to the flat off the Edgware Road, where, like an emissary, I handed over my envelope, tactfully accompanied by Miss Lawlor's biscuits, I was too young and also too inexperienced to read Dolly's admirably disguised signals. Her set of assumptions was so radically different from the ones I accepted as natural that she generally contrived to surprise me every time. My mother, in her naïvety, imagined that my visits would be welcomed, that interest would be shown in me, that a certain goodwill might prevail. In fact I was tolerated, as was indicated by Annie's absence of any sort of conventional greeting, and by the appearance of Dolly only some minutes after I had been seated in the drawing-room and left to read a magazine, for all the world as if I had an appointment with a doctor or a dentist. This did not worry me: I preferred reading anyway. In this fashion I failed to be insulted by Dolly, although I recognised that the potential was always there.

The invitation to lunch did not materialise. Nevertheless I was invited to sit down and watch Dolly eating her own lunch, which took place early, sometimes just before midday. Annie made her delicious and unfamiliar food, which she ate rapidly and cleanly, as if picking the bones of an animal, in itself an animal procedure. I remember a leek tart; I remember a plate of *langue de chat* biscuits with a little Bordeaux poured over them. I often assisted at these lunches with a lingering sense of fascination. To me they were pure spectacle, for I could see that Annie was jealous and would only cook food for one. These lunches were workmanlike, refueling stops before the business of the afternoon, which was usually bridge, either at home or in someone else's house. Once the food was eaten I was permitted to join Dolly in a cup of strong black coffee. Annie too was present; this was their moment of intimacy, after which she went back to the kitchen and tidied up. I can still see their fine teeth closing identically over the lumps of sugar dipped in the staggeringly strong brew. As if to demonstrate their physical imperviousness to the stimulant properties of the coffee, which set my own heart beating, both then retired to their rooms to take a brief rest. Annie's rest was more sombre and more prolonged, after which she would rise and change out of her overall into her black dress and prepare for the afternoon's entertainment. Often she accompanied Dolly to other people's houses to lend a hand. This she never minded doing. My feeling is that she hated to be left out.

If I called when Dolly was engaged in more active preparation for her role I was not always treated with the appropriate formality. *'Madame fait sa toilette,'* said Annie, and a voice from the bathroom would call, 'In here, Jane.' Once I caught her towelling herself after a bath and blushed red with embarrassment. She gave a mocking laugh at such puerility, but the mockery held a jeer with little indulgence in it. The jeer was not only for myself, a pale English schoolgirl, whose adolescent body was still that of a child, but for herself, for the widened hips, the coarse dark pubic hair, and the no longer buoyant breasts. Indifferent to my confusion, or even made provocative by it, she lifted one leg, rested her foot on the rim of the bath, and towelled the inside of her thigh. Then she sighed and said, 'I want to get dressed. Go and wait for me.' I was dismissed. If she had hoped for confidences, either given or received, she was disappointed. I felt the weight of her disappointment, which would soon turn into disapprobation. I sat in the ugly drawing-room and waited for her, although I had nothing to say. I felt she needed some sort of consolation for what I thought of as the awful state of her body. But when she bustled in, in her black and white silk 'afternoon' dress, she was the aunt again, impatient for sensation, hungry for action, myself forgotten.

Two pointers here to the state of her affairs, though not fit, I thought, for my mother's ears. The scent she used was powerful, though agreeable; it did not smell inexpensive. I inhaled it appreciatively, for I have always been sensitive to fine odours. This apparently met with her approval. 'I always use it,' she confided. 'I always have. People know me by it. "We shall know what to give you for Christmas, Dolly," they say. I have quite a stock of it. I'd rather go hungry than go without scent. Remember, Jane, it is so important not to lower one's standards. I have never lowered mine, I'm glad to say.' She turned complacently to one of the many mirrors and patted her hair. Her image of herself once again relegated me to the periphery: I never, during the years of my adolescence and young womanhood, managed to impose my presence on Dolly. I was the equivalent of those donor figures in religious paintings who look clumsy and out of place and whose presence seems barely justified, beside the saints and the madonna, except for the consideration of spot cash.

Another indication of Dolly's resourcefulness: one day as Annie was setting out the tea trolley I admired the cups and saucers, which were exquisitely thin and adorned with painted birds. Dolly, always responsive to admiration, said, 'Those cups are by Porthault, my dear, *c'est la fin du fin*. They belonged to Adèle Rougier. She knew how much I loved them. I always remarked on them when I had tea with her, poor dear. In the end she said, "If you like them so much you'd better have them." So I asked her maid to parcel them up and send them over. They are pretty, aren't they?' They were pretty, and so were the plates, and the silver teaspoons, which presumably were her own, and the fragile cargo of appetisers — tiny rounds of black bread topped with a mousse of smoked salmon, glazed fruit tartlets small enough to disappear in a single mouthful — which Dolly would serve with tea before the main business of the afternoon got under way. Dolly's guests were greedy: she never underestimated their appetites. In this way she was an excellent hostess.

'And how was Dolly?' my mother would ask, when I got home, oddly flattered to have been offered a cup of strong black coffee, if nothing else. 'How did she look?' For she took a wistful but utterly selfless interest in Dolly's health and appearance. Both were in excellent shape, as far as I could see. Dolly's health was robust and pleasingly apparent in her clear dark eyes, the red flush under the olive skin, the pouter pigeon bosom, of which she was clearly proud, and the fine unspoilt hands on which she wore Hugo's diamond ring and her platinum wedding ring. She had an agreeable faith in herself and in her attractions. So confident was she of what she would have called her charm that she refused to wear any make-up other than a thin and glistening thread of lipstick or to dye her hair which was rapidly going grey: the grey in fact softened the black and framed a face which contrived to look on the world with an eager and expectant expression. Once or twice I caught a hint of what she must have looked like as a girl, and I commended her silently for not clinging on to a semblance of youth. In fact, although Dolly claimed to have said goodbye to 'all that', she was still interested in men, but interested in them as consorts rather than as lovers. Though a robustly physical woman she still had something virginal about her; with a little encouragement, that of her mother, perhaps, she would have set out once again to have a good time. My own mother perceived this, and felt all the pathos of which Dolly seemed unaware. For this reason she played her part as an admirer, an adherent, without once demonstrating anything less than perfect good faith.

Dolly was an annexe of our own small family, a footnote, never part of the main text. We all felt this, Dolly included, but as Dolly considered herself to be more interesting than our largely uneventful and so united selves she was happy to accept us as peripheral to her world and to her interests. She descended on us more rarely than she had done when first making her way in what she clearly thought of as more superior company: when she did it was in a spirit of public service, as if to spread a little gossip and glamour into our colourless preoccupations. It was important to her to be admired, and my mother genuinely admired her, not, as Dolly thought, for her social brilliance, but for her uncompromising sense of reality. Thus is it possible to admire someone of whom one disapproves, for having gone further than the distance one is prepared to travel oneself; in such situations it is even possible to admire immodesty, vanity, ruthlessness. In this sense my mother loved Dolly, listened with forbearance to the stories in which some friend received her comeuppance, applauded Dolly's munificence as she continually rose above some quite genuine snubs. In her heart my mother was too aware of her own good fortune to be other than sympathetic to those to whom a similar good fortune had been denied. Yet it must have jarred on her own honesty and humility to express unmitigated acceptance of Dolly's bravado. She chose silence, or muted encouragement, which merely confirmed Dolly's suspicions that my mother was dull, a limited bourgeoise with a bourgeois husband and no social life to speak of. As her own social life grew more resplendent the visits became more distanced; my mother telephoned her regularly, to be given an account of her invitations and her triumphs. Only at the end of these conversations did Dolly issue a peremptory, 'And what about you? All well?' 'Oh, yes, dear,' my mother would reply. 'We are all quite well.'

But we were not. The first indication of a change in our fortunes was mysterious. One night my mother woke up to find the other half of the bed empty. 'Paul?' she queried. 'Paul? Where are you?' Receiving no answer she put on her dressing-gown and went into the drawing-room, where she found my father sitting in a chair in the dark.

'What is it, darling? Have you got indigestion?

125

Shall I make you a hot drink?'

For some reason she did not put on the light. She was no doubt intimidated by the fact that my father did not immediately answer her. In the face of his silence she chose to sit down, and for a silent five minutes they sat in the dark, with no sound but that of a late car on a wet road and no light but that of the faint glow which is always present above a sleeping city.

'Perhaps the cheese?' my mother said finally. 'Perhaps you shouldn't have had the cheese?'

She told me later that she half believed that this was the case. Or perhaps she chose to believe it. My father had given no hint to her of any malaise, and in view of his excellent general health she had no reason to suspect any. Although thin and slight they were moderately resistant, and never seemed to catch colds or be subject to passing infections. It seemed reasonable to her — and the emphasis at this stage was all on reason: fear came later — to suppose that he had eaten something unwise, no doubt at lunch, for she was meticulous in the preparation of food and careful with her menus. After a while he gave a great sigh, and then perhaps she felt the first flicker of anxiety, for he was an equable man and not given to public expressions of downheartedness.

'Won't you come back to bed, darling? You'll catch cold sitting here.'

It was then that he said, 'I am no longer comfortable.' He did not address her by name, which was unusual. In the light of subsequent events this

126

oracular statement took on something of the aura of a declaration and of a warning. At the time, however, my mother merely took his hand and led him back to bed.

In the morning he gave no hint that anything untoward had taken place. He ate the toast and drank the coffee that my mother put in front of him, greeted Miss Lawlor when she arrived, kissed me, and prepared to go to work as usual. In the light of this normality my mother decided to ignore the events of the previous night, that strange colloquy in the dark, and indeed it was easy to ignore, for in retrospect it took on something of the quality of a dream. It was even impossible to estimate how long it had lasted. Five minutes? Half an hour? The uneasiness caused by any episode which takes place in the middle of the night remained below the surface, and to all intents and purposes the day proceeded as it usually did. In the evening my father came home, and we all sat down to dinner. He ate sparingly, which was unusual; what was more unusual was the care with which he raised his fork to his lips, his look of preoccupation as he masticated and swallowed the food, rather as if he had not eaten for a long time and as if he were learning to eat again: his eyes were downcast, and he seemed to study his plate, as if he were unfamiliar with the pattern. When he laid down his fork it was with a hand which very slightly trembled.

Perhaps it was a week later that I became alerted to the situation, which was not yet a situation.

I awoke to hear footsteps in the corridor that separated my bedroom from that of my parents. In a half doze I waited automatically to hear them come back, but in fact I heard a second set of footsteps, the lighter footsteps of my mother. I sat up in bed, and faced black silence. For a time, that incalculable time in the middle of the night, nothing happened. Then I heard what sounded like weeping, but whose I could not make out. I got up and ventured into the passage: empty. Then I made my way, still in the dark, to the drawing-room, where I found my parents sitting hand in hand, my father's head resting on my mother's shoulder.

Whatever had taken place was not apparently to be discussed, at least not between my parents and myself. I felt excluded from this mysterious sorrow, and chose to be indignant, impatient; thus does one disguise one's apprehensions. For a short while it was possible to believe that my father had been ill and was now better. He looked no different. Only the meals we took together became fraught with tension, and we watched with imperfectly disguised anxiety as his trembling fork negotiated a fillet of fish and conveyed it with terrible care to his mouth, and how that same fork was laid down again with evident relief.

'Perhaps a cup of tea?' he would say cheerily, avoiding my mother's sad eyes. 'Tea is better than coffee in the evening. Put the kettle on, Jane.'

And again we would watch the tremulous fingers close round the handle of the cup. Both hands were used to guide the cup to his mouth. This evidence we could no longer ignore. My father's table manners were delicate; in all matters of eating and drinking he insisted on correct usage. For him to hold his cup with both hands and even to drink noisily, with a kind of hunger he had not shown for his food, was an indication of how far he had departed from his normal self. When I see natural history programmes on television I am reminded of my father at that stage of his illness: the eagerness, the desperation of animals feeding and their alertness to danger are all reminiscent of his condition, glimpsed in that microsecond when, all unconscious of my eyes on him, he devoted all his living energies, what remained of them, to drinking the hot sweet liquid, while my mother turned away and wiped her eyes.

At last the doctor was called, the consultant alerted, and the whole dreadful business put in train. He was advised to enter hospital for what was known as treatment but what was in effect pain relief. The cancer, which he had concealed for so long, had reached his spine, and the consultant warned my mother that the pain might be severe. My father chose to be cheerful, although by now he was shaking and grey with the effort of appearing normal. Now that his illness was known he collapsed into it. His one thought was for my mother, whom he entrusted not to me but to Miss Lawlor. This was on the morning of the day on which he left home for good, my mother by his side. I remember the pitifully small suitcase she carried for him, and his arm through hers, for comfort.

Yet in the hospital he seemed to improve. His small room looked out on to the hospital garden, and when I went to see him, in the mornings, before those last days at school, his eyes, now huge, would be filled with the light from that window, as he pointed out to me, with childlike eagerness, a robin, or a sparrow, or occasionally a blackbird. The blackbirds, in particular, gave him pleasure. I would call in again in the late afternoon, after school, to take my mother home. She had of course been with him for most of the day. She was by now as thin as my father, but thin from grief, and I think I knew at that stage that she would not long survive him. I forced myself to be practical, gathered up the increasingly soiled pyjamas, and put them into a bag which I would later empty into the washing machine when my mother had gone to bed. In this way I spared her the worst manifestations of his illness, for he was peaceful in her company, one hand in hers, the other attached to a morphine drip. He seemed content to lie there with his hand in hers, his eyes filled with light and with longing. They did not speak much. Once he told her that he loved her, and once he mentioned John Pickering. For there would unfortunately be business to be carried out, and he knew that my mother would be too bereft to think clearly. Having made these two pronouncements he never spoke again. I would come upon them, in the darkening spring evening, so wordlessly close that I sensed their exaltation, as if they were twin spirits divested of earthly form, as if never could they have achieved such closeness while still imprisoned in their mortal bodies. For a time I feared that they would die together, and I felt coarse and practical as I collected the dirty washing. He died one night while my mother was profoundly asleep in a chair beside him. When I answered the telephone at home in the early morning, my mother's voice said, 'Our darling has left us.' Then the receiver was gently replaced. I went to the hospital to collect her, still feeling clumsy and earth-bound. She let herself be led away quite peaceably, but seemed to have nothing to say. It was only when we got home and were faced with Miss Lawlor's tears that she began to cry, but by then I had warned the doctor who came and gave her a sedative, so that she slept for the remainder of the day.

The rest of the time — for those days and nights which followed were somehow the only authentic time, in comparison with which my own activities became negligeable — was baroque, bizarre, oddly acceptable. The flat was intermittently filled with people who drifted in and out and seemed to congregate in the evenings. Some of these people I hardly knew; some were our friends and neighbours. People came from the bank, the doctor came, my friend Marigold came with her mother and father, even some of my grandmother's surviving cronies came, making their way across London in their ancient fur coats, their sticks tapping their way along the pavement under a late spring sky of palest green. I was totally inadequate to this influx, although my mother seemed grateful for it. I had not prepared any refreshment, nor had Miss Lawlor, who was quite badly affected. My mother sat quite still in a corner of the sofa and tried to listen to what John Pickering was telling her. 'Lean on me, Henrietta,' he said. 'I am the executor. Yours as well as Paul's. Everything is in order. There is no need for you to worry about a thing.' I could have told him that my mother would never worry about anything again, not even about myself, and I began to grow faint and weary with the task ahead of me. And then the door opened and in rushed Dolly, who took my mother in her arms and let her sob, and then ordered her to stop, and put her back on the sofa oddly comforted.

This was Dolly as I had rarely seen her, attentive to the task in hand. In that instant I saw her as a woman of infinite capacity, betrayed by meagre opportunities and perhaps too suspicious an attitude to the world in general. Had fortune favoured her with a more ample background she might not have looked on her acquaintances with such envy and scorn. Her strong passions were compromised by the limited nature of her objectives. My mother had seen this at an early stage; it was to Dolly's advantage that she had never seen it at all. She needed a guide and had never found one; she needed a benevolent elder, who would watch over her and correct her. Tact would be needed for this task, for Dolly was not humble and tended to consider herself more intelligent than her contemporaries. What energies she had, and these were considerable, were devoted to consolidating her own position in the world, an undertaking which might involve many a volte-face. Although not consistent she was single-minded, and this single-mindedness conferred on her an iron confidence. It was her confidence that she brought with her into our crowded and desultory drawing-room on that strange evening, and my mother was grateful for it.

'Now Jane, now Violet,' said Dolly, divesting herself of her fur coat. 'We need refreshments. Violet, make some coffee; make it strong.' Nobody called Miss Lawlor Violet except my mother, but in these circumstances possibly none of us minded. 'Take these, Jane, and put them on plates,' she said, handing over two bags of what I assumed to be left-overs from one of her parties: cheese twists and *petits fours* and the tiny savoury pastries that Annie made so well. Suddenly I was hungry. I helped Miss Lawlor in the kitchen while Dolly held court in the drawing-room. When I went back with the trolley the atmosphere was quite convivial. Dolly was particularly gracious to John Pickering and the men from the bank. I have to admit that she behaved well. She appeared to think that any expression of grief was out of place in such a gathering, and of course people were relieved by such assurance. When conversation had become general, and cigarettes were being lighted, and ashtrays sought, she sat down on the sofa beside my mother.

'Now Etty,' she said. 'I hope you're going to be sensible. There's no point in being anything else. I know what you're feeling; I went through it all before you, when Hugo died. At least you've got the flat.' I waited for her to say, and you've got Jane, but this did not take place. 'And I'm sure you're provided for.' She paused for a moment, a look of returning rancour beginning to dawn. 'Mr Pickering says you've nothing to worry about on the financial side. And of course you've money of your own, haven't you?'

When contemplation of my mother's good fortune became too much for her she turned to me.

'Well, Jane, this has altered your plans, I dare say. You won't be going to Cambridge now, I suppose?'

'Oh, no,' I said, for I had already told my headmistress of my decision.

'But darling,' protested my mother. 'You must go. You've always wanted to go. And there's no reason for you to stay here. I don't want you to ruin your life.'

'She won't be ruining it,' said Dolly promptly. 'She can find herself a job and look after you. After all, she's got to face the world some time. And you've protected her, Etty,' she reproached my mother, who had begun to weep again as she contemplated my ruined life. But although the decision had been mine, and had been freely made, and although I did not really resent Dolly's intervention, I suddenly felt lonely, as if nobody wished me well, and very very tired. We were both tired, my mother and I, and I longed for us to be able to go to bed. It was Marigold's mother who came to my rescue. 'I think we should let these people get some sleep,' she announced. She was a primary school teacher; her voice carried. Within five minutes the room had emptied. 'Come along, Mrs Ferber,' said Marigold's mother, in her firm keen voice. She had resented Dolly's intervention, and was protesting on my behalf. At the door she kissed me, and said, 'If there's anything you want, Jane . . .' But I had heard this from so many people that it no longer meant anything. Perhaps it never had.

I put my mother to bed but once again she was estranged from me, bound up in her own silence and in contemplation of her so recent communion with my father. For as long as she dwelt on this she was euphoric. It was only when recalled to the real world, the world in which I unfortunately existed, that she became distressed. My task henceforth would be to spare her the sight of me, for as much as I decently could. I was seventeen, nearly eighteen; I was an adult, but it was then that I understood how children feel, and how they go on feeling all their lives. When I wrote my first book for children, designed to give comfort to any child who has lost a parent, it was with this insight in mind. The book enjoyed some success: I was hailed as a talented newcomer. But I remembered how the book had been written, and took little pleasure from it.

5

After the school choir had sung the last school song ('On with you, Chronos, onward Charioteer') I gathered up my possessions, said goodbye to form mistress, music mistress and headmistress, and left with Marigold. She was a sympathetic friend at this time, as she has been ever since, but her sympathy was always limited by her intense practicality, which was to make her such an excellent nurse. We wandered down the King's Road to her house in Bramerton Street, where I had looked forward to spending such time as I felt entitled to, although I was aware that I had fewer claims on my own time now than I had had in the past, when I was free to wander all day, if I felt inclined to do so, and when this ruminative behaviour was accepted as entirely natural by my ruminative parents. They themselves seemed to spend their lives in a state of delicate preoccupation, emerging from this only to bestow distracted and loving smiles on each other, as if they shared a spirit life which had no need of words.

Although benefiting from their intense and genuine if absent-minded sweetness I had always felt myself to be made of somewhat coarser material, liable to make more noise, to have more subversive thoughts than either of my parents were likely to entertain, and to be excluded from their particularly rapt communion, which to me (and I am almost sure to them as well) was untainted by any gross manifestation of sexuality. If they ever came together, as I imagine they must have done from time to time, it would have been in the nature of a pre-Raphaelite painting, in which two almost identical figures, barely distinguishable as a man and a woman, fully dressed, and with abundant flowing hair, press their faces together intently, and gaze into each other's eyes as if sealing a pact, as if after long travail, and as if attaining that unity which is the stuff of legend, of myth, and of religion too, whereas most lovers desire a certain otherness in their partners, and would look askance on the fairy sadness of these debilitated creatures, whose silent closeness they would nevertheless envy once their own more robust appetites were satisfied. I have seen couples in the Tate Gallery looking at such pictures with intense irritation, as if they set an impossible standard of behaviour, which of course they do, since such behaviour lies in the domain of courtly love, which few can sustain. I have followed such couples through the gallery to the entrance hall, and seen them choose their postcards. For a second, their postcards in their hands, they look like disappointed children, until cheered up by the thought of tea, to which they walk with a brisker step and a renewed confidence. Such is the faith one places in the body, after a disconcerting confrontation with the soul.

My parents never expressed a need for anything which they did not already possess, from which I deduce that they were perfectly happy. In their inability to imagine other partners, other forms of felicity, other appetites — and I emphasise that this was a genuine inability — they were truly innocent, Adam and Eve before the Fall and the Expulsion from Eden. Now my mother had been expelled, but without having eaten of the apple: expelled in a state of disastrous innocence, and therefore doubly vulnerable. I saw that it would fall to my lot to protect her, and I felt unequal to the task. I loved my parents dearly, and contemplated their life together as a miracle which I might never be able to reproduce on my own account, but once my father had died I knew that something was finished in my life as well as in my mother's, for I had lost my freedom, or rather exchanged that freedom for perpetual anxiety. I did not then know that anxiety, of an existential kind, can attach to freedom itself. I was too young for metaphysical speculations, although I had read Simone de Beauvoir and had a vague sense of the wrongs done to women, particularly to daughters. Thus I was not quite equipped to deal with my mother's grief, and felt perhaps a certain impatience. The impatience was a useful strategem for disguising my most unmanageable sensation, which was one of dread.

'What will you do?' asked Marigold, as we turned into her street.

'Get a job, I suppose,' I replied, as negligently

as I could. I felt obliged to meet her practicality with some of my own, although I did not see how I was to be practical all the time, and would have welcomed a discussion of my feelings, of which I was ashamed. I was acutely aware of the division between what I really felt and what I thought I should feel. I affected a cynical despair over my renunciation of three years at Cambridge, whereas what I really mourned was the loss of a protected childhood: I did not know that this was permitted. Cambridge had never had more than a token reality for me, for I had always imagined that life would continue unmodified by either time or distance. That is the proper attribute of the limitless world of childhood, whereas I was, at the time of my father's death, a belated adolescent. I still looked young, as the child of such parents was perhaps bound to look. I had no beauty to speak of, for I was thin and pale, with only hair of an unusual light, almost white blonde, to distinguish me. My intense inwardness gave me a disconsolate air, which had prompted many hissed reprimands and instructions from Dolly. I was aware that she disliked me: I was also aware that she was genuinely ignorant of this fact. If she had been questioned on this point she would have replied that she was very fond of me, but that she wished I would do something about my appearance. I was so used to this sort of genuine subterfuge — always an interesting indication of character — that I took no more notice of Dolly than she did of me.

Nevertheless my attitude towards her hardened

at this time. I felt that she should be taking on certain family duties instead of amusing herself. I felt that instead of entertaining my mother with stories of her bridge parties she should have been communing with her, listening to her, enquiring of her health and her feelings. This was to misjudge Dolly's capacities and her desires. Dolly was a working woman, as I came only later to understand. She had never ceased to be a working woman. Her work consisted of bettering her situation, making her way in a world which she rightly judged to be hostile. My mother's feelings — my own feelings — did not come within her remit. If questioned on this point (but I was not old enough, was never old enough to pose such a question) she would have shrugged and replied that she was a widow herself, that most of her friends were widows, but that there was no point in dwelling on the matter; it was a fact of life. Her opacity served her well: no one was in a position to criticise her, for as she constantly reminded one she had had a hard life and had refused to burden others with her misfortunes. Her irritating optimism was, she thought, a hallmark of endurance, indeed of excellence. Besides, she was too busy to linger over our situation, which she continued to view as relatively benign, as I suppose it was. While she was making herself agreeable to her acquaintances we continued to sit at home, stricken, as she saw it, by a fate which was no more or no less than the fate common to all mortals. She had been there before us. This, she seemed to think, conferred on her a natural superiority, a superiority which could never be called into question.

Her busyness was mysterious, and given her circumstances, meritorious. At any event it kept her in good spirits. At times it struck me that she was actually happy, yet I did not see how this could be. The company of women, to whom she was indifferent, seemed to elevate her mood to a point at which I even suspected that she had made the acquaintance of a man, and that a second marriage was in the offing. She said nothing of this, but had acquired a new liveliness, which was painfully out of place in our reduced household. Yet who would grudge her this new vivacity? Certainly not my mother, with her touching faith in marriage, any marriage. Certainly not myself, who longed at that time for someone — anyone — to be happy. Yet Dolly said nothing, merely gave out unimportant signals, such as an increased attention to her appearance, and by association to ours. I found this irksome, but had to concede her the right. She was a handsome woman, and the contrast between her full-blown expansiveness and my mother's shrinking pallor was too plain for me to ignore. I longed for the breath of life that Dolly brought in with her, yet within minutes of her arrival she had managed to annoy me all over again.

I was grateful to her for visiting my mother from time to time. She would arrive in her hired car, with a full complement of uplifting thoughts and examples, rather like an old-time evangelist. The whole cast of my mother's grief was foreign to her, and I think slightly repulsive to her, as it was even to me. This did not mean that there was a *rapprochement* between Dolly and myself at this time: indeed, I went to a great deal of trouble to be out of the house when she was expected, leaving Miss Lawlor to cope with the bags of Annie's leftovers which were thrust into her hands and my mother to listen meekly to Dolly's stories of her own triumphs over adversity. In this way my mother got to hear of every good deed that Dolly had ever performed, and in addition of every compliment she had ever received. This afforded my mother a certain gentle amusement, although she soon fell into a morbid habit of censuring any sign of an unbecoming levity. For her part Dolly eventually ran out of inspirational material, and even felt a whisper of annoyance that her own example was not being followed and her own advice not applied. This may have been why she took to timing her visits to coincide with the weekends, when I could hardly pretend to be out looking for a job. It was not desire for my company which prompted these weekend visits so much as intense irritation. The irritation was felt for my mother but was passed on to me as being a more worthy recipient. 'If only you'd do something with your hair!' she would complain. 'After all, Jane, you're about to go out into the world; you'll want to look attractive. Men don't like a glum expression.' There would follow the admonition to wear an expression of rapturous enjoyment. 'Singing and dancing, Jane! Always let them think of you as singing and dancing!'

I have no idea where this image came from, but it was dear to Dolly's heart. I think it dated from her youth, from her nights at the Crillon with the Americans; I think she looked with pity and contempt on any young person who did not enjoy such a youth. Dolly's saving grace, the key to her confidence in herself and her message to the world, was her faith in pleasure. Where the possibility of pleasure was seen to be non-existent her valiant optimism dwindled into impotent annoyance, and she could be seen to be making active preparations to leave the scene, her hands grasping her bag and relinquishing it, or adjusting the pearl studs at her ears or the neckline of her dress, at which she directed a complacent downward glance from time to time. My impression was that she could have been appeased if I had in any way resembled Dolly herself, which meant being greedy, alluring, and prompt, given to discussion of female concerns, sexily provocative, generous with stories of boy-friends and boyfriends' prospects. For mention of sex or love — on her part, not on mine — always led to some sort of speculation as to financial advantage. Her interest in money was fathomless. Although living well herself, she was, in her view, not living well enough. What frustration she felt at this state of affairs came my way with increasing regularity.

'Time you found work, Jane,' she would say. 'Time you brought some money in. Not that you need it, of course.' This remark would be followed by a little laugh, which contained both resentment and anticipation, for it became clear to me that she regarded herself as my mother's eventual legatee, by which time I would have a job which would satisfy my modest needs and make me providentially self-sufficient. Since I was so deficient in sexual attraction, her argument might have gone, I could be relegated to that unfortunate subspecies which devoted itself to getting on with the world's work. I would no doubt wear cardigans and flat shoes, and Dolly could safely wash her hands of me, since I had proved to be so backward in taking her advice.

Oddly enough my mother did not read between the lines of Dolly's concern but chose to trust only that part of it which was genuine. For there was a certain rough affection there, for my mother at least, although this affection was mixed with an almost intolerable condescension, which my mother would not have recognised even if it had been brought to her notice. She seemed to regard Dolly as a source of life, the life which was no longer permitted to her to enjoy, and on Sunday evenings she would rouse herself from her almost permanent position in a corner of the sofa and go into my father's study to telephone Dolly. I would hear the vigorous clacking of Dolly's voice, interspersed with my mother's wistful interrogations. As far as I could judge Dolly was as perfunctory as ever in enquiring after my mother, regarding the fact that she was on the other end of the telephone as sufficient proof of her concern. She had almost no curiosity, and like many obtuse people prided herself on her knowledge of human nature. She was certainly conversant with the murkier wellsprings of natural conduct. Thus she never asked me any questions more searching than whether I had found work or boyfriends, preferably both. When I purposely offered a blank face and a negative reply she would turn away in something like disgust.

For this reason I preferred to spend the remainder of that summer in Marigold's house, where her great-aunts were in monumental but ever-active residence, spring-cleaning the bedrooms over the family's protestations, turning out daily batches of delicious cakes, willing to cook chips for Marigold's brother Oliver if he came in looking hungry, or sometimes, formidably arrayed, having a day in town, which meant a day at Selfridges, from which they returned by public transport, despite being weighed down by several shopping bags. These excellent women regarded me with the deepest concern, which I found shamefully acceptable, since it was accompanied by a desire for my wellbeing which I no longer found at home. 'Sit down, dear,' Kate or Nell would say. 'Marigold, give Jane that wee cushion for her back. Will you take a scone, Jane?' To take was their favourite verb, although no two people could have been more giving. 'Will you take a cup of tea, Mary?' was a question regularly put to Marigold's mother when she came home from school. 'Will I put the kettle on?' By the same token one of them might remark to the other, 'I hear Mrs Wishart took another stroke,' to which Kate or Nell might reply, 'Poor wee thing,' although the Mrs Wishart in question might have been seventy-five years old and a menace to her unfortunate neighbours.

They were such good women, so tireless on everyone's behalf, so blameless in pursuit of their duty. Even when exhausted by a day's shopping, and resting swollen ankles on small footstools, they congratulated everyone on their time well spent. 'Such a good day,' they would reassure their nephew, Marigold's father, as he sat becalmed by further scones. 'We managed to match those pillowcases at Selfridges. We took our lunch there.' This meant that they had eaten their lunch there, not that they had carried it in with them. 'Have you had a sufficiency, Peter?' Swallowing a last mouthful of superfluous scone, their nephew would assure them that he had. 'Then we'll away to bed. Just give me that cup and plate, Mary. No, no, Nell will put them under the tap. Will you be taking anything more this evening? No? Then we'll away to bed. Goodnight, then.'

It was a giant step from this affecting cordiality to the new loneliness of my home, where my mother sat virtually silent in the corner of the sofa. For a time I endured this with her, until my natural energies reasserted themselves. Then I devoted myself to cheering her up, and for a while, a brief blessed interval in our reduced life together, I succeeded. In this I was greatly aided by television, that friend of lonely hearts, that comfort of the oppressed and the depressed. In the daytime, when I knew she was safe with Miss Lawlor, who would see that she ate lunch, I was free to roam around London, with or without Marigold: in the evening I would ask her, 'Is there anything good on to-night?' 'Jane does so love television,' I heard her tell John Pickering, who came to see us from time to time. He looked at me strangely, as if he understood my manoeuvres. 'I watch for her sake, really. As you know, John, my husband only cared for the news, and sometimes not even for that. We listened to music, mostly. But Jane is young; she needs a brighter life than the one I can give her. And sometimes the programmes are quite entertaining.' For her sake I sat through game shows and quizzes, in which she seemed to take an innocent delight. This disturbed me, as if I had detected an advancing puerility. I kept a watch on this, and at times of lowered morale, or when I was very tired, my suspicions were confirmed. My mother seemed to go straight from one condition to another, from the obedient debility of the day-time, when she would creep about the flat, exchanging mild words with Miss Lawlor, to the factitious excitement of the evening, when she could look forward to entertainment at a level which made no demands on her and which all too frequently treated her as the child she was fast becoming.

I would get home at about six o'clock to find a lavish meal prepared for me. I would be bustled into the kitchen, as if there were little time to lose. A plate of chicken stew or some elaborate casserole would be put down in front of me, while my mother went into the drawing-room to switch on the television, as if my homecoming were merely a pretext or a signal, after which she could enjoy the rest of the evening undisturbed. But this is not quite fair: she would make the odd journey into the kitchen to see if I were enjoying my dinner. At these times there was a look of girlish love on her face. 'Is it nice, darling? Violet and I thought you needed something hot after your day out.' This referred to my idle and almost unbearably aimless day, which my mother chose to believe was an honourable occupation, in much the same way that my father had left home for the bank in the morning and returned at six in the evening. My timetabling therefore reassured her, although the day was as often as not spent in the National Gallery or the British Museum, or simply wandering over vast tracts of London, as if seeking another home. It was at times like these that I would wonder how I would manage to live the rest of my life, for even getting a job seemed to be beyond me, as was any other kind of realistic endeavour. I was sore at heart and fatalistic; my main preoccupation was my mother's state of mind, and I held myself in readiness in case she should need me. And yet my anxiety was so great that I had to leave the flat in the morning, and the diversions I thought I could legitimately award myself would calm me sufficiently to ensure an equable return and the faintly sinister evening that awaited me.

My mother's mental state alarmed me. In this way I was able to overlook her physical state, which was not good. By living such a reduced life she was able to contain her condition, and never referred to it. In this she was like my father, who only confessed to illness when it had become too conspicuous to ignore. My mother rarely left the flat; I had no idea what she did all day. My own survival depended on my being absent. When I returned in the late afternoon or the early evening I found her buoyed up merely because the day would soon be at an end and she could retire to bed. I see now that she did battle all the time with her failing heart. She complained of the cold, although the weather was mild and the flat well heated. It did not occur to me that her brain was being slowly starved of oxygen. What I thought of as her increasing childishness had a physical cause, but because it made her so easy to please I did not question it. Her odd exaggerated excitement, which would collapse all at once into trembling fatigue, I put down to the change wrought by grief. I thought that she would eventually return to normal; in the meantime I joined her in her little distractions, which were harmless. It cost me a certain amount to do so; I was aware of something unusual in her behaviour. Yet I wanted her to be happy, and there was enough loving communion in our moods, however disparate, to satisfy us both. We loved each other. Neither of us wanted to disappoint or to give pain.

My mother prepared for me an elaborate meal in order to disguise the fact that she ate nothing herself. After a cup of tea and a biscuit with Miss Lawlor she thankfully renounced the task of eating until the following morning. This was not too serious; she had had lunch; she was therefore nourished. What was more worrying was the primacy of entertainment, with which eating dinner could only interfere. She would settle herself with anticipation in her corner of the sofa, sometimes having run a comb through her hair and put on a little lipstick in honour of the ceremony, while I sat in the kitchen, stolidly eating the heavy food which I no longer wanted. I would have thrown it away, were it not for the lightning visits my mother paid to see the gratifying look of appreciation on my face. For that was what she now required: appeasement, reassurance. She ardently desired to have no more serious preoccupations than the choice between one serial and another, although in reality she preferred programmes which made no demands on her at all. Thus through the kitchen wall I would hear a cacophony of pop music or the triumphant catch phrases of a compère or quiz master. Sometimes, most terrible of all, I would hear my mother laugh with delight and thus become one with the moronic audience. She might pay a further visit to the kitchen as I slowly washed up. 'Aren't you coming to watch?' she would ask. 'Aren't you coming to watch the show?' For the unbroken stream of programmes had become 'the show', and she had become infinitely younger, almost a girl again, and reacting as children do when taken to the pantomime at Christmas.

My heart broke for her, although she seemed oddly happy. Grimly I took up my position next to her on the sofa, until I saw that she was tired, although she protested that she was not. In this way she believed that she was neither tired nor hungry, even when her eyelids were drooping with fatigue and her thin hands were restless in her lap. 'Come on,' I would say. 'I'm sleepy, even if you aren't,' and I would get up and switch off the set. This was the signal for her to come down to earth; a tired or painful smile would replace the factitious enthusiasm which had greeted me at my homecoming, and for a brief interval we looked into each other's eyes with total understanding. 'I'll come and see you to say goodnight,' I would assure her, and indeed those colloquies which took place in her bedroom, while she lay becalmed in the big double bed which my parents had always shared, constitute my most precious memories of that unhappy time, although in retrospect I see that I came to treasure even the memory of her eager face at the kitchen door, and her artless question, 'Aren't you coming to watch the show?'

In the morning she would once again be the woman who had been married to my father, neat and correct, as she always was, but now weary, as if beset with problems. In fact she was beset with memories, which did not appear to give her pleasure. 'I shouldn't have insisted on going to the Isle of Wight,' she said. 'Paul wanted to go back to Étretat, but I thought you were too small. I was frightened of the rocks.' Another time she said, 'That case of vintage champagne is for you. It is for when you get married. He put it down when you were born.' Or again, and more worryingly, 'That was a lovely concert at the Wigmore Hall, the one when I met your father. Such a pity you couldn't have heard it.' But when I got up to go, picking up some vague approximation to a briefcase, she got up with a smile on her face and kissed me, for all the world as if I were my father and she were seeing me off to work. I would wait until Miss Lawlor had taken off her hat and coat, and when I heard the comfortable murmur of what seemed like normal conversation, I would make my escape, striding out with gratitude into the increasingly misty mornings, away from the dread which afflicted me at home, and into the reassuring bustle of the working world.

I was grateful that we had no visitors, or that when we did, as when John Pickering looked in once or twice a month, my mother behaved normally. Indeed I think she was normal, but was subject to the abnormal states which follow the loss of the one who has given one's life its meaning. From being repressed and overlooked as a girl my mother had been awoken to life by my father: I truly think that my birth was of lesser importance to her than my father's wellbeing, although they

153

both loved me dearly. Fortunately, or unfortunately, I resembled my father, with his pale hair and aquiline face, so that my mother, in looking at me, was constantly reminded of him. At no time was my mother deluded or deranged, but she had the deep sadness and the childish gaiety that prefigure derangement. I trusted John Pickering to be discreet, to pick up only those signals which he alone could discern, without any corroboration from myself. When I saw him to the door after these visits we did not indulge in those whispered consultations which turn the one left in the other room into an unwitting patient. He did not even ask me if I could manage, for which I was grateful. For after all I could manage. I was managing. But all the time I was aware of the silence of the flat, a silence broken only by the witless jingles of television commercials, which my mother particularly appreciated. I was aware of the relief with which I left the flat every morning, and of my watchfulness when I returned to it in the evening. When I was particularly downhearted I even thought of invoking the help of Dolly, but when I got round to telephoning her, from a public call box, there was no reply, not even from Annie, and I was forced to assume that she had gone back to Brussels for a visit, perhaps to dear Adèle Rougier, with whom Dolly was once again on the best of terms.

At last, when I could no longer bear my own aimlessness, I confronted the possibility of finding work. Marigold had gone off to begin her training at St Thomas's, and I only saw her on her odd weekend off. Her house seemed oddly silent after the departure of the great-aunts, who, according to custom, had lavished on their hosts a hospitality which they naturally assumed to be in their gift. I bought the local paper, sat down in a café in the King's Road, and scanned the Personal Columns, looking for that oblique out of the way message that would cause me to rise from my seat and go blindly to where the message would lead me. There was no message that day; on the other hand a small office of an indeterminate nature in Holbein Place was looking for a trainee: good reading skills necessary. Holbein Place was off Sloane Square and therefore a short distance from where I was actually sitting. Moreover, whatever else I could not do I could certainly read. Rather than telephone I walked, not too unwillingly, to Holbein Place, where I mounted the stairs to the first floor of a dark brick building, and knocked on a door marked 'ABC Enterprises'. 'Come in,' sang a female voice, and I went into a small office in which a rather distinguished looking woman was seated behind a desk and talking on the telephone. 'Be with you in a moment,' she said and went on with her conversation, which appeared to be with a son or daughter and was to do with arrangements for the coming weekend.

'Daddy can't be expected to assume entire responsibility, you know,' she said severely, tapping on the desk with a pencil. 'I should think you could at least get yourselves to Winchester *and* do the shopping. If you don't want to drive take the train.'

There were muted sounds of argument from the other end: a daughter, I decided.

'There are taxis,' said the woman. 'I should have thought it not beyond the wit of man to have worked that out. Well, I can't discuss it any further now; there's someone waiting to see me. I'll ring you tonight. Goodbye, darling. Now,' she said, apparently refreshed by this exchange. 'What can I do for you?'

'I've come about the job,' I said.

'So soon? But this is marvellous, although we've paid for three days.' I worked out that she meant the advertisement. 'How old are you?'

'Eighteen,' I said, although I was not eighteen for another six weeks.

'Splendid. There's not a lot of money, you see, although the work is pleasant. You know what we do, I suppose?'

'Not really, no.'

'How could you? We are a press cutting agency. Do you know what that is? We have a list of subscribers and a lot of newspapers and journals and we extract the pieces that refer to the names on our list and send them out. Do you think you would be able to do that?'

I said that I thought it sounded very interesting.

'In that case,' she said, rising from her desk and smoothing down her tight check skirt, 'shall we agree on a trial period? I am Barbara Hemmings, by the way. This is my little concern. I run the business, although I'm not here every day. Shall we say a fortnight on trial?'

I said, quite sincerely, that I should like that, and that if agreeable to her I could start right away.

'In that case,' she said, leading the way into an inner office, 'I shall introduce you to Mrs Swarbrick and Mrs Cassidy. They will tell you what to do.'

After a few initial moments of shyness and panic I settled down at a small desk of my own with a list of names and a pile of trade papers such as the *Draper's Record* and the *Hairdresser's Journal*, which apparently nobody else wanted, preferring to stick to something a little more newsworthy or glamorous. When I had marked up the relevant passages I asked Mrs Swarbrick or Mrs Cassidy — I did not yet distinguish between them — what I had to do next.

'Call me Margaret,' said the comfortable blonde woman, who might have been either but who was henceforth to be indelibly Margaret. 'And I'm Wendy,' said the other, no less comfortably.

'I'm Jane,' I said.

'Well, Jane, we usually have a cup of tea about now. Do you think you could make us a cup? Kettle and teapot in the bathroom, stove and fridge on the landing. Not that way, dear, that's Mrs Hemmings's office. Out the back. You'll find all you need there.'

The cup of tea was my rite of passage. When it was found to be sufficiently strong I was accepted. After that the morning became very convivial. I was shown how to cut out the relevant articles (Cutting out! Shades of the nursery!) and how to fix the identifying tabs. This was a job I was prepared to do beautifully, expertly, rapidly, but this apparently was not what was required.

'Slow down, dear,' said Margaret. 'Slow and steady wins the race. Mark out in the morning and cut out in the afternoon, that's the way. You'll find you concentrate better in the morning, and the afternoon always seems more peaceful, doesn't it? Now, tell us something about yourself. You've got lovely hair, for a start.'

'Unusual,' agreed Wendy, who reached into a cupboard and brought out a tin of biscuits.

So I told them how my father had died and I had given up the idea of going to university, and how I lived with my mother, about whom I was rather worried. All this came tumbling out, and I realised that I had not previously spoken of such matters.

'Well, you poor girl,' said Margaret, and Wendy added, 'Hard on a young person, that.' After which I willed the tears to stay in my eyes, while Wendy got up and put her arm round me. And after that we were friends for life.

They were the dearest women, although my contemporaries would not have immediately identified them as the efficient and loyal workers they turned out to be. They were not fashionably slim, did not wear tight suits with big shoulders, did not arrive and depart with briefcases. We are talking here, rather, of the Liberty printed oilcloth shop-

158

ping bag, of the viscose dress from John Lewis, and of the modest heel on the spacious court shoe, wide fitting for extra comfort. They were both in their late fifties and had long said goodbye to the illusions of youth, but as they said, they liked to look nice, and on Saturday afternoons they would go to Oxford Street and treat themselves to something new to wear. To my eyes they looked splendid in their royal blue or dusty pink patterned dresses, with the neat bow at the neck and the self-covered belt. These dresses were invariably the same, with the smallest possible variation. 'Well, you've got to look nice for work, haven't you?' they assured one another, and to this end sported finely groomed heads of hair, silver blonde and chestnut brown respectively, silk scarves, and inexpensive though not unpleasant scent. To these modest women going out to work was an adventure; after years at home bringing up a family a job like ours was an invitation to enter the world once more. The job was not demanding, but they did it thoroughly, as I did, and we took a pride in our work, simple though it was. The day was agreeably broken up by snacks and cups of strong tea, but the work got done, and as the afternoon wore on and the light faded the pleasant sound of scissors cutting paper replaced our normal friendly exchanges, with full complement of the news of Margaret's husband's back and of Wendy's grandchild (Fiona Kylie). I can hear that sound now. At five-thirty Mrs Hemmings would fling open the door between her office and ours, and say, 'All right, ladies? You can get off now.' I learned that she did very little, having inherited the business from her father, and was out for most of the day, but she seemed well-disposed, and soon accepted me as the others did, completely.

My days in the office, and the constant snacks I was offered, prepared me better for a return to the flat, although not the meals which continued to await me. In time, and rather to my relief, these dwindled, first to a slice of meat and some vegetables keeping hot between two plates on top of a saucepan of simmering water, and eventually to a rather sad assemblage of ham and salad which I ate while my mother communed with the television. As time went on she appeared less excited, less anticipatory, as if sense were returning, and with sense pain. Often I found her in a dream, while the succession of images unrolled unnoticed before her eyes. I tried to tell her about the work, about Margaret and Wendy, but she did not seem to want to know, as if these late additions could be of no interest to a life now lived mainly in the past. She was still neatly dressed, but her hair had turned quite grey. Finally she would let me lead her to bed, and we would sit for a while hand in hand. Once she said, 'I love you, Jane,' but I found myself too sad to reply that I loved her too, and in any case at such moments reassurance of my love for her was unnecessary.

'Poor soul,' commented Margaret, to whom I was something of a godsend, since her own daughters were married and far away. 'If there's anything we can do, you only have to say, dear. Is there anyone else in the family?' It was then that I thought of Dolly, although only as a last resort. I dreaded her comments, but I thought she should know of my mother's condition. Perhaps I remembered her vigour and enthusiasm, perhaps I placed some faith in her survivor's common sense. I telephoned her from the office and she promised to come over at the weekend, 'if I can fit it in'. I thought that cavalier of her, but was relieved that she did not appear to be taking the matter seriously.

On the Saturday I put some biscuits on a plate and cut some brown bread and butter, all of which proved to be superfluous as the bag of slightly broken delicacies was handed over. She arrived out of the greyness of a foggy afternoon, a positive embodiment of health and durability, in one of her exquisite short-sleeved dresses, now decidedly tight. I thought I detected a change in her, although I had not seen her for some weeks. In comparison, my mother looked weak, faded, although this Dolly appeared not to notice. Dolly, by contrast, was resplendent, with an eager alert look which nevertheless seemed to see nothing. I noted that certain modifications had taken place in her appearance. Her fingernails were now red, as were her lips, and there was a flush, either of excitement or of rouge, on her cheeks. She seemed to gaze towards the window rather a lot, and once or twice went over to see if her car was still there. Apparently she had told the driver that she would not be long. 'Never keep a man waiting, Jane.' Once or twice she referred, rather offhandedly, to 'a friend of mine'. When I told her that I had telephoned and got no reply, she said that Annie had gone to Ostend on a visit and that she had been out rather a lot. After which she twisted the rings on her left hand and assumed an unconvincing look of insouciance. Then I realised that what had formerly been a vague and ludic suspicion on my part had become reality. Dolly had a man friend. Quite possibly, although this seemed grotesque to me, Dolly was in love. And the object of her affections was the man in the car downstairs, although as far as I knew she still used the same car-hire firm in the Edgware Road. All became clear when she said, in response to my mother's question as to how she had managed the journey to our flat — always a hazardous undertaking, as they both professed to believe — 'My friend drove me over. Actually, he owns the firm. You could say he was combining business with pleasure. Harry,' she added, with deep satisfaction. 'Harry Dean. A dear friend.'

Dolly must have been sixty-one or sixty-two at the time of which I speak. Certainly she looked good for her age. She had the Frenchwoman's air of defiant belief in herself, although there were certain give-away signs, such as the feet now crammed into painful-looking shoes, and the bluish rinse on her greying hair. I have to say that she had in addition the aura of romance, although I have reason to believe that this was produced largely by her own expectations. The humid eye, the wandering smile, the quick glances towards the window almost rendered us irrelevant. These were indulged without mercy, though unaffectedly. Dolly's good fortune had made her careless of others, as love tends to do. But could it be love? I thought it must be, since there was no mention of money, her constant preoccupation. Only love could have freed Dolly from this care. Above all there was a new sense of enjoyment and a new sense of self. Her friends, if friends they were, were not mentioned; there seemed to be no visits to Nice or Brussels in the offing. Even a call on such relations as we were was undertaken lightly, since this involved the company of Harry on the journey. It was quite clear that there was to be no sharing of my problems, no solicitude for my mother's welfare. Dolly had moved beyond us into undiscovered country — undiscovered by me, that is, and probably even by my mother — where flirtatious skills were the order of the day.

It was to her credit that these skills did not make her seem ridiculous. In fact they were native to her, but had remained unused for a very long time. At heart she was still a girl who enjoyed the admiration of men. At least this may have been true when she was a girl, when admiration seemed of a higher order of attainment than desire. But now the vulnerable girl had become a confident woman, her wits sharpened by years of making do, of financial bluffing, of social insincerity. Her way of life may have been more restricted than we knew:

her small income from my grandmother had not kept pace with inflation, and my mother and I had tended to neglect her needs in the light of our own recent and current misfortunes. What Dolly wanted, of course, was to marry again, for to be dependent on a man was a far more honourable course than to be dependent on a bunch of women. I saw that Dolly despised us, although she would never have admitted as much, even to herself: she thought of us with a sort of familiarity which she no doubt took for affection, but she had nothing but contempt for the poor use we made of our money, which in her eyes had reached astronomical proportions, as if it were a limitless shower of gold, whereas, as far as I knew, it was a fairly comfortable but fairly modest income quite boringly invested. Dolly even despised the fact that it was invested; if it had been hers she would have blown the lot, on clothes, on parties, on hotels, on the fantasies of her starved youth, when she sat in her mother's workroom and dreamed of the wider world.

I also saw that Dolly would make quite a superior business woman, and that if she married this Harry Dean would run his car-hire business without prejudice, exchanging her afternoon bridge parties for regular spells in his office. In time she would own the business and make quite a prosperous concern out of it, Harry Dean being relegated to the golf course and sundry leisure pursuits. She would look after his interests, she would look after him, but quite possibly she would once more be disappointed, for the promise of glamour would have evaporated and been replaced by a security which she found humdrum. For the essence of Dolly was her longing: it was expressed in that ardent hopeful smile which had captivated my uncle on the dance floor long ago, and which, before that, had left so many American soldiers with a disarming, and disarmingly misleading, impression of a typical French girl. Led by her need for money she had perhaps overlooked or even buried that longing, that desire for fulfilment, for obedience, for a man's protection, archaic female longings which will not be banished, but which survive long after compromises have been reached and reality acknowledged. Many a woman knows that on the level of her most basic imaginings she has not been satisfied; hence the look of cheerful forbearance which is the most recognisable expression on the face of the average woman, whereas if questioned she would confess to a certain mystification. Why must it be like this? A more romantic way would have been so much better.

I doubt whether Dolly was aware of the buried layers of her make-up. It was entirely to her credit that she refused to make a fairy story of her life, that she accepted each successive phase of it without question, that she adapted to each new set of circumstances with such remarkable facility that one tended to forget her previous incarnation. She now believed herself to be living the life of an average Englishwoman, although in fact her life was far from typical. Her accent was English, her good sense was English, her endurance was English. Yet she had a look of readiness, of adroitness, that was not English, and which led back to her early need to make her way in the world. Above all it was easy to discern from Dolly's now evasive, now conspiratorial gaze that she was a woman of passion, whose senses, long dormant or long diverted to other goals, had been stirred, and who was living the experience of a new excitement as if it were the bliss of fulfillment itself, and in whom the old archaic tremulous longings had been reborn, in the hope, the last and final anticipation, of a happy end.

My mother noticed nothing of this. I could see that she was concentrating all her resources, by now drastically diminished, on giving an impression of normality. To this end she made vague routine enquiries, of the kind she had made many times in the past, to which Dolly gave abstracted answers, her mind evidently elsewhere. Their meeting was a dialogue of the deaf, for Dolly was too preoccupied to see that there was anything wrong with my mother or with our little household, which, in the light of her new awakening, must have struck her as intolerably lifeless. I viewed this incompatibility with despair, for it seemed to me that I was too young to bear the burden of what I knew was to come. If I had placed any faith in Dolly's seniority, which I thought must endow her with a certain wisdom, I was to be disappointed, for she now appeared to me as undeniably frivolous, with her mysterious smiles and her ill-concealed excitement. I cannot, in my defence, say that my attitude towards her was changed by this last manifestation. She had always made me feel uncomfortable, as if proposing for my benefit a model of behaviour which I had no desire to emulate. I was always aware, in her presence, of a subtlety, an astuteness, which nevertheless failed to disguise an emotional clumsiness. She was a heavyweight, a demanding presence, a force to be reckoned with, yet I was never entirely on her side. Indeed I felt myself resisting her, as I did now, when she returned briefly to the matter in hand and asked me whether I liked my job.

'I love it,' I said truthfully, for I could not wait to get back to it, and to the comforting presence of Margaret and Wendy.

'Any men?' she asked, as I could see she would now never fail to ask, since as far as she was concerned I had reached the age of consent, when more recognisable behaviour could be expected of me.

'No, we are four women,' I replied, at which she looked at me curiously, and remarked, 'Then perhaps you should look for something a bit more promising. You'll never get anywhere in a roomful of women.'

We were a roomful of women and we were not getting anywhere. It was a dreary Saturday, the day Miss Lawlor did not come, although she usually looked in on a Sunday after church, and my mother was left to my ministrations. I had managed to cook lunch, had put the chicken in the oven

167

at the time Miss Lawlor had indicated in the page of instructions she had left for me, and had added creamed potato and a salad. My mother had eaten with application, as I had; the food tasted of metal in my mouth. Then my mother had drifted towards her bedroom, saying, with a return to something like her usual manner, 'If Dolly is coming I shall need a rest.' I had been left alone, as I so often was these days, and for this reason had perhaps entertained unrealistic hopes of Dolly's visit. And it had come to nothing; worse, it had merely ushered in a new chapter in Dolly's life which rendered us invisible to her. If she turned her attention momentarily to my mother it was to deplore her appearance, as if detecting in her some unbecoming act of wilfulness.

'Such a pity you've let your hair go, Etty. It does so age a woman. Why not have a rinse like mine? Or you could have a proper tint. I would if I could afford it.' As always at the mention of money she gave an annoyed little laugh. 'And you really shouldn't let yourself get so thin.'

But my mother merely said, 'I'm well enough, Dolly. And my darling looks after me.'

This was how she had always referred to my father, and I felt the old heart-soreness and fear, but she got up from the sofa and put her arm round my waist. 'My darling daughter,' she said. So the afternoon was not entirely wasted.

At the door Dolly said to me, in an undertone which was clearly audible to my mother, 'She has no business to let herself go like that, Jane. She

168

is *giving way.*' It was in her eyes the worst crime a woman could commit. Then, with an intake of breath, which seemed to be indicative of appetite, and a lifting of the head, she sailed off to the possibility of new adventures. She had been with us a little less than an hour.

It was November and the afternoons were dark. After Dolly's departure my mother drifted off again in the direction of her bedroom, where I found her half an hour later sitting motionless in front of her dressing-table. When she saw my ghostly presence in the twilit glass of the mirror she picked up a pearl necklace and said, 'This is for you.' I took it from her and kept it coiled in my hand, ready to return it when she was not looking, for these days she hated any break with routine and let her hands stray to her possessions as if seeking an assurance that they would not change. Then she got up quite calmly, and said, 'You must be tired. Shall we sit quietly for a little while?'

'Do you want to watch television?' I asked.

She merely smiled and shook her head. Then she took my arm in hers, and together we walked back into the drawing-room, and sat in the dark. I moved to put on the lights but she restrained me, and I was grateful even for this show of authority. I was reading *David Copperfield* at the time and was aware that my mother, like Barkis, was going out with the tide. I felt no more fear, only sorrow. When the afternoon expired into evening she stirred and said, almost normally, 'I'm rather

169

tired. Dolly has tired me. I think I'll go to bed now. Will you come and say goodnight to me?'

I left her at her bedroom door, then went back and gathered the dirty cups and plates. In the kitchen I poured away my mother's untouched tea, and washed up. Then I opened the window and leaned out into the darkness of the park. A late bird was singing, unusual for that time of the year. 'Why haven't you gone away like everyone else?' I wanted to say, but I was aware of giving way, as Dolly would have said, and composed myself into that state of impassivity which was almost natural to me. Thus I frequently gave rise to the accusation that I was unfeeling, which has persisted into my adult life, so that people constantly wonder how I can identify so closely with children, as I do in my stories. Then I went into my mother's bedroom and slid the pearl necklace back into the glass tray on the dressing-table. I kissed her, and she smiled at me. I was aware that a long night was beginning. I went into my own bedroom, and lay down on my bed. That night I slept the deepest sleep of my entire life.

With perfect symmetry my mother died while I slept. I found her in the morning, Sunday morning, when I took in her tea. I was not surprised: it seemed fitting. She had died in her sleep, as I would have wished her to do. I felt quite sober, and sat in the drawing-room, in her place on the sofa, until I heard Miss Lawlor's key in the door. I went into the hall to meet her, but I had no need to tell her what had happened. 'She's gone,

170

then?' Miss Lawlor enquired, her lips pale. I nodded. She took off her hat and coat and went in to my mother.

Miss Lawlor was a religious woman, with a profound faith in the world to come. I had no such faith myself, nor did I see any point in a spiritual sanction for what had happened. Indeed I fought against such an interpretation. As far as I could see what had happened was in nature, and therefore subject to a superior law. I had always known that my mother would not long survive my father; therefore it seemed entirely natural that she should die. I was aware only of a deeper silence than I had ever known before; I was aware too that the silence would deepen throughout my life. In this I have not been wrong.

After a while Miss Lawlor came back into the drawing-room, where I was sitting, still in my mother's place. I felt no desire to say an elaborate farewell, for Miss Lawlor's benefit, or for mine. She made us a cup of tea, which we drank together. Then she said, 'You'll telephone the doctor, Jane? And Mr Pickering?' So I did that, and after a while people came, but I paid them no attention, for my mind had gone out to meet my mother's, and for a brief blessed time we were at one again, as if few moments had passed since the days when I ran to her, and she was always there.

6

And so I lost her. David Copperfield's words, not
mine, but never bettered. During the days which
followed I read the book urgently, obsessively, in
order to reassure myself of David's eventual victory over circumstance. Every time he suffered
a mishap or a reversal of fortune I suffered with
him. I grew impatient with those who wasted his
time: I saw nothing amusing in Mr Micawber,
while Uriah Heep afflicted me with a sort of des-
olation, as if evil might just this once be allowed
to triumph. But Dickens was on the side of Betsey
Trotwood, and so was I. Had I had an aunt like
her I should have been as valiant as David. But
the likes of Betsey Trotwood were in exceedingly
short supply — perhaps Marigold's great-aunts
came nearest to that ideal model — whereas all
I had in the world now was Dolly. When this became borne in on me I realised why I was so impatient with Mr Micawber. And Dolly was not
only Mr Micawber, she was Mrs Micawber as well,
hinting that she had come down in the world, as
she no doubt believed to be the case. At this stage
I knew little of Dolly's inner life, but was merely
acquainted with my mother's account of her various misfortunes. My mother made allowances for
her, as she did for everyone. But to reflect yet

again on my mother was to invite pain, and I simply read on, willing myself to reach the end of the story, and promising myself an easing of the heart when David finally achieved happiness. When I got to the end I went back to the beginning. Miss Lawlor dusted silently around me, but took to leaving earlier than usual. She missed my mother's modest companionship and found me cold in comparison.

The emptiness of the flat oppressed me, and I wished I could be out of doors, as I had been in the late days of summer, before the world turned dark. It was now physically dark as well, a mild dusky late November, leaves falling quietly in the windless air, evening setting in earlier and earlier. These evenings frightened me and found me at the window, which I opened wide to inhale the leaf smell of the park: I would stand there for as long as half an hour, my hands gingerly patting the hot radiator, until my face was numb with the cold. Then there was nothing left to do but go to bed, which I did earlier and earlier. I would get rid of the television; I would give it to Miss Lawlor. I would never watch it again. Sometimes I turned on the radio very softly, and it made me feel less lonely. I paid no attention to the programmes, but I found the sound of all those well-meaning voices comforting. But most of the time I slept, deeply, greedily, voluptuously, as if sleep were the only pleasure to which I could legitimately aspire. I now know that grief, like pain, is immensely tiring, and am less harsh on my eighteen-year-old self than I was at the time. At the time I merely felt unworthy of the catastrophe which had befallen me and took refuge in sleep from the decisions which would have to be made.

One decision I managed to make quite easily. The funeral was delayed because my mother's doctor, for some reason, insisted on a post-mortem. He saw no physical justification for her death, apart from an increased weakness of the heart which he had failed to diagnose. Indeed, apart from providing a sedative for my mother on the day of my father's death, he had not been in attendance, let alone regular attendance. The funeral was therefore delayed for a week until the various certificates could be produced. When John Pickering told me all this on the telephone I listened humbly; when he asked me if I would trust him with the arrangements I thanked him with the sincerest gratitude.

'Whom do you want me to notify, Jane?' For he saw that I was inexperienced and wanted to spare me what he correctly thought of as embarrassment.

'I don't want anyone at the funeral, John. Just myself and Miss Lawlor. And you, of course.'

'I should in any case be present,' he reminded me gently. 'In my position as executor. And I was very fond of your mother. Paul, of course, was a dear friend. I have known them both for many years.' He paused. 'Just the three of us, then? You won't want a friend to stand by you? It will be quite an ordeal, although it will be over quickly.

That is the advantage of a cremation over a burial. Any family?'

'No,' I said. 'No family. Miss Lawlor will see me through.' For I considered Miss Lawlor to be the last remnant of our little family, and knew that with my arm through hers I should not falter. I even hoped that I might absorb some of her faith in her Saviour, but there was as yet no sign of this, and when I lay down in my bed at night I stared into the darkness, knowing that it would not be lightened by any supernatural agency, and that what faith I had would be in Miss Lawlor's prayers rather than in any of my own.

But the mention of family led me to telephone Dolly, who had as yet no knowledge of my mother's death. This was a shameful omission on my part, which put me in the wrong, from Dolly's point of view and from my own, for many years. Quite simply, my instinct told me she had no part in this event; she had shown little compassion for my mother, whom she regarded as more fortunate than herself. According to Dolly's reasoning, my mother's inheritance had made her fortunate in perpetuity. That she chose not to spend it consigned her to the ranks of the meek, whom Dolly despised. For myself she had not an ounce of feeling, except perhaps for a certain irritable dislike. Nevertheless, she insisted that I make a show of feeling for her own person, that I accord her deference, and concern. A fiction of affection must be maintained; she must be credited with sentiments which she had not previously thought to entertain.

When I told her of my mother's death — after three whole days had passed — her shock seemed to me entirely genuine, but overlaid with indignation.

'How could you, Jane? I would have come over at once if I'd known she was so ill. How could you be so unfeeling? After all, you're all I've got.'

She meant, and we both knew it, 'I'm all you've got.'

'I could come over now,' she said doubtfully, sniffing and blowing her nose. 'There'll be her things to sort out. I dare say I could help you dispose of them, though we weren't the same size, of course. She'd managed to let herself get very thin.'

'The funeral will be on Friday morning,' I said, with as much calmness as I could muster. 'But no one is to come.' To make quite sure of this I refrained from giving her the time, which was eleven o'clock. 'Only Miss Lawlor and myself will be there. And John Pickering. No one else.'

'What a strange girl you are, Jane! Not like your mother. Oh, well, if you've made up your mind. But of course you must come back here afterwards. You and Mr Pickering.'

'And Miss Lawlor.'

'Oh, Miss Lawlor, of course. She can give Annie a hand.'

'A hand with what?'

'Really, Jane, don't be ridiculous. It's customary to offer refreshments on these occasions, you know. Violet can make herself useful. I dare say she'll be glad to.'

'But there will only be four of us. Four of us with Miss Lawlor,' I said pleasantly. I was very angry.

She gave an elaborate sigh. 'As you wish, Jane. I'm not going to argue with you.' She managed to leave me with the impression that nothing would have given her greater pleasure. Then there was another sigh, more tremulous this time. 'Poor Etty. Poor girl. She didn't have much of a life, did she?'

'How can you say that? She was happy. She had my father.' I managed not to say, she had me, but Dolly gave a forbearing little laugh, as if she had heard the unspoken words.

'Yes, I dare say she was happy in her own funny way. What will you do with the flat, Jane?'

'Live in it, I suppose.'

'But it's too big for one person. You could get yourself a little studio somewhere. I might be able to take the flat off your hands. Or one of my friends might know someone. Not that it's very conveniently situated. I always wondered why Etty lived in such an out of the way place. And I don't think it's very suitable for someone of your age. You shouldn't be living alone anyway. Why don't you move in with a girlfriend?'

'Miss Lawlor is here with me. I'm not alone.'

'Oh, Miss Lawlor, Miss Lawlor. I'm hearing a lot about Miss Lawlor today. Anyone would think you cared more for her than you do for me.'

Since this was an accurate observation I said

nothing. I did not yet know how to lie. At the other end of the telephone I could almost hear Dolly's temper rising, but all she said was, 'I'm very upset, Jane. You might consider my feelings when you've got a moment. Very well. I'll expect the three of you on Friday. I dare say you'll be quite glad of me then, if at no other time.'

This was said with surprising bitterness and left me thoughtful. As far as I knew I did not need Dolly, although it occurred to me that the gifts my mother had made so discreetly would now have to be made by myself. I had in a sense inherited Dolly from my mother, just as my mother had inherited her from her mother. This did not worry me unduly, but Dolly's bitterness made me feel somewhat ashamed. She did not care for me, and yet she wished me to care for her, or perhaps to make a show of caring for her. In what abyss of non-feeling did Dolly dwell? She made careful placements of affection, always ready to be withdrawn in a fit of indignation. Her world was loveless, and she craved love as others crave sugar, and for the same reason: to replace a sudden lack, of which she would be abruptly and fearfully aware.

Her needs were primitive, immediate, and therefore pressing; they appeared to her to be entirely natural and justified, so that it was difficult to indicate caution, or wariness, certainly not disbelief or disagreement. Those who were not with her were against her, nor were one's own feelings of any interest to her. She no doubt saw my news, or rather the announcement of my news, as shocking, and would be swift with accusations of coldheartedness. Of my own situation she remained unaware, and even indignantly unaware. I did not underestimate her own feeling of loss. She knew that my mother had been a true friend to her, and would have registered a sensation of sadness at her disappearance. Yet she had not noticed — had genuinely failed to notice — my mother's obvious decline, engrossed as she was in delightful speculations of her own. These, naturally, were uppermost in her mind, and I emphasise, as she would have done, had she thought about it, the word naturally. When I had last seen her she was flirtatious, impatient: I had thought her in love, then. Now I see that my reasoning was frivolous, that Dolly's need for love was more archaic than this, that what she wanted was to be thought of as a loveable person. She wanted to demonstrate that she was worthy of love, of any kind of love, of all kinds. And if she clung to this supposed lover of hers, she was willing to cling no less to myself, grotesque though this may seem. And had been repulsed. I now saw that she had detected my lack of affection with her fine adventuress's instincts, and was ready to punish me for life.

Because we both considered this telephone call to be disastrous, revealing too much on both sides, our farewells were cold, subdued on my side, unforgiving on hers. To my already great distress was added a feeling of unworthiness; I was not only deficient in family solidarity, I was deficient in feminist solidarity (a far greater crime at that time). Because I had considered Dolly well able to take care of herself I had failed to ask certain questions. 'What do you need? Whom do you love? Whom do you miss? What do you share? And with whom do you share it?' Because I needed someone to ask these questions of me I became aware of the questions themselves. 'What do you lack?' I thought; that was the most fundamental question of all. Yet how could one ask such a question of others? It would be almost impertinent, as if one were in a position to dispense charity. But if charity meant love, as it did in some translations, should one not dispense it anyway? But what regard should one have for the sensitivities of others? If I had asked such questions, crudely, of Dolly, she would have bridled with indignation, with justifiable outrage. 'You look after your affairs, and I'll look after mine, thank you, Jane.' She might add that she had never asked anything of anyone, and no doubt believe it. To a certain extent this was true. Dolly did not ask; she merely indicated that others were in a position to give. That was quite different from asking. And the burden had already been placed on my shoulders by Dolly, who was in one of her periodic states of lack. I say lack rather than need, for need could be rather more easily dealt with. The burden Dolly placed on me was but a pale reflection of the burden she placed on the world. Love me! Save me! Already I had let her down. But how could I not? This last question, I am sure, she never formulated. She simply knew that I, like many others, had disappointed her, and that she, so gifted for pleasure, so ardent and so apt, must henceforth deal with a sullen girl, who showed no signs, and would never show any signs, of understanding or of sympathy with the life that Dolly so longingly desired.

These reflections made me so uncomfortable that I slept badly that night. The following day I went back to work, although I had been given the week off and was not expected to return until after the funeral. My arrival in the office seemed to cause a certain amount of surprise, as well it might, and was judged to be tactless. In the outer office Mrs Hemmings was on the telephone as usual, and no doubt to her daughter, who seemed to be causing a great deal of trouble. She raised her eyebrows at me in an attempt to express both astonishment and sympathy: as I shut her door behind me I could just hear her say, 'Daddy was *tremendously* disappointed . . .' and then I was where I longed to be, with Margaret and Wendy, in whose infinite commiseration I had unconsciously placed a good deal of trust. This, however, was not forthcoming, at least not to the extent which I had perhaps rashly anticipated.

'Why, Jane,' said Margaret. 'We didn't expect to see you here.'

'Our deepest sympathy, dear,' said Wendy, but her heart was not in it.

'I just couldn't stand being in the flat any more,' I said. 'Have you had your tea? Shall I make it?'

'That would be kind, dear. Will you have a cup

yourself? Were you thinking of staying?'

'Of course. If that's all right.'

'We didn't think you'd want to, after what had happened to your poor mother, going like that. No, no sugar, dear; I've given it up.'

They drank their tea in silence, clearly disapproving. I had come in for so much disapproval of late that I was nearly sunk under the weight of it. Fortunately or unfortunately, I have a good deal of self-control, and although I wanted to cry and sob my eyes were quite dry and my face composed. Besides, I reflected, only my mother and I knew the truth of the matter, and I had only to remember our oddly tranquil last night together, or even our last weeks together, when there had been no panic, no impatience, and, more important, no disapproval, to feel reassured. What sadness I felt had to do with the fact that no one else had shared or witnessed our accord, so that I would be eternally censured for my lack of feeling, when what had happened had involved a plentitude of feeling, of a nature to leave me denuded in the future and almost affectless in the present. I was aware of the coldness and darkness of the day, of the hissing overhead neon light, of the crammed wastepaper baskets. I would find no comfort here.

Margaret and Wendy continued to drink their tea in silence, eating their biscuits with constrained good taste.

'Is anything wrong?' I asked. 'Shall I go home?'

Margaret stirred from her trance.

'It's not you, dear. It's just that we've had a bit of a shock.'

'She dropped a bombshell,' said Wendy, rolling her eyes towards the outer office. 'Didn't even wait until we'd taken off our coats. "Relocating," she said. "The lease is up and I can't afford a new one." Not that it affects *her;* she could shut up shop entirely, as far as I can see, probably wants to. We all know about her place in the country, taking off on a Friday and not coming in till Monday afternoon, sometimes Tuesday morning, sometimes Tuesday after*noon*. She won't be affected. But what about us?'

Handkerchiefs were brought out; eyes were dabbed.

'Five years we've been here,' said Margaret. 'And now I suppose it's early retirement. Not what we expected. And just to let us know like that! And then she was on the telephone again, straight away. Her precious family: that's all she ever thinks of.'

'Just a minute,' I said. 'If she said "relocating" that means she's taken another office somewhere.'

'Warwick Way, she said, but that's not convenient. We're used to catching the 137, door to door. We can't do a long journey, not at our age.'

'It's not that far,' I said. 'You could catch the tube from Sloane Square to Victoria, and walk the rest of the way.'

This suggestion was met with a certain amount of scorn. Dissension was in the air, and it was they who wanted sympathy.

'When do we have to go?' I asked.

'She's shutting down at Christmas, so that's when we'll leave. I might think about coming back, but Wendy's dead against it. She's got our telephone numbers, if she wants us. I might consider part-time, but I don't know. It's just that it's so quiet at home, with the children gone. Not that you'd know about that.'

'And nothing to dress up for. I can't see us getting dressed up to go shopping at Clapham Junction. You're young, Jane; you can walk it. We can't.'

I thought this ridiculous but said nothing. I realised that a slight class difference was emerging. As far as I was concerned we all lived in Battersea. Now I was aware that Margaret and Wendy lived in council flats in a part of Battersea I had never visited and was now not likely to, whatever faint hopes I had entertained of being invited for Christmas, a festival I approached with the purest horror. Margaret and Wendy had no doubt observed among themselves that our flat in Prince of Wales Drive had seven rooms and two bathrooms, with an extra cloakroom, for so I had innocently described it in answer to their seemingly casual questions.

'The money's not going to be easy either,' sighed Margaret. 'This way we always had a bit in hand. Not that we did it for the money. It was the interest of the thing. And going out to work, well, it gives you respect, doesn't it?'

It had not given me respect, but rather a childish

pleasure in being included, an alibi for the daytime, just as sleep was my alibi at night. And I realised that I had not really needed the money, and that Margaret and Wendy knew this and would not forgive me for my relative affluence. It was clear to me that no work would be done that day, for Margaret and Wendy had already downed tools, regarding Mrs Hemming's bombshell as a calculated insult to which they were responding with hauteur.

'And what will you do, Jane?' asked Wendy distantly.

'I don't know,' I answered. 'I might stay on, if she wants me. I've got nothing else to do.'

It occurred to me briefly that I could now go to Cambridge, but I dismissed the idea. I felt too committed to the memory of the past few weeks to give my mind to anything else. I also felt too frightened. It was one thing to read *David Copperfield* in comfort, in my own bed at night, but quite another to produce a clever essay on withholding in Dickens's narratives, or the technique of the *mise en abîme* in Dickens's later novels (I had seen these subjects, or something like them, in specimen Cambridge entrance papers). Instinctively I rebelled against such investigations, which seemed to me clever and coldhearted. Self-conscious, too. And I should never be able to read again with childlike pleasure. I rejected Cambridge out of hand. I may have had some misty attachment to my domestic background: I may have thought I would be all right if I could go home every evening and sleep in my own bed. What I would do in the daytime was less clear to me. It was obvious that Margaret and Wendy would consider it treachery if I continued without them.

'Oh, I dare say I shall leave too,' I said weakly.

They brightened at this, and nodded to each other.

'We thought you'd say that, Jane. It's no less than she deserves, after all. Two highly trained workers, and you were coming along quite nicely, dear. Will you tell her, or will you leave it to us?'

'I'll write to her,' I said, after a moment's hesitation. 'We're here until Christmas, you said?' Christmas was a bare four weeks away.

'Hardly worth coming in, though, is it? Might as well take our money and go. I'll work out a few days' notice, that's all I can say. You won't have to do that, Jane. I reckon you can leave as soon as you like. Did the funeral go well, dear?'

'It's tomorrow,' I said, desolate once more.

I left after washing up the teacups, as they expected me to do. I wandered home through the park, with a sense of everything ending. I reflected that our exchange had taken no more than an hour: I could easily have stayed and cut up *Country Life* (something of a promotion, which Wendy had handed over after some hesitation) but the atmosphere had been silent and uncomfortable, and I had known that I was expected to go so that they could get on with their ruminations undisturbed. I was aware that I had become something of a class enemy, for my financial situation had been accurately assessed; not for me the happy shopping afternoons in Oxford Street which they had so enjoyed. My own shopping would be subtly differentiated from theirs. Awareness of this was almost palpable. I marvelled at the swiftness with which the change in our fortunes had been registered, but was too saddened by this sudden loss of affection to defend myself. In any event no defence was available to me, since there had been no accusation. Indeed, it seemed almost natural to me that I should lose everything, so utterly bereft did my situation appear to me. I was to remember this situation for some time. In an odd way it served me well, for it rallied my reserves of courage, such as they were. In later life I was to refer to it whenever I needed extra strength to deal with the exigencies of my not very onerous life. My importance in the scheme of things seemed to me minimal, even negligeable, yet a certain obstinacy, of which perhaps others were conscious, though I was not, kept me afloat.

I kissed them both, at which they bridled slightly, for I had committed the sin of not observing my mourning. I had no need to observe it: I was inhabited by it, but it did not seem worth trying to explain this. The outer office was empty, so I was spared the dilemma of whether or not to announce my resignation. In fact I was determined not to resign, for I might eventually want to do the job again, and I decided that I would write to Mrs Hemmings and ask her to let me know whether or not she might need me. I had a cup of coffee in a sandwich bar, envying the workers who had begun to crowd in on their lunch-time break. Then, since there was nothing else to do, I went home.

I walked through Battersea Park, as I had done so many times before. It was misty, and already growing dim, the weather I liked the most. London parks are at their best in this type of weather, and I lingered in the shadows, aware that the only figures I passed were, like myself, thoughtful, or merely unemployed. That way I managed to use up most of the afternoon. When I got back to the flat I found that Miss Lawlor had left. My supper, between two plates, was on a tray in the kitchen, as if I no longer needed or deserved the formality of a table and its proper accoutrements. Under the top plate I found a slice of meat loaf and a tomato salad, a perfunctory meal which in-creased my feeling of sadness. It was not that Miss Lawlor was neglecting me: I knew that she was given to tears and did not want me to see her crying. Besides, she was as unhappy as I was, and we found it difficult to comfort one another. I had always taken her for granted; it was my mother who was her true friend, although she had the company of the church ladies on Monday evenings. But with my mother she was an equal, and was able to discuss her affairs over the teacups. I dare say my father helped her with her tax returns and scrutinised any bills when she thought she had been overcharged. Now there was only myself, and I could do none of these things. In fact I could do very little, and as well as sorrow I felt an immense perplexity, as if I had no idea how to behave in this new cold world.

When it got properly dark I went to bed, regardless of the time. I slept immediately and profoundly. I dreamt not of my mother but of my father, who appeared before me, dressed as if to leave for the bank, but with tears running down his face. I woke after that, aware that the night had turned colder. Then I slept again, and when the morning finally came I got out of bed and went to the window to see mist, a mist that might lighten into sunlight later in the day, and a hard white frost. Now the last leaves that fell made a tiny clatter, and it was bitterly cold.

I dressed in the sad dark colours of mourning, and waited in my bedroom for the day to start. When I could wait no longer I went into the drawing-room: it must have been ten o'clock, and Miss Lawlor and John Pickering were already there. Both seemed unnaturally grave; in comparison I felt as weightless as a leaf. We greeted each other with great politeness and muted concern. Then they stood up with a sigh and came towards me. One arm firmly clasped in each of theirs I went down to the waiting car. Of the actual ceremony I registered little; I kept my eyes cast down and was only aware of the supporting arms. At the noise of the closing doors Miss Lawlor sobbed; I did not raise my eyes. Outside, in the day which had become sunny, John Pickering wiped his mouth with his handkerchief, while Miss Lawlor wandered off and pretended to look at the terrible flowers. Then she recovered herself and came resolutely back, putting away a handkerchief smelling of lavender water. I cannot now smell lavender water without thinking of that day.

'Come, Jane,' said Mr Pickering. 'Mrs Ferber is expecting us. I'm sure she will understand if I leave rather sharply. I have to get back to the bank. But I shall call on you this evening, and perhaps Miss Lawlor would be kind enough to stay with you until I arrive? It will be about six o'clock.'

'Certainly,' said Miss Lawlor. 'I shouldn't dream of leaving her.'

'Then we had better go and drink the coffee Mrs Ferber is so kindly preparing for us. Are you ready, Jane?'

'Quite ready,' I said.

I felt a sudden shameful hunger, and I needed that cup of coffee. What I did not need was Dolly, an impression confirmed when Annie opened the door on to a hum of conversation. Dolly's drawing-room, when we entered it, seemed to be full of people I had never seen before, highly scented women of a certain age, all tremendously dressed up. These women were introduced as, 'My dear friend, Rose. Dear Meriel, who didn't want me to be alone on such a sad day. Dear Phyllis, who insisted on coming to comfort me. And Beatrice, who is goodness itself, and who flew to my side.' I shook hands dazedly with these people. Beatrice, who had flown to Dolly's side, was a tall distracted-looking woman, possibly a latter-day avatar of dear Adèle Rougier. She held out a long cold hand: I wondered if I was expected to kiss it. 'Such a beastly day,' she said vaguely. 'Have you come far?'

I was aware of a shadow rising to its feet somewhere behind me. 'And this is Harry,' said Dolly, 'who looks after us all.' She gave a little laugh, as if to imply that the others need not necessarily feel themselves included. A man, the only man in the room apart from John Pickering, crossed the carpet on silent expensive shoes, shook my hand, and then sat down again. Harry: so he existed. I took him in, glad of something on which I could concentrate.

He was a coarse, sly, attractive man, and he was clearly at home. He wore a dark suit and a silver tie, which he caressed from time to time. The expression on a face which I registered as excessively tanned, as from a sunbed, was amused, aware of the farcical elements of the situation. A surprisingly small hand occasionally wandered to his sleek silver hair, which he smoothed, before returning to his tie. He looked like a dance band leader of the Thirties, jovial, expansive, and very slightly testy. He lounged in his chair, revealing an expanse of silk shirt, one leg crossed over the other, his foot wagging rhythmically, as if to music. At no time after he had greeted us did he rise to his feet. When Annie came in with the trolley — the Porthault cups, I noticed — he remained firmly seated, allowing Dolly to wait on him. Almost im-

191

mediately his plate held a careful selection of *petits fours*. This was all right, as the ladies protested that they were on a diet. In due course they relented, although it was Annie who was allowed to serve them, I noticed. Dolly, while taking the opportunity to return a few outstanding invitations, was not inclined to let the occasion slip away from her, as was evident from her oddly festive expression. John Pickering was also allowed a certain amount of attention, but the hierarchies were clearly to be observed.

I contributed nothing to the conversation, but merely sat with Miss Lawlor, drinking coffee. After a while Miss Lawlor got up and collected the empty cups. Dolly made sympathetic comments to John Pickering, as if he were the chief mourner. I was the only one out of place. Harry, to do him justice, noticed this, and cocked his head at me. 'All right?' he queried, and without waiting for an answer, said, 'That's the ticket. Don't let it get you down.' 'That's the way,' said Dolly ardently. 'One must never give in. Heaven knows what this has done to me. But I sing and dance, and I won't let anyone feel sorry for me.' Harry favoured her with a glance. I realised that he was no fool. I also realised that he was some years younger than Dolly, although to me he looked old. He was probably fifty-seven or eight, on the right side of sixty, at any rate, whereas Dolly was on the wrong side. I revised my estimate of her age: she must have been sixty-three or even sixty-four. But she looked well, was flushed, and obviously exhilarated. Maybe she was always like this when her friends were around her. But I thought that the exhilaration was due to Harry's presence, and so did the others, for they had realised that they were there as spectators, a role which they did not fully accept or appreciate.

'I'm afraid I must be getting back,' said John Pickering. 'I hope you will excuse me. This has been most kind of you. Jane . . .'

'One moment, Mr Pickering,' said Dolly. 'As we are all among friends I'm sure you wouldn't mind putting our minds at rest about Jane's future. I believe you are the executor? The will,' she added delicately. 'Poor Etty's will.'

'I'm afraid I couldn't possibly . . .'

'But it would put my mind at rest, Mr Pickering. May I call you John? I do so worry about Jane. And I am her nearest relation.'

He hesitated, clearly embarrassed. 'Well, if Jane has no objection . . .'

'None,' I said.

'One moment, dear. Annie, just take the trolley out.'

She seated herself in a wing chair, next to Harry, who was seated in a slightly lower chair. They looked like the Queen and the Duke of Edinburgh at the State Opening of Parliament.

'This is most irregular,' fretted John Pickering. 'And of course I don't have the document with me.'

'Just the outline,' said Dolly. Her tone was tranquil, agreeable.

'Everything goes to Jane, of course. There is quite a substantial amount. I will give you the details this evening, Jane. That is what I intended to do anyway. But you will be comfortably off, I might even say very comfortably. There is no need for you to worry about her, Mrs Ferber.' Dolly smiled.

'There were two other bequests,' he went on. 'One of five thousand pounds to Violet Lawlor, "in consideration of our long friendship". Those were the exact words. And a gift of one thousand pounds to yourself, Mrs Ferber.' He seemed embarrassed at this, as well he might. We were all embarrassed. Out of the corner of my eye I saw the smile frozen on Dolly's face. I saw Harry give her an ironic but not unsympathetic glance. I saw one or two of Dolly's friends exchange the briefest of looks, and then consult the interior of their handbags. Miss Lawlor was flushed and evidently ill at ease. Most faces were flushed, as if after an indiscretion. Dolly, when I could bear to look at her, was the most flushed of all, still smiling, but obviously boiling with rage, and, I thought, looking rather magnificent. Despite her setback this was perhaps Dolly's finest hour. Hastily regrouping her forces she stretched out loving hands to Miss Lawlor and myself.

'Dear Jane,' she said. 'I'm so glad for you. Could you ask Annie to make some more coffee, dear? I'm sure we could all do with some. And there are some smoked salmon sandwiches, and one of Annie's fruit tarts. Just put it all on the trolley, dear, and bring it in. Lucky girl,' she added winsomely. 'But I am so relieved. I do worry, you know.'

I escaped from the uncomfortable atmosphere in the drawing-room and wandered off in search of the kitchen. As I did so I reflected that this flat was quite large and must be rather expensive. I remembered Dolly telling my mother she had taken it on a short lease 'for a song', and supposed that the money obtained from the sale of the flat in Brussels, supplemented by my grandmother's allowance, was enough to cover it. But if this flat were only rented, as I knew it to be, then Dolly must be nearly at the end of her resources. And the money seemed to flow out, on bridge parties, and Annie's exquisite refreshments, and a wardrobe which seemed static but must have been renewed from time to time, and the recent refurbishments to her appearance . . . This last I could understand. It was painfully important to Dolly to make a show of affluence to her friends, one or two of whom may actually have obliged her with a loan but had then taken fright and had never renewed their one offer of help. I could imagine the scene: Dolly sighing over some luxury which she could not afford, or standing in a trance of admiration in front of one of her friends' possessions. 'And I've seen one just like it!' she would say. 'I've gone back a dozen times to look at it, and it's still there. But my allowance doesn't come through until next month. Oh, I don't know what to do.' At which point Rose or Phyllis might,

195

rather reluctantly, take out a cheque-book, reflecting that Dolly seemed to make enough out of her bridge games to buy the pretty object for herself. And the money would be paid back, of course, but after some delay, and an occasional reminder. 'Dear Rose' (or Phyllis), Dolly would muse to Beatrice or to Meriel. 'She does look after her money, doesn't she? *Elle est assez près de ses sous.*' For a French phrase or two went down rather well in the company she was now obliged to keep.

There was also the crucial business of Harry, who might turn out to be Dolly's last chance. Apart from his creditworthiness — the expensive clothes, the expensive lizard face — Harry had another function, which was to stir Dolly's heart, which was in danger of becoming atrophied, and to revive her desire. To judge from her demeanour she may have been genuinely in love with him, overlooking her age, which her friends shared and which they had decided should be given over to dignity and respectable pastimes. Dolly's friends were shocked at her behaviour, and here she may have been imprudent, for she could not resist her moment of glory. For Dolly now possessed a woman's prime asset: a man. Never mind the fact that all knew that this was a last throw of the dice, that Dolly might not bring it off, that it might end in tears. Never mind the fact that Harry was socially not quite what they were used to (an East End background? they queried, looking concerned for their friend). None of this mattered, as Dolly knew. For Harry had his attractions. His lazy body, lazily at ease in Dolly's drawing-room, had purpose. It was not of the same order of laziness as, for example, Rose's husband's, or Beatrice's: inert, the chest sunken into the stomach, the trousers riding high. No, Harry looked at women keenly, and if he did not look at Dolly it was because he had already seen what there was to see. A survey had been carried out, and had been found to be satisfactory. And although he might occasionally bestir himself for the other women and convey them in person from door to door, it was obvious from his attitude towards them that he found them of no conceivable interest. The occasional sexual innuendo might fall from his lips, but would be properly non-committal. 'Be a good girl now,' he might call out, as he started up the car again. 'Behave yourself.' With Dolly he did not bother. Therefore all were given to believe that Dolly and Harry behaved like grown-ups and did what grown-ups usually did. Further explanations would be superfluous.

I sincerely hoped that Harry would marry Dolly, for she was in many ways an old-fashioned woman, apt to hang on a man's words, brought up in any case to flatter, to placate, to cajole, as if this were a profession in itself, as it must have been before women worked and earned their own money. And although the money — Harry's money — would be a consideration, it was the prestige of the thing that mattered. Not only was it of prime importance to a woman like Dolly to have a man of her own, but that same man, if he were willing (Barkis again), would, in marrying her, confer on her a status which she had not enjoyed for many years. And by her own standards she had been very gallant, for I have no doubt that she disliked the company of women, with whom she had no choice but to consort, and not only to consort but to entertain, to ply with Annie's exquisite delicacies. Her mind was sharper than theirs: she found them stupid and confused, unable to give an account of their own money. 'Dolly, look at this for me, would you?' they would say, pulling a sheaf of papers — sometimes a bank statement — from their crowded handbags. No doubt she performed little services for them; no doubt she despised them utterly. Therefore the arrival of a man in her life was an epochal event, for thus she would repair her damaged reputation, and at the same time take her revenge.

When I went back into the drawing-room she was holding court, her cheeks still flushed, but her hand occasionally straying to Harry's arm. Thus she signified that the paucity of her legacy was but a temporary setback. I had to admire her. I only hope that if ever I suffer what amounts to a public humiliation I react as magnificently as Dolly did on that day. I realised, soberly, that she was enabled so to do by the presence of a man at her side, and was forced to revise certain feminist tenets and articles of belief. At the same time I also realised that I had inherited Dolly's financial problems — for I doubted that Harry was of an impressionable nature — and that I must work out the best way of tiding her over, as I should no doubt be shortly called upon to do, for our roles were now clearly defined. Then I reflected that she had a thousand pounds, which might give me a brief respite; as far as I was concerned, never having had so much money, a thousand pounds could last a long time. And now I was rich, I thought, and I had never wanted to be. What I wanted was to go out to work, and I somehow thought that my presence at ABC Enterprises would no longer be welcome, for were not wills published in the newspaper? Who, in future, would want to employ me?

I now understand that what I wanted to be was not independent, but its very opposite: dependent. I now understand — but of course did not at the time — that Dolly and I had something in common, an age-old ache that may have been no more and no less than a longing to be taken in, to be appropriated, to be endowed with someone's worldly goods whosoever they might be, for in that extremity of longing it might hardly matter. But I was young then, and unfeeling, as they all thought, and so, although I was not shocked by Dolly's behaviour I was sincerely disapproving. She knew this, of course. 'Dear little thing,' she mused, laying her hand fondly on my cheek, before whirling away to see to her guests.

'I really must be going,' said John Pickering. 'I will take you both home, if you are ready. The car is still downstairs.'

'How much is he charging you?' called Harry.

Mr Pickering ignored this. 'Must you go?' said Dolly. 'The girls are staying.' Indeed the atmosphere was relaxed. Crumbs were being brushed away, make-up repaired. I did not doubt that there would be a game of cards, and a little mild gambling, later on. None of this was anything to do with me. 'If you're sure,' said Dolly, marshalling us quite smartly to the door. 'You've been so kind, John. I'm sure you won't mind if I consult you on the best way to invest my legacy, tiny as it is. Goodbye, Jane. I'll be in touch.' To Miss Lawlor she said nothing. That was the only sign of her displeasure. When the door shut behind us we avoided each other's eyes. The coldness of the weather in the street made us gasp.

Oddly enough I was grateful to Dolly for lightening the gloom of that grim day. I reflected that she could always be relied upon to provide a diversion from one's own thoughts, the only things that could rightly be called one's own. By the same token she would separate one from those thoughts, so that in Dolly's company one was eternally dispossessed, forced to concentrate on her needs of the moment, as if these were paramount in a world of conflicting claims. On that journey back to Prince of Wales Drive I therefore felt empty of thought, and even of sadness, yet as we approached the flat I was overtaken by a terrible reluctance, even a superstitious horror, of what was awaiting me. I think Miss Lawlor felt the same, for her pale lips moved silently as if she were praying for strength. We stood on the pavement for an unnecessary moment, bidding farewell to John Pickering.

'I will see you both later,' he assured us. 'You're all right, Jane? You bore up very well.'

Then he got back in the car and was driven to the bank. The funeral must have been hard on him, I reflected. He was a lonely man, or seemed to be. After his wife's desertion he had sold his house in Chelsea and moved into a bachelor flat, determined never to marry again, although my parents had gently urged him to change his mind. He was a man of deep feeling and the utmost reserve. Unfortunately the reserve did not advertise the feeling, and he was looked upon as a cold fish. He had made a virtue of necessity and fashioned a solitary life for himself, observing a strict and unrelenting routine: the bank, a little rudimentary housekeeping, lunch at his club, and dinner at a local restaurant. On Sundays he had sometimes joined my father for a long walk, but as time went on he seemed more and more determined to endure his own company and set off on his own. Very occasionally he would join us for tea, looking as pale and unemotional in his weekend tweed jacket as he did in his formal suit for the bank. My father had admired him greatly; he in his turn had been fond of my father and indulgent towards my mother. He was very slightly awkward with myself, for he had no children of his own and was uncertain about the variations of childhood or adolescence he might be called upon to observe. He viewed the fact that

I was eighteen with relief, for technically I had become an adult and could be treated as one. I was extremely grateful to him for his precision and his coldness, which precluded the possibility of tears or despair in his presence. Nevertheless both Miss Lawlor and I felt the resurgence of both as we turned into the dusky hallway. The afternoon would, we felt, present a problem. Lunch was out of the question; neither of us could have eaten anything.

'You'd better have a rest, Jane, a sleep if you can manage it. I'll go out and do some shopping. And then I think I'd better make a cake for when Mr Pickering comes. He might want something with his coffee.'

We were both too unsophisticated to think that he might prefer a drink. In that sense Miss Lawlor and I were perfectly attuned, although I did not realise until later how deeply shocked she had been by the events at Dolly's. Nevertheless I suspected her of using the shopping as a pretext for going round to the church to say a prayer for my mother. This I in no sense begrudged her, wishing for her a peace of mind which might be denied to me.

I wandered into my bedroom, lay down on my bed, and watched the light fade outside the window. Sleep eluded me: I was wearily awake. If I were conscious of any wish it was for the energy to take a long walk in the park, but I did not think Miss Lawlor would approve, and so I continued to lie on my bed, where Miss Lawlor expected me to be, and waited for her to call me and tell me that tea was ready. I was aware of a golden smell of cake baking for the visitor, but the visitor was myself. I felt like a visitor in the house which I now supposed to be mine.

I got up, washed, and changed my clothes. Miss Lawlor had made a small additional cake for our tea, which we ate together, both rather silent. Our silence was nevertheless companionable, for we took one another for granted. Miss Lawlor was very slightly agitated by the impending visit of John Pickering, for the details of her legacy now appeared to her to be illusory, and she feared that he would now tell her that he had made a mistake, that there was no money for any of us.

'Will he want dinner, do you think? If so, I could make a cheese soufflé — I've got some eggs.'

'No, I don't think so. And anyway you must go home as soon as he leaves. You must be worn out.'

She smiled tremulously. 'I am, Jane, I will confess. I felt quite breathless this morning. Funerals are no good to the elderly. Well, it's over, just this one more ordeal to get through, and then I hope we can have a good night's sleep. You'll be all right on your own? You won't be nervous?'

No, I assured her, I would not be nervous. I was less confident than I made myself sound.

This time Mr Pickering came with an official-looking briefcase, so we knew we were in for some sound instruction.

'As I said, Jane, everything goes to you. There is quite a substantial sum.' He mentioned a sum so substantial that I was appalled. 'Most of it comes from the sale of the house in Maresfield Gardens, which your father invested for your mother. Then there were her own endowments from her father, and your father's pension from the bank, as well as his own small income from his mother. You follow?'

I nodded. 'What about Miss Lawlor?' I asked him, longing to put her mind at rest.

'Miss Lawlor, as I said, gets a sum of five thousand pounds, which I am empowered to pay her immediately, or to invest for her, whichever she prefers. And now, Jane, I believe Miss Lawlor has something to say to you.'

Miss Lawlor put a trembling hand on mine. 'I can't work here any more, Jane. I decided this afternoon, although I did ask Mr Pickering's advice earlier, when he called on us before the . . . this morning. I'm too old, dear. I'm seventy. And that little attack of breathlessness was a warning. I believe our dear one thought of all this when she decided to leave me all that money.' She dabbed at her eyes. 'She was my dear friend. Forgive me, Jane, but it wouldn't be the same without her.'

'How will you live?' I asked her, my lips numb.

'I'll be all right, dear, at home with Fluff.' Fluff was her cat. 'And I've got the church. I won't be alone. But I do worry about you here in this flat. It was different when she was alive. Now it seems so big.' And so empty, was what she meant.

'Here I have a suggestion which you might think

about, Jane,' said Mr Pickering. 'As you know I live in Dolphin Square.' I had not known this and did not immediately see its relevance. 'There is a small flat going on the fourth floor of my building, that is two floors above me. It is, as I say, small: two rooms, bathroom and kitchen. But the advantage is that it gets the sun all day and is very easy to maintain. I believe you should sell this place and make a move across the river. You will be quite comfortable there.' He gave a small constrained smile. 'And I shall be able to keep an eye on you.'

In a day of dispossessions this seemed the most final. But I was daunted by the prospect of living in our flat entirely on my own, without Miss Lawlor for company. I had asked her how she would live, but how would I live? I would find work eventually; indeed I would work desperately hard at some humble employment in an effort to forget my swollen inheritance. But to come back from wherever that work would take place (I was still thinking in terms of ABC Enterprises) to an empty flat, each room of which would resonate with other presences, was perhaps more than I could endure. The question was whether I could endure my loneliness any better in a small flat in a large anonymous block, whether or not it got the sun all day. How much sun was there in England, anyway? Would I sit at the window on eternal winter days and wait for it to return? Was that how I should spend my time? Or should I be meticulously well organised and turn myself into a facsimile of John Pickering?

He smiled encouragingly. 'It is a big decision, I know, but now is the time to make it. I can arrange everything for you, sale, purchase, removal, everything. And you have only to call on me if you need anything, you know.'

'What do you think?' I appealed to Miss Lawlor.

'Mr Pickering is right, Jane. Start afresh. You're only young; you've got your life ahead of you. Don't stay here, dear. You'll be too sad. I haven't been comfortable here myself since . . . It's too big, Jane. It needs a lot of work doing. Make a fresh start, dear. I'll come and see you. It's only across the river.'

But we both knew that she would not come and see me, or rather that she would come once to satisfy her conscience, and then thankfully return home to her own tea-time and her own comforts. And after that I would visit her, for as long as would be necessary. Since they both seemed to want me to move I said I would, although the loss of my only home would grieve me. When John Pickering left, with assurances of his help in all eventualities, I realised that I had agreed to go and see the flat in Dolphin Square on the following day, Saturday, when he would be at home to show it to me. I did this to please Miss Lawlor, who now looked exhausted. I saw her off, washed up, and went to bed. That night I did not sleep. I felt inhabited by ghosts, and could not wait for the following day, and the changes it would bring.

7

I was to move into the new flat after Christmas. I decided to take nothing with me except my bed, a chest of drawers, a table, and my parents' armchairs. The rest could be picked up as and when I needed it: I had done with bourgeois accoutrements. A considerable quantity of glass and china went round to Miss Lawlor, who also undertook to dispose of my mother's clothes. Although most of the looming furniture was still in place the flat began to look denuded. I ate hastily from the cups, saucers and plates I had reserved for myself and took my improvised meals on a tray in the kitchen, for there were no more tablecloths. This grand expulsion of my parents', even my grandparents', effects was accomplished with a cold determination which was intended to be an antidote to sorrow. At the back of my mind lurked the spectre of homesickness, which would no doubt come into its own once I lay in a different bedroom watching different lights flickering over a different landscape, so removed from the dark silent mass of the park, which took on a venerable aspect at night, and which no sound, apart from the muffled squeak of an animal, ever disturbed.

Soon there would be a busy road outside my window, and cars, and the impenetrable barrier of the dirty river, which would symbolise my separation from my old home. I had visited the flat and found it unobjectionable: it had been sunny, and the view from the window was quite distracting. The walls were solid, the rooms were functional and already carpeted and curtained by the previous tenant; it was very warm, with the dry, slightly stale warmth of a heated building when the weather outside is still mild. One thing had worried me: the noise of the lift going up and down and the unseen presence of so many people. In our old flat it was easy to avoid the neighbours because they all went out early in the morning, leaving my mother and Miss Lawlor, and myself if I were at home, undisturbed all day. The only couple who seemed to keep the same hours as we did consisted of a curious brother and sister who were never out of each other's company, both tall, both distinguished-looking, clad in identical Burberry raincoats over identical trousers, who murmured to each other in a language we could never identify, but who nodded and smiled and bade us 'Good-morning' in perfect unaccented English. My father had entertained a fantasy that they were deposed aristocrats from somewhere in central Europe and had embroidered this story until it became one of the set pieces of my childhood. Each encounter with them, as they silently and conspiratorially descended the stairs, revived our speculations. 'Latvian? Serbian?' my mother would ask, to which my father would reply, 'The bone structure is too northern — those long jawbones, you know. And that pale hair. Possibly Icelandic. Does anybody know them? What do they do all day?'

'They go for a walk in the park, as we do.'

'Suspicious. Are they waiting for the call?'

'If they are Icelandic they can't be waiting for a call. Iceland is a democracy.'

'Have you considered Hungary? What about Bulgaria? We haven't heard the last of Bulgaria. I think we must widen our parameters.'

'They are always perfectly pleasant. They say "Good-morning", and remark on the weather. I feel we should invite them to something.'

'And reveal our ignorance?'

'I'm sure there's nothing political about them. We would know if they were Russians. And anyway Russian spies seem to be a thing of the past. I dare say they can't afford them any more.'

'They may be members of the Israeli secret service. They are masters of disguise, I believe.'

The truth, when it was casually mentioned by the porter, was an anticlimax. The name of the couple was Dix, and they were French Canadian. So extremely subtle were their appearances and disappearances that I did not think to say goodbye to them. Apart from Miss Lawlor there was no one to whom I need say goodbye, a fact which filled me with relief. Miss Lawlor knew where I should be, John Pickering knew, Marigold knew. I telephoned Dolly to give her my new address, expecting a torrent of criticism, but she sounded detached, even indifferent. This I put down to the credit of Harry Dean, who must, I thought, be keeping her occupied, or at the very least pre-occupied. I had no idea how a couple of that age would amuse themselves. If I thought of them at all it was with a vague pity for their supposed infirmity, as if pleasure were beyond them, or should be. Indeed I did not think in terms of pleasure, which I identified with a certain slimness of build, whereas Dolly and Harry were both plump, as if after a lifetime of indulgence: I could still see Harry lolling in Dolly's armchair, his foot wagging in time to invisible music, and Dolly, important at his side, her bosom straining against a dress which was now, as it always had been, slightly too tight. I imagined them restricted to the indulgence of overeating, as if that might be how they spent their time together. I was aware of my own lack of experience, for at that stage I had no physical life of my own, but I was sure that my instincts were correct. I saw that what united them was greed. In this I was fairly pre-scient. Unfortunately I was not yet in a position to identify that greed. Therefore I was both right and wrong, but I did not give the matter much thought. Indeed I viewed it with some distaste, as a taboo which should be preserved intact. I was simply grateful to Harry for taking Dolly off my hands.

As far as I was concerned I was under an ob-ligation to Dolly. It never occurred to me that she might be under an obligation to me. I am quite sure it never occurred to Dolly either. Despite the gulf in our respective ages it was natural to me to think of Dolly as the younger of the two of us, for she laid claim to so many pleasures which as yet made no appeal to me, and which I, in my wisdom, considered illusory. Even her injunction to sing and dance I took as an indication of juvenility, not recognising it for the desperate stratagem it was in reality. In this way I managed not to take her seriously, although I found her disturbing, and for this reason never enjoyed her company, although Dolly did not doubt that she was bestowing pleasure wherever she went. Her visits to my mother were conceived with this purpose in mind, as if compensating her for the negligeable advantage she enjoyed by virtue of the mere fact of her private income, an advantage which did not render her interesting but which Dolly sought to alleviate by accepting her benefices from time to time. When pocketing my mother's cheques Dolly never doubted that she was doing my mother a favour. 'Poor Etty,' one could imagine her saying to herself in all good faith. 'Such a dull girl. Sitting at home all day in that mausoleum. And all those wasted assets! What wouldn't I do with her money! But she means no harm, poor dear, she just wants a bit of gumption. I'll cheer her up. I always do.'

She might reflect, without any sense of incongruity, that it was time to send some money to Nice, to the mother whom she now rarely visited, or to Lucette, who looked after her mother's affairs. She saw no harm in mentioning this new outlay. Her great strength was that she felt no shame in talking about money, whereas to my mother the whole subject was fraught with guilt. To Dolly money was a commodity like any other: she needed it, others had it. She could have it simply by pointing out the discrepancy. A more spirited woman than my mother might have said, 'But if I hand it over to you I won't have it any more, and then what will you do? For there is no doubt that you will go on wanting it.' But my mother was ashamed of her money; hence the furtive cheques, for which she seemed to want to be forgiven. If anything she was reassured by the magnificent equanimity with which Dolly stowed the cheque in her bag. 'I hope she didn't feel insulted,' my mother would worry, but even I, even as a child, could see that her worries were unnecessary.

Now that I was between homes, in a sort of no-man's-land, I found that I had a great deal of unoccupied and unattributed time. This frightened me, and I was hard put to fill the day. In desperation I went back to ABC Enterprises, to find Margaret and Wendy gone, and the builders dismantling the inner office, but Mrs Hemmings still on the telephone and not much incommoded by the open doors and the sound of Radio One.

'Ah, Jane,' she said, when she at last replaced the receiver. 'You're lucky to catch me; I shall be gone by tomorrow. My husband has booked us both on a Caribbean cruise, did so without telling me. Of course it's massively inconvenient. On the other hand I've no staff, as you may have noticed. So I'm leaving it all behind me. You weren't expecting to do any work, were you?'

'I was, actually.'

'As you can see, there's nothing to do. This is the official end of ABC Enterprises. I thought of keeping the name, but then I thought, why not make a clean break? So I've given the business to my son, and it'll be James Hemmings Enterprises in future. Or JH Enterprises, I suppose. He'll want to make changes, of course. But I'll take your number and let you know. There's not much going on before Christmas anyway. Where are you living now? Still in the same place?'

'Dolphin Square.'

'In that case Warwick Way would be quite convenient for you. I'll let you know. It depends on my son, of course. At the moment all I want to do is get on that ship and into the sun. Well, goodbye, Jane. Nice of you to come and see me. Perhaps we'll meet in the New Year. Oh, and Merry Christmas!'

I wandered out into Holbein Place. It was a beautiful day, cold and sunny, and the Christmas tree was up in the middle of Sloane Square. I had not, until that moment, considered Christmas. I supposed that I should spend it with Miss Lawlor, but reflected that Miss Lawlor would certainly be in attendance at church and almost as certainly would be visited by one of her elderly friends. Marigold, I knew, would be on duty. I did not as yet feel any panic at the thought of Christmas, or rather I did not feel any extra panic, for all the days were equally burdensome to me. But the day was so fine that it seemed idle to anticipate a day which might not be so fine, and I walked over the bridge to Prince of Wales Drive, aware that in reality I had already said goodbye to my old home, and even appreciating that the flat in Dolphin Square would, on a day like this, be bathed in winter sunlight.

My malaise, I decided, was now caused by the fact that I had no work, and I thought that to be deprived of work was a shameful thing, even more shameful than being independently wealthy. I needed work, but I also needed an education, and the thought occurred to me that I could take a degree without going to Cambridge, and that I could enrol at Birkbeck College in the following October and attend the evening lectures there. Then if I kept on working at the agency and studied in the evening I could fill my time most profitably, and in three years, or however long it took, be in a position to do real work and thus feel exonerated. What I wanted to do was write, but then so did everyone else. I liked stories; I had the gift of fabulation, but I always imagined an audience of children, sitting cross-legged on the floor in front of me. I might become a teacher, I thought. This decision reassured me, and I reached the old flat without more than the usual sadness. It did not occur to me to seek any guidance as to my future. I conceived of it as one long lonely effort, and was a little frightened. My world was underpopulated: I did not see how I was to make new friends. I only knew that I did not want the future to start straight away. Therefore I decreed for myself a holiday, albeit a sad one, which I would try to fill as best I could.

After a morning spent circulating with the crowds in the National Gallery and eating a meal in the restaurant there, sharing a table with three lively young women who apparently worked in the same office and to whom I longed to speak, I reflected that this experience had not been too bad, and that I might just repeat it on the following day, when I might look more closely at the Sienese school and perhaps attend one of the lectures, but that it could not be repeated *ad infinitum* because I would eventually see it for what it was, a pretext. I was no David Copperfield: I did not gather round myself a cast of fascinating characters, nor were there benevolent elders in the background, happy to recognise my gifts and my promise. I came out of the Gallery and leaned over the balustrade, gazing with puzzled eyes at an indifferent Trafalgar Square. It was not yet three o'clock, but already the day was dying; the sun, the colour of a blood orange, was shrinking in the sky, and an expanse of whitish cloud, soon to turn grey, and then to darken, dispensed a more palpable cold than I had noticed in the daytime. That moment of going home was for me always fraught with difficulty. Although self-sufficient by nature I hated the silent evenings, for the television had gone to Miss Lawlor and the radio was already in Dolphin Square. And perhaps I lacked resource; perhaps

I simply lacked company. On the evening of which I speak I felt the onset of a deplorable weakness, which was augmented by the prospect of Christmas, as, I have since discovered, is the case with others, even those more fortunately placed than myself.

When the telephone rang I ran to it with the purest gratitude.

'Dolly here,' said a brisk voice. 'I notice you don't bother to keep in touch these days.'

'I suppose I was waiting for you,' I said, immediately regretting the criticism implicit in this remark.

'What else am I doing, you funny girl?' Funny, in Dolly's parlance, was a synonym for selfish, dreary, stupid, and similar terms of disparagement. Since she used it all the time, of everyone, one could not challenge her on it, although her meaning was always perfectly clear. Being funny meant being relegated, as having revealed a sordid disposition. 'Funny woman,' she would say wonderingly, after unleashing a diatribe against one of her dearest friends. I took it that I was where I had always been, in the wrong.

'I was thinking about Christmas,' Dolly went on. 'You won't want to be alone, and I don't either. Everyone wants me to go to them, but I don't fancy it, not this year.'

I thought she was referring to my mother's recent death, and said eagerly, 'Shall I come over to you?'

'Good heavens, I'm not staying here. Anyway

I couldn't. Annie's gone to Ostend, to her daughter. No, I thought of a hotel. Somewhere on the coast. I thought you might like to join me. It would get you out. Of course it's ridiculously expensive, although not for you.' She gave her familiar little laugh.

'I could treat us both,' I said. I was grateful to her for thinking of me, for including me in her plans.

'You could, of course. Well, that would be very nice of you, Jane.'

Praise from Dolly! I began to experience a family feeling that I had never, even at my most desolate, connected with Dolly.

'Had you anywhere in mind?'

'Bournemouth,' she said. 'The Grand. I went there with Mother when we first came to England. It's where I met your uncle, as a matter of fact. I'll book, shall I?'

'And I'll look up the trains.'

'What a funny girl you are. We'll go by car, of course. I hope you've got something decent to wear. One is expected to make a bit of an effort. And I dare say there will be dancing.'

'Do we really need a car?'

'Well I certainly do, Jane. There's my luggage, my make-up case, my heated rollers. Good heavens, I certainly need a car. I don't suppose you'll take much. You can take a cab over to me — I'll hire the car. Be here at midday on the twenty-third. We should be there in time for tea.'

My case was packed by the twenty-second. I

was timidly delighted. I watched the weather, as if we should be out all day, walking by the sea, although as far as I knew Dolly never walked anywhere. In the evenings there would be dancing, she said. I would not dance, for I doubted whether I should find a partner, but I should be quite content to watch, even though it might mean seeing the equivalent of one of those television programmes my mother so enjoyed coming to life. Coming to life! I was young; I was ready for pleasure. And maybe Dolly and I could use this occasion to become on better terms with each other, for as she had once so nearly remarked, she was all I had.

On the day on which we had agreed, or rather Dolly had agreed, that we should meet, I found her standing in the hallway of her flat, in her fur coat, surrounded by various pieces of luggage. I had time to notice that the flat looked dusty: Dolly, by contrast, was heavily made-up, her face enlivened by various colours which heightened her expression of appetite but looked harsh on this grey day. She seemed morose, as if regretting the necessity for my company. Her manner was equally distant; in fact her disposition seemed sombre, even brooding, as if she desired nothing more than to be left to herself, as if she had urgent calculations to make, as if her normal vivacity, however irritating it occasionally was, had been laid aside in favour of a sudden access of cold reason.

I did not see why she should be so bleak at the

outset of what purported to be a holiday, but I noted with relief that I was not the occasion for her strange humour, that I had in effect done nothing to provoke it, that my presence did not even register very strongly, and was in any case irrelevant to Dolly's mood. This had its origins in circumstances then unknown to me, although I was to approach an understanding of them later on.

I followed her down the stairs, noting how easily she lifted and carried her suitcase, watching her glossy fur back with its obedient muscles, reflecting that she was essentially durable. Yet there was a suspicion of age — the merest suspicion only — in the very slight hunching of the shoulders, the shortening of the neck, half submerged in, and therefore even more drastically shortened by, an expensive silk scarf. When a woman can no longer straighten her neck and throw back her head with ease she had better see that she performs neither action inadvertently. Dolly's newly coiffed head disappeared down the stairwell in front of me; her footsteps seemed heavier, or merely more determined, as if she were undertaking a mission which might have something perilous about it, but which she was pursuing with her usual courage. For Dolly had courage, had in fact never lacked it.

'I hope you will be able to amuse yourself, Jane,' she said, settling herself in the back of the car, which immediately filled with the smell of her scent. 'And now, if you don't mind, I'm going to close my eyes. I shall need all my energy for this evening.'

She handed me a brochure which showed a Jacobean-style mansion in a sunlit snowy landscape. Inside was another photograph of a log fire in a marble fireplace wreathed with holly. The first thing to register was the price charged for this three-day Christmas break, which struck me as excessive, although this apparently was what people were prepared to pay for the privilege of being taken in at a problematic time of the year. The object seemed to be to create the atmosphere of a cruise, with the accent on food, entertainment, and dancing. There was to be a welcome champagne reception, I read, that evening, with local carol singers, followed by dinner in the French style. A full range of diversions, including cards and a quiz in the television room, would be available. On Christmas Eve, ladies were advised that the hairdressing salon would be open until five o'clock. Another champagne reception would be followed by dinner in the Italian style. There would be dancing until midnight, when hot punch and mince pies would be served. Feeling slightly sick I noted that Christmas Day would be marked by full English breakfast, morning coffee, with a visit from more carol singers, traditional Christmas lunch, followed by tea with Christmas cake. Dinner would consist of a Scandinavian smorgasbord. On Boxing Day one could take brunch in the restaurant, after which one was expected to make oneself scarce until the evening cocktail party, followed by a grand gala dinner, with dancing and cabaret. On the following day, I noticed, no food other than breakfast was provided; after yet another cocktail party one was expected to depart, while the hotel geared itself up for what was announced as a magnificent New Year's break.

The grim professionalism of these people astounded me, for surely there could be little pleasure in any of this for the staff. Or even for the patrons, stuffed to the gills with smorgasbord and Christmas cake. But then I reflected that lonely people, widows especially, might wait all the year for the opportunity of meeting others in a festive atmosphere, and for three or four days manage to give an impression of high spirits and fulfillment, overlooking or even forgetting the circumstances in which they lived. In this category I was forced to include Dolly, yet it worried me that she had to descend to this sort of amusement which seemed inferior to me, commercial, if not downright cynical. But people went on cruises, I thought, and sometimes made friends, and although Dolly seemed to have plenty of friends I could see that she might enjoy a holiday from her real life.

I stole a look at her from time to time. Her bluish eyelids were tightly shut, and her thin lips, painted a dark red, were clamped together in a downward line never before witnessed by me. She looked old; she looked ill. She also looked resolute, as if about to undertake a difficult enterprise. She remained asleep, or else communing with herself, for two hours, at the end of which she opened her eyes, relaxed her mouth, looked thoughtful, then enthusiastic, then joyous, in a progression so natural that I wondered how I had ever thought her old. A layer of scented powder was applied, lipstick was renewed, the social persona was refurbished and ready for action. Yet somehow I was left with that impression of determination, as if Dolly were a professional herself. Maybe this was an element of her natural behaviour, faced, as she had been, with many precarious situations.

This glimpse behind the façade of Dolly's life made me uncomfortable. I did not like her, yet I had no wish to see her humiliated, and I sensed that she was ripe for a humiliation of one kind or another. She had lost her natural sense of festivity, which was in fact her most attractive characteristic. Her spontaneity I had always doubted, since I had become aware of the enormous amount of calculation behind it. Now there was a watchfulness about her; I was seeing an older, more effortful Dolly. Yet when I looked at her again I was surprised by a dazzling if meaningless smile, one of the smiles by which I had first known her, and I determined to afford her as good a time as possible, since that was what she wanted. 'Singing and dancing, Jane', I could almost hear her say. It seemed to me something of a defeat that she had been reduced to the manufactured entertainment advertised in the brochure. As for myself, I hoped for nothing from this excursion. The only saving grace was that neither of us would be on our own.

The car approached a looming pile which bore

only the faintest resemblance to the illustration in the brochure. The weather, moreover, was mild, grey, and overcast. We entered a ferociously heated lobby which seemed full of people whom Dolly surveyed with an expectant eye. From time to time a voice on a loudspeaker, prefaced by a crackle, announced that tea was now being served in the lounge. 'Come along, Jane,' said Dolly, in her normal brisk and emphatic voice. I followed her into a huge room smelling of cigars, where waitresses sped about with silver teapots and plates of pastries. I prepared to chaperone Dolly to the best of my ability, but her eyes were sharper than mine. 'Why Harry,' I heard her say, in a delighted and infinitely honeyed tone. Harry rose to his feet from a chair beside a log fire: that at least was genuine. 'You got here all right, then,' he said. 'The others are over there.' He seated himself again, as if he had fulfilled his social duty, and returned to the newspaper, in which he was checking the racing results. I followed Dolly across the room to where Phyllis, Beatrice, and the other two were seated, with their amiable but unimpressive husbands. All uttered delighted noises of appreciation. 'Jane, do ask Harry to join us,' said Dolly, who was now restored to full vivacity. 'Oh, yes, do,' said Phyllis, or Rose, or Meriel. 'A party's not a party without Harry.' 'And order tea,' added Dolly, whose face had lost any suggestion of age, even less of the bitter reflections which seemed to have assailed her in the car. I was self-conscious as I crossed the floor, although I felt invisible in this middle-aged company. 'Dolly says, won't you join them?' I asked Harry. He gave me a hard look, not altogether well-meaning. I was slightly afraid of him. 'Ordered tea, have you?' he said. I recovered a little of my composure. 'Perhaps you could do that for me,' I told him, and rejoined the group.

Harry's presence stimulated the ladies to gales of laughter, at which their husbands permitted themselves an absent-minded and indulgent smile. It was as if Harry were relieving them of a duty which had become onerous. His talk was invariably suggestive, and I felt there was something slightly professional about Harry as well. As the flat-chested Phyllis helped herself to an éclair Harry remarked, 'Better weigh yourself this evening, darling. I think you'll find you need a bigger size. I'd offer to do it for you, if Jack weren't here.' They loved it. I reflected how easy it is for a man to reduce women of a certain age to imbecility. All he has to do is give an impersonation of desire, or better still, of secret knowledge, for a woman to feel herself a source of power. Dolly, although deploring the concessions Harry was making to her friends, was radiant, succumbing not only to Harry's presence but to the *louche* atmosphere. I was too dazed to feel any sense of outrage. I realised that all this had been conjugated without me, that one friend had indicated the hotel as a possibility for Christmas for the others to join in, and for Dolly to be determined not to be left out. 'Where are you going, Jane?' called Dolly, as I got up to leave them.

'I'm going for a walk,' I said. 'I've got a slight headache.'

'Don't forget dinner's at seven-thirty. Oh, and the champagne reception. Don't forget that.'

But in fact they were uninterested in my movements. I wandered out into the dusk, and down in the direction of the sea, although the tide was out and the sea was silent. There was no one about. In front of me spread a colourless emptiness; behind me the hotel blazed with all its discordant light and heat. Although it was nearly dark I descended the steps to the sand and walked a long way. I was unaware of distances, forced myself to notice only the chill of the air and the whisper of the waves. I was alone, and less angry than sad, sad to have been duped, sad to have been disappointed, sad even to have been denied the opportunity of befriending, or being befriended by, Dolly, to whom I was now irrelevant, having performed the only service for which she judged me apt. I might have given way to tears, but my native obstinacy reasserted itself, and I walked on, in the growing darkness, and under an empty sky, willing myself back into some sort of composure. I must have walked for well over an hour and a half. In that way I was able to avoid the champagne reception, which took place without me. I only had time for a quick bath and change before joining Dolly and Harry for dinner.

They were both too greedy to flirt at the table. Both ate in an intense and businesslike manner, as if not willing to waste words when there was nourishment to be had. All around me middle-aged and elderly couples devoted themselves to dinner in the French style. 'We're paying for it', their attitude seemed to say, although they tried to be restrained, and often indulged in a little mild conversation with husbands for whom they generally answered as a matter of course. Against this gentility Dolly and Harry, mouths glistening, gave an impression of superior appetite. A clue could be read here to their more intimate behaviour. As an unwelcome guest at their table I was not able to ignore this.

I escaped and went to bed early, my stomach heavy with the unwanted food. Because I hated the room, with its pink lampshade and its cynical minibar, I took one of the sleeping pills the doctor had given my mother after my father's death. I slept dreamlessly, woke easily, and was the first down to breakfast, which I ate alone. All around me was evidence that the day had not properly started. Waiters looked pasty, and did not bother to lower their voices as they passed through the swing doors into the kitchen. I was alone in the dining-room, apart from a couple of elderly men eating All-Bran at distant tables. The air smelt of the dinner of the previous evening. On an impulse — and I was thinking more clearly this morning — I decided that I owed Dolly no more than a token presence. I got my coat and left a message at the desk that I would be back for dinner. I would have been absent even for that but could not think of a sufficiently convincing excuse.

It was Christmas Eve, and as I left the hotel the loudspeaker was crackling into play. I retraced my steps of the previous evening and walked in the direction of Sandbanks, or so a notice with an arrow informed me. The day was mild and slightly overcast, a good day for walking, although there were few walkers about. The coastline seemed to me unresolved, neither hilly nor flat but occasionally both, and not brought into focus by the strange tentative misty light which hinted, or seemed to me then to hint, at forlorn destinies, lives lived in silence, desolate villas with gimcrack balconies, gardens filled with mournful laurels, cautious promenades with subservient dogs, widowhood. I felt oppressed by the silence, and even thought kindly of Dolphin Square, wishing I were there already, unpacking my books.

I walked on until the tide began to come in, and then I turned towards what was to become the town. I ate a lunch of fish and chips in a café crowded with school-children being treated by their parents. Children again: I began to feel better. Undoubtedly my destiny was to be coloured by children, and I felt a distaste and an impatience for those elderly revellers waiting for me back at the hotel. I wandered about the town in the afternoon, bought a pair of gloves for Dolly, for whom I now felt my usual mixture of pity and exasperation, drank a cup of tea in another café, and then, when I could no longer avoid it, made my way back, through streets now crowded with last-minute shoppers, to the glistening lights of the monstrous and menacingly hospitable hotel.

The only evening wear I possessed consisted of a black top and a black and white check taffeta skirt. This had always seemed adequate for the few parties I had attended at home, but here, I realised, as I joined the others for the champagne reception, I was out of my depth. All the ladies were tremendously coiffed, having evidently spent the afternoon in the hairdressing salon, and they were dressed as if for a gala evening at Covent Garden. Perfumes mingled and clashed; ear-rings were constantly adjusted. The mild husbands circulated goodnaturedly in ancient dinner jackets which revealed their owners' ages. Dolly and Harry stood out clearly as the most handsome couple, for both had that air of busyness and appetite which their contemporaries could only envy. Everything about Harry gleamed: his shirt, his silver hair, his narrow shoes on his small dancer's feet. Dolly wore black, but there was nothing modest about Dolly's black: it was a shameless satin sheath moulded to her opulent figure, the tulip skirt parting from time to time to reveal her still excellent legs. She looked resolute, outrageous, and magnificent, like a star giving what might turn out to be her final performance. So filled was she with her defiant belief in herself that all eyes were upon her. And I did not begrudge her her triumph, for however much I had contributed (unwittingly, a hidden voice reminded me, but I silenced it) I had to concede that I had given her pleasure.

And Dolly's desire for pleasure was so profound that it seemed only natural to provide it. When in a state of pleasure — and there was no denying this — the years fell away from Dolly, making her real age and its disadvantages irrelevant. It was almost possible to wish her well in whatever she undertook. I learned something in those few moments; mainly I learned that not everyone felt as I did. I saw and applauded the energy of a temperament in every way opposed to mine; I saw — and even understood — the thrill of the chase. That Harry was the prey seemed to me unimportant. That I was there under false pretences seemed equally unimportant. Momentarily I was Dolly's faithful ally, with, at the back of my mind, the memory of her bitter European face, as revealed in sleep, in the half light of the car, the effervescent mask for once cast aside and the grim working woman revealed. I was both frightened and determined for her, as she must have been frightened and determined for herself.

My indulgence cooled slightly in the course of the evening, when it became obvious that Dolly had forgotten all about me, and that Harry regarded my presence as a joke. This became even more apparent when the loudspeaker, after a preliminary crackle, announced that dancing was about to begin. Although rendered almost comatose by dinner in the Italian style I followed Dolly and Harry into the ballroom, where I caught the eye of an otherwise impassive teenage saxophonist who immediately looked away. The music was predictable and slightly out of date: selections from the Beatles' early albums, selections from *Fiddler on the Roof*, selections from *Brigadoon*, and once every hour, with a wail from the saxophone, 'Moon River'. Dolly and Harry sped across the floor, weightless and at one, still businesslike, but expert, as if they had been doing this all their lives. It occurred to me, as I waited silently for the evening to end, that this was what they did in their spare time. There must have been afternoon tea dances in various London hotels, or maybe they had joined a club of some sort. A club was where a predatory man or woman would look for a partner, and Harry and Dolly were both predators. I shifted uneasily as Dolly's tulip skirt swung open and her triumphant laughter rang out. I doubted whether on that previous occasion, in this hotel or one like it, when she had subjugated my uncle, she had been more sexually aroused than she so obviously was now. Others became aware of what was in any case obvious: applause which had been enthusiastic became desultory, faces relapsed into disapproval. At last Dolly noticed this, and led Harry off the floor to where I was seated. 'Give Jane a dance, Harry,' she said.

'I'd rather not,' I protested.

'Don't be ridiculous, Jane. Off you go.'

Harry's fingertips moved intimately to my upper arm. Longingly I gazed back at Dolly who glared at me. As the band struck up 'Moon River' for the third time I heard the last instructions I was ever to accept from Dolly. Harry smoothed his hair: I gave Dolly one final glance. 'Charm!' she hissed, and then I was on the dance floor, far from human aid.

Harry was a good dancer; he was even too good. He was certainly too good for me. His tiny feet sped over the floor while mine trod hesitantly after them, occasionally a step behind. Humming jauntily he issued instructions which, coming from him, sounded dubious. 'Let it go,' he ordered. 'Easy now,' and again, 'Let it go.' I had lost weight and my skirt was slightly loose. I was aware of his hand, which he turned fastidiously outwards, shifting the waistband. When my ordeal was over I was obliged to adjust it, in full view of Dolly and her friends. 'Harry up to his tricks again,' tittered Phyllis, but Dolly, I could see, was put out. When I said that I was going to bed, she said, quite shortly, 'Yes, do.' Evidently my increasingly agonised presence was no longer to her liking, if it ever had been. I was only a pretext, I reflected, and none of it was important. But I woke in the night to hear delighted laughter in the next room — Dolly's room — interspersed with Harry's slow chuckle. Looking back now I realise that what was taking place may have been merely anodyne; then it sounded like an introduction to the world's corruption. I put the pillow over my head and somehow struggled through until morning.

I was up far too early. I went down into the stale-smelling restaurant, where there was no one about. There was a sound of hoovering from the lounge. I date my horror of hotels from that morning. When a waiter finally appeared I coldly requested coffee and toast. 'Full English breakfast at nine, Madam,' I was told. Even more coldly I repeated my request. At nine o'clock Dolly appeared, alone, in a rather unfortunate trouser suit which was ill-suited to her odalisque's figure.

'A word with you, if you don't mind, Dolly,' I said.

'Well?' She was no better disposed than I was.

'I'm going home. There's no point in my staying. You've got your friends, and I've got mine.'

'Oh, really? And who are your friends? Miss Lawlor? Pickering? Your mother?'

'I thought you were fond of my mother.'

'I loved her! But she wasn't a real woman to my mind. She just sat and read. Real women are alive, Jane!' Here I anticipated her views on the desirability of singing and dancing, but she was too angry for that. 'Real women attract men, Jane! It's no good your looking at me like that. It's true. How do you think life goes on?'

'I didn't expect to see your friend here . . .'

'Why not? He is my friend, after all. I'm not going to apologise because he wants to be with me, because we want to be together. You'll find out one day, although at the moment I wouldn't bank on it.'

'I'm going home today.'

'Yes, go! Go back to your books! Go back to Pickering! You're no good to me here.'

'But I wasn't ever going to be, was I? You planned to be with your friends all along. I was just here as an afterthought.' To pay the bill, I knew, but that seemed too outrageous a thing to say, even now.

'My dear, you were never of the slightest importance to Harry and me, or the girls. I thought to do you a good turn, show you a bit of life, take you out of yourself. Instead of which you sulk!'

'Excuse me,' I said. 'I'm rather tired. I didn't get much sleep last night.'

There was the tiniest pause.

'Then perhaps you know a bit more about life today than you did yesterday.'

'Perhaps I do.'

There was a silence.

'Go home, Jane. You're no good to me here. In fact if anything could spoil the pleasure it would be you.'

'Unfortunately there are no trains until tomorrow.'

'And you're too mean to hire a car! Just like your mother, with her little skirts from Jaeger! Oh, go home! I don't care how you get there. *Bon débarras!* Of course, you know what's really wrong, don't you? You're jealous! Harry was saying to me last night, what that girl needs is a man.'

I doubted whether Harry had put it as delicately as that. We were both so terribly angry that I thought we must never see each other again. There remained the matter of the bill, a matter which had also occurred to Dolly.

'Pay your bill and go,' she said. 'Harry and I

will look after ourselves.' And with that she turned on her heel and went upstairs, having effectively had the last word.

I checked out, in the horrible hotel parlance. 'Checking out already, Madam?' the clerk enquired, relieved to see at least one of us leave. He ordered a car for me — at least hotels were used to this service, and at the moment it was the only service I required — and we slid silently away into a deserted town, where everyone was at home and would be worn out by lunchtime. At the hotel the carol singers would soon be arriving, to be served up with the mid-morning coffee. And no doubt my shortcomings would be discussed by Dolly and her friends, all of whom would be delighted to have a new and scandalous topic of conversation. The husbands might feel a little sorry for me, but would prudently say nothing. Harry would repeat his opinion as to my real requirements, but here they would laughingly shriek in protest and the atmosphere would be restored to something like normality. I had, if anything, done them all a favour.

My thoughts were so discordant that I hardly noticed the countryside, through which we intermittently passed. Eventually my sadness became qualified by a certain resignation. Dolly's almost unbelievable crassness I put down to age, and perhaps something else. What was it? Desperation? A sense of time running out? For although things had gone according to plan — her plan — there was a bitterness about her which surfaced from time to time, in the grimly closed mouth perceived on the journey down, and the force of her anger, which was no longer her more easily recognisable impatience. There was a coarsening there, as if all her instincts had deteriorated. She had not always been so blatant, so complacent in her demands: indeed my father had frequently shaken his head in admiration over her obliquity. Now she had become cynical, like a blackmailer. Yet here perhaps I began to glimpse a deeper reason for her behaviour, for she knew that however silent we remained on the matter, we — my mother, my father, and myself — considered her excessive, and that she was thus destined to remain something of a stranger among us.

For our exclusiveness we were required to pay a penalty. And so uncomfortable were our own feelings in this matter that it never occurred to us to demand something as simple and straightforward as an accounting. If my father had cheerfully sat her down, and said, 'Now, Dolly, let's find out exactly how much money you have. Let's look at your outgoings and see if we can save something.' Instead of which he had regarded Dolly's visits as comic interludes, and demanded to be entertained with descriptions of her performance. After all these years nobody knew exactly how much Dolly had to live on, how much rent she paid, what Annie's wages cost her. She was not in need; that much my mother, and before her my grandmother, had seen to. But they may have felt a fundamental distaste for one who exploited them so conscientiously, more, for one who put exploitation to work for her as others engage in a profession, and this distaste may have been perceived by Dolly, whose judgements were usually kept hidden but whose instincts were far from misinformed. We had held her at arm's length and she had made us pay for the privilege. And because I was the last in line I had to be the last victim, for I had inherited not only the money but the moral high ground. For this I would not be forgiven.

Nobody loved Dolly: that was her tragedy. Nobody even liked her very much, and she knew that too. She was accepted as a friend by women inferior to herself because she was vigorous and clever, because she entertained and fed them, because she sorted out their affairs, and listened with every appearance of interest to their feeble gossip. Unnerved and enervated by years of this company she had succumbed to the first man to make a show of virility in her presence, and thus, like any victim, had cast herself under his spell. And he had partly compensated her for many humiliations by allowing her to reassert her right to be a normal woman, with a normal woman's expectations, love, certainly, even marriage. This far-distant goal had been approached more nearly than at any other time in her long widowhood. Her present coarseness spoke of feelings long held in check by what had in fact been an unwanted chastity. She was a woman of her time and of her age, idle but enterprising, passive but demanding; she would have

236

made an excellent wife. Women of my own generation are expected to accumulate love affairs throughout the years until they are Dolly's age, although this may be as distasteful to some of them as the idea of celibacy is supposed to be: they have 'rights', usually described as rights over their body, and they are expected to exercise them. But Dolly was in her sixties; she still thought in terms of marriage, and for this reason she was chaste, as her own mother had been in that previous widowhood, and whose shyness and humility she may have cherished as an ideal, in default of any other.

There remained the business of Harry, and his effect on her, all the more dangerous because of her circumstances. She had been encouraged, or had encouraged herself, to think of permanence, whereas what he offered was the most cursory of interludes — even I could see that. To Harry Dolly must have seemed an original personality, the kind which did not normally come his way, but for her age much too impressionable. The temptation to make love to such a woman, and to reduce her to gratitude and passivity, was very real but essentially cruel. Harry offered a ration of lovemaking, to an extent which would cause him no inconvenience. He was even amused by her ardour, which confirmed him in his own high opinion of himself. He had not once in my presence exchanged a gentle word with her, expressed pleasure, or even offered her a conventional greeting. 'You got here all right, then?' he had said, looking up from his newspaper, which was not even cast aside. Harry, in short, was the worst kind of man, the kind who fails to recognise his own cruelty. Coarsely attractive he may have been, physically vigorous he undoubtedly was, but he regarded his willingness to make love to lonely women in as professional a manner as others lay claim to an ability to manipulate bad backs. Harry was the sexual equivalent of an osteopath or a chiropractor: he offered 'relief', and gave, as he thought, satisfaction all round.

And in her heart Dolly knew this, just as she knew that he did not love her, that he was the sort of man she would have treated with disdain in former happier times. For Harry did not make Dolly feel safe, and safety was the only condition she now sought. She knew perfectly well that among her friends her status was uncertain, but that all could have been rectified by the presence of a man at her side, or even in the background, provided that his presence was permanent. She may even have reckoned, in her desperation, that if she had a husband, however humdrum, she could afford to be as stupid as Phyllis or Beatrice or Rose, those dear friends by whom she was so profoundly bored. After years of living on her wits she looked on stupidity as a luxury she could not afford, but which she craved, now more than ever, because it held a promise of the peace which had so far been denied her.

So that the coarseness of her own behaviour, towards myself in particular, was in reality the outcome of despair, as if her defences were giving way, her pretences as well, and as if she no longer had the faith in herself necessary to carry out her difficult task. I had seen her at a turning point in her affair with Harry. Despite having spent the night with him (and who knows whether it might not have been the last?) she had been discontented on the following morning, the morning of our argument. She may have sensed that the affair had ended, for Harry would certainly not bother to explain himself, and would have expressed astonishment if she had been unwise enough to challenge him. There had been a tired asperity about her; she had already made the mistake of wearing that tight trouser suit, which did not become her. Would she commit further imprudences, plant a man's cap roguishly on her greying head, like the lady in Colette's story? I was painfully glad that I would not be present to witness this, if indeed it were to take place. At the same time I felt profoundly unhappy for Dolly. Even the matter of the hotel bill upset me. It was then that I had the idea of making her an allowance out of my own money. It was the old equation: she wanted it, I had it. On this silent Christmas afternoon, when Dolly would be tucking in to whatever food the hotel judged appropriate to the occasion and which would no doubt run the gamut down to the very last mince pie (here I became aware that I was hungry), I made a vow to endow Dolly as she would wish to be endowed. There was no doubt in my mind that if I did not do so I should have bad dreams.

It was already getting dark when I reached home. Throughout the journey the driver and I had not exchanged a single word. My thoughts had been so searching and so uncomfortable that I had not noticed this, nor had I noticed the time passing. The sky already had a lightless look, although one could not expect it to get properly dark for a couple of hours. Prince of Wales Drive lay under a silence so profound that it might have been an enchantment: not a car passed in the street, nor were there many lights in the windows. Maybe everyone had gone away, as I was supposed to have done. The sound of my key in the lock was an anomaly, even an indiscretion. I unpacked my bag, made coffee, which I had to drink without milk, and ate an apple. Then I lay down on my bed, not to sleep, but to reread the last chapter of *David Copperfield*, to give myself encouragement.

Yet I must have slept, for when I awoke it was properly dark and the phone was ringing. For a brief wild moment (and how enriching that moment was) I thought it must be Dolly, apologising, even wishing me well. It was of course Miss Lawlor.

'Jane? Are you coming over for a slice of my Christmas cake? You know how you always enjoy it. And Fluffy and I would be very glad to see you.'

So I went round to Parkgate Road, through streets which were now black and silent, and sat in Miss Lawlor's bright little sitting-room, where the Christmas cards were draped on strings over the fireplace, and there was even a small tree, decked with presents for the cat, 'and for you, dear,' said Miss Lawlor, handing over something soft, which turned out to be handkerchiefs. Fortunately I had given her a silk square before departing on my great Christmas adventure. I ate slice after slice of cake, at which Miss Lawlor looked on approvingly.

'I telephoned you earlier,' she said. 'But there was no reply. Then I realised you must be with Marigold.'

'Marigold's on duty today.'

'On duty?'

'She's a student nurse now, Miss Lawlor. She's on duty at the hospital.'

'Good heavens. She's still a little girl to me. As you are, Jane. Have you given some thought to the future?'

'I'll probably go to college,' I said. 'In London, so I'll still be here if you need me. And I can work part-time.'

'That's nice, dear.' She frowned. 'But if you weren't with Marigold where were you?'

'I was invited out,' I told her. Nothing could have been further from the truth, but her face cleared. 'And what about you?' I said quickly, for I wanted her peaceful images to replace my own discordant ones.

'A lovely day, dear. After church I went on to Mrs Cronin's and had lunch with her. Then we watched the Queen, and then I came back here

241

and had a rest. I do that now.' She smiled. 'I've got old all of a sudden, Jane. Maybe it's retirement. I feel it won't be long now before I won't want to go out. But I'm quite happy, dear, so don't worry about me. I've got the ladies from the church, and they'll look in on me. Not yet, of course; that day is still some way off. And I'll see you from time to time, not that I want you running over here every five minutes. You see, dear, I'll be all right because I've got my faith. If only you could believe, Jane! It's like a whole new life being given to you. When I put my light out at night I feel perfectly safe. Do you think you might like to come to church with me one Sunday?'

'Perhaps,' I said, for I did not want to offend her.

'Just read a psalm occasionally, Jane. You were always a good girl. I'm sure you'll come to the light one day.'

As this was profoundly embarrassing to me I said that it was getting late and that I must go. Then when I was at home and had unpacked all the small parcels of foodstuffs Miss Lawlor had put into a bag for me I did what people without faith do, and made practical arrangements. I drafted a letter to the bank, asking for a certain sum to be paid monthly to Dolly. I may have over-estimated; I could have waited and consulted Pickering, but I wanted this to remain unknown, a secret, so that Dolly would not have to pretend to me (I was after all less impressionable

242

than my mother), and that when she taxed me with being cold, and lacking in charm, as she almost certainly would, my conscience would be almost clear.

8

It pleased Dolly to be displeased with me, in order to camouflage her bad behaviour. She never forgave those who criticised her, and my criticism, although not stated, had been implicit. I telephoned her several times, only to be told by Annie that she was out. I accepted that she no longer wished to be in contact, posted my letter to the bank, and when I received no acknowledgement from her came slowly to the conclusion that our relationship was at an end. This caused me disappointment, as well as a degree of relief. I was young, and unwilling to suffer an injustice which I had done little to merit. As time went on it no longer became possible for me to think of Dolly as other than backlit by the lurid illuminations of the hotel ballroom, locked in connivance with the awful Harry, and deaf to all the calls of decency and reason. I hoped that she was happy: I was sure that she was defiant. I saw no way of breaking the deadlock. Therefore, after those unavailing telephone calls, to which there was no response, I did nothing.

Two years passed, during which I was not entirely inactive. I enrolled at Birkbeck, and was allowed to sit in on lectures until the beginning of the following academic year. I chose to study German, largely because of my interest in the Brothers Grimm, although they were not in the syllabus. I returned to the fairy stories I had read in my youth and found them frightening, as I had not done when I was a child. They have to do with ordeals, and an ordeal is less frightening to a child than unfairness, an arbitrary decision rather than a trial undergone. The reverse is true for adults, of course. I did not see how these stories could be bettered, and I got to know them almost by heart. By virtue of some unconscious process I was familiarising myself once more with the world of children, with whom, in my unguarded moments, I still identified. It seemed to me that one could perform a service to children by gently exploring their interior life: in that way one could neutralise their fears before they developed. I had not yet begun to write, but it seemed as if the task of writing was waiting for me, biding its time until I felt myself to be ready.

I was thus rather busy, for the days were spent at James Hemmings Enterprises, where I had graduated to the *Financial Times* and similar economic forecasts, by virtue of being the oldest inhabitant. I spent my time cutting out in the company of Carol and Lynda, two women in their forties, rather sharp, rather knowing, and markedly less convivial than Margaret and Wendy. Although married, they seemed to have a healthy contempt for men, and advertised their availability in a way which bordered on the burlesque. This was their way of winning the war between the sexes, by treating men as victims, or rather by treating them as they thought men treated women. I was rather frightened of Carol and Lynda, who in any case had no time for the likes of me. I annoyed them in ways I could not altogether change: they branded me as a snob, simply by virtue of the fact that I was rather silent, whereas they were given to gales of reminiscent laughter, and the kind of teasing — of each other, fortunately — which made me uncomfortable.

Again I was perceived as a class enemy, taking the job away from someone who needed it. They were not entirely wrong: unemployment was a new feature of working life. I was not invited to accompany them to the pub at lunchtime, while at the end of the day I left sharply to have a quick bite to eat before going on to Birkbeck. Nevertheless, although I tend to be impervious to hostility, their unfriendly behaviour made me feel lonely. Their conversation ceased abruptly when I entered the office, and they exchanged looks when I remarked that we should need to hurry if we intended to catch the post. I no longer enjoyed the work and would leave the office with relief. Naturally, the fact that I was at college antagonised them even further. Their intimacy with the printed word during office hours did not predispose them to read for either pleasure or profit when they were off duty. They worked mechanically, exchanging remarks from which I was excluded. This began to depress me, and I thought at several points that I might give in my notice, but refrained from doing so from inertia, a certain loyalty, and a mild but persistent fear of the future.

I was saved from this necessity by J.H., as he liked us to call him, who sat in the outer office with his friends Roger and Gavin, former university friends whom he had co-opted as fellow directors. What they did was a mystery, although we had a growing list of subscribers. J.H. sat behind a computer, stylishly dressed, and ostentatiously engaged in work. I think he was terrified that his mother might come back to see what he was doing. He was not doing very much. The computer was used for compiling lists, which could have taken half an hour out of his working day, if that, since the lists were constantly updated by either Roger or Gavin, whose workload was only marginally more impressive. They appeared to think that they were in advertising, an infinitely more glamorous calling, and talked about campaigns and concepts; letters were referred to as mailshots. They had learned the jargon ahead of the expertise, but as the business ran itself, and as they had a hazy idea of what it was supposed to do, there was little opportunity for a difference of opinion. I was regarded as possessing experience and was therefore treated warily by J.H., who was a harmless youth only a few years older than myself. He avoided my eye whenever we met, unlike the other two, who were to be found leaning back in their chairs, their hands clasped behind their heads, discussing the previous night's party. J.H. was aware of being less astute than either of them.

I believe he thought himself less astute than I was. That may have been the case. He did, however, produce one master-stroke, for which I was forced to salute him.

'Jane?' he said, putting his head round the door to the inner office. 'Could I have a word?' I followed him through to his own office, where he seated himself behind his desk. He was deeply flushed, for some reason. The other two silently got up and left.

'I don't know how to put this, Jane. You've been with us for so long.' I had worked for James Hemmings Enterprises for nearly two years, an unimaginable length of time for J.H. 'The fact is, we're restructuring.' He sat back, relieved to have made himself clear.

'I don't understand,' I said.

'A merger,' he went on. 'Well, actually, not quite. I've sold the business, Jane.' He mentioned a larger and more active concern which had been interested in our lists for some time.

'Does that mean you want me to leave?' I asked.

He flushed even more deeply. 'They'll want to bring in their own people, I suppose. In fact they'll eventually shut us down and move us over to their offices in Hammersmith.'

'So we've all got to go?' I asked, reflecting that the press cutting business was proving more volatile than I had previously suspected.

'I'm afraid so. They've taken me on: they're offering short-term contracts to Roger and Gavin to transfer the lists and generally monitor the take-over.' It had become a take-over, I reflected. 'I'm sorry, Jane. I know you've been happy here.' I had not, particularly, not since leaving Holbein Place. 'Perhaps you could tell the girls?'

'I think it would look better coming from you. When do you want me to go?'

He looked even more unhappy. 'Perhaps a week or so?'

The next day was a Friday. 'Would you mind terribly if I left tomorrow? The girls can stay on until the last minute. They'd prefer it if I left first.'

'What will you do, Jane?'

'I'll get my degree, I suppose. And then I don't know. I've got a little time to decide.'

'Perhaps I can see you again, Jane? Perhaps we could have dinner?'

'You've got my number,' I told him.

I doubted whether I should ever see him again. In this I was wrong. We had dinner several times, on the evenings when I had no lectures. When I saw the burning flush increase, and when his glance became unmistakably intense, I would make an excuse that I was very caught up in my work and would not be free until I had finished my degree. Oddly enough this was not an excuse, although it sounded like one. J.H., or James, as he had now become, was hurt, but sufficiently good-mannered to behave rather well. He dropped my hand, which he had been clasping, and signalled to the waiter for the bill. We went home in silence. Outside my flat, which I did not invite him to enter, he offered me his cheek to kiss. The gesture was so completely dismissive that I knew it for what it was, the gesture that indicated the end of the affair.

I wanted no one. Short of a man's faithful friendship I wanted nothing. I had had brief liaisons with men I had met at the college and they had left me dissatisfied. I came to the conclusion that I was destined to remain alone, for I was not good at dwindling affection or growing estrangement. I preferred to be precise. The word went round that I was cold — that old accusation — and I accepted it, for that was how I seemed to be. When I came home at night and stepped into the silent warmth of my flat I was grateful that no voice would be raised from the bedroom, reminding me that I was not alone. I resolved then that no one would ever again take up residence, as one or two had tried to do: the word had also gone round that I was well-off. I was a cold rich pretty girl with whom it was difficult to become intimate, which of course encouraged many more to try. I was perhaps unconsciously influenced by Pickering, who was courtesy itself, and who seemed to offer that *gravitas* which was so lacking in my contemporaries. My contemporaries I saw as children, like myself. For all my coldness I ached when I saw their childish necks, their long bony wrists. Had I been the Brothers Grimm I would have sent them off on a hazardous journey, which they would undertake, bright-eyed, and all unknowing. And I would bring them home again, no wiser. And then the story would be ended. My women friends still sought to appropriate men, in the old manner. I preferred my single state, and the silence of my little room.

At weekends John Pickering would invite me out to dinner. I would accept one invitation in three, for I knew that he valued his solitude as much as I valued mine. I enjoyed his company, while for his part he found me increasingly sensible. 'Sensible' was his highest term of praise. He was in his late forties at this time, and had decided that he was too old for me. That was his sensible decision, never openly referred to, but understood by us both. Neither of us suffered. His affection for me was moderate, like everything else about him; I was permitted to feel moderately in return. In this way I passed my youth almost *in statu pupillari*, for he still devoted himself to my affairs and to my income, which to my despair seemed to increase. Sometimes I felt like the sorcerer's apprentice, when my bank statement showed an even more rounded figure. I began to think that I had not made ample enough provision for Dolly, from whom I still had not heard, and mentioned this to John, who was horrified.

'It is more than generous,' he said. 'In fact it is excessive. If you had consulted me I should have advised against it. But you acted on your own. That was not sensible, Jane.'

'What worries me is the fact that I haven't heard from her.'

'She is well,' he said, with a wry smile. 'She bombards me with letters, you know. She seems to think of me as her confidential clerk, or her man of affairs. She mentioned buying the lease of her flat, but that is out of the question: it would mean a substantial loan, which I could not authorise. You need not worry about Mrs Ferber. She invites me to her bridge parties when she can't persuade me any other way. I never go, of course. We have very little in common.'

Which was his moderate way of letting me know that he disapproved of her, and had done ever since the day he had been forced to disclose the contents of the will.

'There is no need for you to worry,' he repeated, but I was annoyed that Dolly was in touch with Pickering rather than myself. At the same time I did not want to have to deal with the recriminations I suspected would be forthcoming. Why else would she ignore me, and in so obvious a manner? I had probably been drafted into the ranks of those dear friends in whom she had discovered some unforgiveable fault. I had become 'funny'. Dolly's 'funny' was at opposite poles to John Pickering's 'sensible'. Neither of them chose to be explicit, or to make themselves known. Therefore, I reckoned, they could deal with each other; it would do them both good. In due course I should make another approach, but it would be a final one. I did not care to be put in the wrong: I was a prig who needed a clear conscience, but sometimes I felt tired and in need of family affection, and although I had never received any of this from Dolly I somehow occasionally expected it. I had thought that Dolly might have enquired after my welfare. This she had signally failed to do. Given my relative youth I would be expected to make the first move. But if that move were met with accusations of heartless behaviour I would be as heartless as she had decided that I was in reality. I was cold, as she had always accused me of being; I was fastidious; but I was not heartless. Whereas Dolly's heartlessness was manifest, and I realised that she had never spared much feelings for others. I may have entertained some puerile notion of not being the first to give in. *'Bon débarras'*, she had said. Maybe she had meant it. I contrived not to feel hurt by this.

'I believe she went to Nice,' said Pickering, spearing a last leaf of salad. 'I understand her mother died. At a great age,' he added approvingly. This was obviously a sensible thing to do.

'Then I may hear from her when she comes back,' I said. And for a time I managed to believe this, and put Dolly quite out of my mind.

Apart from Pickering my world was emptying, and this suited me well enough. Marigold became engaged to a young houseman who intended to go into general practice; when they both qualified they would get married, and eventually she would work with him in his practice. I liked Alan, a cheerful red-headed youth, or so he seemed to me. I was invited to the engagement party, which was a rather smart affair in a Chelsea restaurant, and I was immensely gratified to see her great-aunts in attendance. They were dressed with solemn magnificence in black, as if to mourn the passing of Marigold's independence and her forthcoming enslavement to a man, but the black was enlivened with a fair distribution of gold chains and enamel brooches, of the sort one sees for sale at high prices in the Portobello Road. They looked both festive and restrained, as if representing an older way of doing things, before London restaurants were considered as suitable venues for family occasions. They seemed mildly melancholy at being removed from their usual setting and their usual activities, but their manners were, as always, impeccable.

They greeted me kindly, enquired after my health, which had never given cause for concern, and from time to time flourished an exquisite lawn handkerchief, drenched in some conservative cologne, as if to imply sorrow for my orphaned state.

'Doesn't she look lovely?' whispered Kate to me. 'We were so excited at the news. Of course we turned to straight away. We found a lovely red pullover for Alan, but Nell said to wait until they were married before setting them up. They'll have nowhere to live, of course. Poor wee Marigold.'

But although I knew that Marigold and Alan were already living together in Alan's flat in Lambeth I said nothing, for it seemed imperative to preserve the aunts in their innocence. They ate their dinner with dainty enthusiasm, visibly regretting the fact that they could not be at Selfridges.

'How long are you staying?' I asked.

'Just till tomorrow, dear. Then we're off home

to our garden. We've had a lovely show this past year. Even the apples were good. Could you take a few home with you, Jane? I know Mary has sufficient. If you come by tomorrow, dear, we can let you have a couple of pounds with pleasure.'

Across the table Marigold flickered an eyelid in a minute wink. The engagement party was a bit of a joke to her, knowing Alan as well as she already did. It was organised mainly for the benefit of Alan's parents, a couple of doctors from Northampton.

'Will you take a little more coffee, Kate?' asked Nell solicitously.

'Not if I want to sleep tonight,' replied Kate. 'And don't you take any more either.'

While this exchange was taking place I managed to return Marigold's wink. Our friendship was too strong and too sincere to change, even though she would marry and I might not. As far as I was concerned we were still those children who crossed the bridge to one another's houses and were taken home again by Marigold's brother, Oliver. I remembered those days with unusual clarity in the unlikely setting of this Chelsea restaurant, and knew that they would stay with me for ever.

On alternate Sundays I had lunch with Miss Lawlor, who had settled down as happily in her solitary life as I had in mine. Because she now could not stand much interruption into her meditative days I left her at three o'clock, always with a large piece of cake for my tea in a paper bag, and walked the long way home, round the park, over the bridge, along Cheyne Walk and back to Dolphin Square. I was more aware of solitude on those Sunday afternoons, as I believe most people are, and I would sit by the window, neglecting my studies, almost frozen into old reveries.

I felt alternately very old and very young. I had not yet learned how best to deal with my freedom, and for a time stayed close to home, fearful of venturing abroad, reluctant sometimes even to go into the street and lose myself in crowds. To break free of this enchantment I knew that I must undertake some drastic action. It was nearly Christmas again, and I resolved to go away. This decision enabled me to make plans, as I had never made them before. I chose Vienna, my grandmother's city, and stayed at a small hotel which suited me very well. I wandered, as solitary travellers do, or looked at the world from behind the windows of Demel's. I ate Sachertorte, which I found disappointing. When I returned home I congratulated myself on a difficult mission successfully carried out.

Thereafter, in vacations, I took off. The trip to Vienna had taught me something about my own resourcefulness, but had not answered my obscure purpose, a purpose too obscure for me to identify but which manifested itself as a steady discomfort. Vienna had been too beautiful, too distracting. I chose out of the way places, out of season: almost any town in France or Germany, however devoid of scenic interest, provided the sort of ruminative space which I seemed to require. One day, seated at a rickety metal table in a side street café in Dijon, I stealthily began to write. Then I knew that it was time to go home.

My first children's book, as this became, was published to some acclaim and was hailed as a great success. I was unimpressed by the small whirl of publicity to which I was subjected, and extremely embarrassed to be photographed for the newspapers. As it was a quiet period in the publishing year the critics gave my book almost more space than it could stand, but this did not bother me either, for I knew that I should write others. I was working hard for my Finals, although I regarded the examinations as something of a formality. Fortunately the problem of what to do afterwards was solved by an offer by not one but two newspapers to review books for children, and other related subjects. There was a great deal of research going on at this time into the meaning of fairy stories and the pattern of children's rhymes and games. Some of this research was feminist; some of it was good. I was happy with these offers, since they meant that I could stay at home with a good conscience, which I would need to do if I were going to write. And so the pattern of my life was set and has remained the same ever since.

As my photograph had appeared in the papers I at last expected to hear from Dolly. This did not happen, and I was puzzled and a little hurt, until I remembered that she never read a newspaper. Her drawing-room was conceived as a salon, in which she welcomed guests and callers;

it was not designed as a room in which to relax, where one could read or sew. I suspected that Dolly read only in the privacy of her bedroom at night: I also suspected that she liked the kind of old-fashioned sentimental stories that she had read as a girl, or had read to her mother. These would have been by Paul Bourget or Victor Margueritte. I did not know what the contemporary equivalents of these might be, but did not doubt that these existed. I also felt oddly sure that Dolly had discovered some kind of refined romance suited to her taste, perhaps of the order of Georgette Heyer, although she had none of the English attachment to a sanitised Regency period which makes that author so perennially successful.

Indeed, if I imagined Dolly reading at all it was from a small hoard of books brought with her to England long ago. I thought I knew what she would like, chaste stories about love, and the marriage which crowns a difficult courtship. There were French writers who specialised in this sort of thing, writers whom no self-respecting Frenchwoman would own up to reading, although most of them did. If I were right in my suppositions, and I thought that I might be, then it was only a small step to picturing Dolly sitting up in bed, restored to the dreams and desires of her distant girlhood, as she followed the spirited and well-born heroine to her fate, which inevitably encompassed a spirited and well-born (but honourable) suitor and a considerable amount of property.

What Dolly wanted was access to a life which

girls of her generation cherished as a fantasy and which they never entirely relinquished: a life in which love became marriage as of right. This was what one was taught; this was what one desired, so that chastity need never be entirely abandoned. Smart Dolly, worldly wise as she undoubtedly was, no doubt partook of these fantasies, undistinguished though they might be. This image of Dolly sitting up in bed and reading her sentimental novel was very different from the bustling predatory figure who entertained her guests in her all too formal drawing-room, and was oddly touching. I found it hurt me to picture Dolly in her moments of solitude. It was three years since our last encounter, and my humiliation at her hands, a humiliation which still made me wince. It seemed longer than that, for so much had happened to me in the intervening time. I did what I always knew I was going to do, picked up the telephone, and dialled her number.

She answered immediately, as if she had been waiting for the call, for any call.

'It's Jane,' I said.

'Jane? Well, you took your time.' Her voice was distant, as if nourished by ancient grudges, rather than by present acrimony.

'I'm sorry I haven't been in touch,' I said, helplessly falling into old patterns of believing myself in the wrong, particularly with regard to Dolly. In any case it was easier to do her bidding than not, for the reproaches she heaped on one's head were tempestuous and out of all proportion to the original offence. They betrayed her impatience with life, with ordinary life, her desire for grander emotions, more extraordinary destinies than those which had come her way or were likely to come her way, as she sat in her rented flat, eternally calculating her expenses. Now, however, she sounded toneless, very different from the usual dispenser of advice, the impassioned advocate of singing and dancing.

'Are you coming over?' she asked, in the same almost disembodied manner.

'Of course, I'd love to,' I said, rather taken aback. 'When are you free?'

'Now,' she said. 'Now's as good a time as any. Come as soon as you like.' And the receiver was replaced.

Obeying some ancestral impulse I took a taxi to a cake shop in Swiss Cottage and bought a few delicacies. I remembered that Dolly had always had a sweet tooth, and I doubted whether Annie made her marvellous confections when no guests were expected. As I hardly counted as a guest there might conceivably be nothing to eat: I remembered how Annie had never provided any food when I called on Dolly in the old days. Besides, the heavenly smell of sugar and cream that I would bring with me would surely make our first difficult moments together less difficult. On impulse, and not knowing quite what made me do it, I added an asparagus quiche and some frozen vegetables to my purchases, and thus burdened with two bags took another taxi to Dolly's flat off the Edgware

Road of evil memory, where she had met her own fate in the person of the owner of a minicab firm, patronised in all innocence before that innocence betrayed her, and was betrayed by her.

'You took your time,' she repeated, as she opened the door on to a hallway which seemed duskier than I remembered it. She had not bothered to switch on the light, economising, no doubt, once the friends had departed. Again I assumed that I was at fault.

'I've telephoned more than once,' I told her, following her indifferent back into the drawing-room. She motioned me to a chair, sat down herself, and looked pensive, abstracted, as if little could come of this interview. When I scrutinised her it took me some time to work out what was different. It was not the hair, now entirely grey, or rather navy blue, for an enthusiastic hairdresser had been at work; it was not the very slightly swollen ankles, or the ancient patent leather court shoes into which she must have recently thrust her plump feet; it was not the familiar black and white silk dress, which now fitted her rather loosely. Rather it was the fact that she was wearing no make-up, that she had completely abandoned colour, even to the smear of lipstick which had always glistened on her eager mouth, and now presented me with a totally expressionless mask, on which the only tones were the tones of age, a heavier shadow under the eyes, the faintest possible adumbration of hair above the upper lip, a thinning of the brows, beneath which her gaze wandered away from mine in an apparently genuine lack of interest. The beautiful olivine complexion, still fine, now had the opaque sheen of candle wax.

'I was sorry to hear about your mother,' I said awkwardly.

At this she stirred. 'Ah, Jane, Jane,' she sighed. 'My mother. She was all I had, ever. And I let her go away from me, when I should have kept her here, looked after her. But I couldn't have done that, do you see? Living as I did. And she wanted to go back to France. She was happy there in the sun, she was looked after, but when I saw her little room, and her little balcony, where she fed the birds, my heart broke.'

Indeed it did seem to me that Dolly's heart was broken, or that some mainspring had been dismantled. Her hands were primly clasped in her lap, her ankles crossed. She looked as though she were in some ante-room to death, some hospital waiting-room, or prison cell, so strong was the impression I had that Dolly was finally without resource, as I had never seen her before.

'I'm sorry,' I said again. There was a silence, as though she could no longer be bothered to reply. I looked round the room. It was getting dark, but only one lamp was lit, its shade tipped up to produce an uncomfortable glare from a bulb which was nevertheless weak. Dust lay quite thickly on the cross-bars of the chairs, although it had been perfunctorily removed from the many small tables which had previously supported the Porthault cups and saucers when Dolly was entertaining. It seemed astonishingly quiet without her guests. I reflected that I should not much like to live here on my own. There was always Annie, of course, but she did not seem to be in evidence.

'Where is Annie?' I asked.

Here a look of pain crossed Dolly's face. 'Annie has left me,' she said. 'Gone back to Belgium. Retired, she says. As if women like us could retire! Always on the go, always on duty.'

It interested me that she classed herself with Annie, however unconsciously. 'How will you manage without her?' I asked.

'Well, I've had to cut down on entertaining, of course.' Here a dark red flush seeped into her cheeks. 'I knew what would happen. Those spoilt selfish women refused to take pot luck. Oh, no, they liked Annie's coffee, her little sandwiches, her *réductions*. They began to make excuses. I still go to them occasionally, but it's not the same. I can't return the hospitality. And I haven't got the energy I once had. This flat is too big; I never liked it. Annie retiring!' she repeated, her flush deepening. 'Did you ever hear such nonsense?' But I suspected that she had been humiliated by her erstwhile friends, whom she now saw more rarely than she had done in the past, and who had abandoned her, like the instinctive but stupid creatures that they were, when they saw her reduced to a badly dusted drawing-room, the usual refreshments only a distant memory.

'I brought something for our tea,' I said cheerfully. And for your dinner, I added silently.

'Shall I put the kettle on?'

She came after me into the kitchen, her hands still clasped, as if to release them would be tantamount to revealing a capacity for work. The kitchen was illuminated by a weak trembling neon tube, which would be difficult to replace when it finally expired. The kettle was an ancient model, with a high straight handle. I opened a cupboard and found some ordinary white cups with a plain gold rim and some glass plates on which I arranged my cakes. I felt immensely sad. I would have given anything to have seen Dolly in her old combative mood.

'What do you do with yourself all day?' I asked, as lightly as possible.

'I go out,' she said, brightening slightly. 'I go to the cinema. I love the cinema. I can get in for half-price.'

'Come now, Dolly, you can't be short of money.'

'Yes I am,' she said, raising her head and glaring at me. 'And it's none of your business why.'

This brief burst of temper surprised me, but I said nothing. I carried the tray to the drawing-room; again she followed me, content for me to take matters in hand.

She ate thoughtfully but greedily, as if there were an intimate connection between her lack of sugar and her downcast demeanour. Strawberry tart followed éclair which in turn followed meringue. And yet she had lost weight, I reflected.

'Do you feed yourself properly, now that Annie's not here?'

At this she looked annoyed. 'Of course I do! I go round the corner, to the Italian, for lunch. Do I feed myself! Impertinence!'

'And for dinner?' I asked.

'Oh, I don't bother with dinner,' she replied, her eyes once more sliding away from mine. 'I open a tin of soup. We always had soup, Mother and I. Then I go to bed. You needn't worry about me.' When she looked at me again I saw that her eyes were full of tears.

'Dolly,' I asked gently. 'What is wrong? Is it your mother?'

'Mother? No, it's not Mother. She was happy enough, in the sun. She had friends. In a way she was lucky, luckier than I shall be. We understood each other, Mother and I; everything was done for the best. I try to think of her there in the sun, and then I think of the old days, when we were together. My life hasn't been easy, Jane.'

'And Harry?' I ventured, with some trepidation, for the answer to this question was all too clear.

'Harry's gone,' she said. 'Harry left me.' Two tears slipped down her face, which she wiped negligently with her hand. 'He meant a great deal to me, Jane. I know you never liked him, but you never got to know him like I did. We were two of a kind; we understood each other. Nobody else did, and that's the truth. That's why I miss him so much. Two years we had, two wonderful years.'

I noticed that she remarked on the understanding between Harry and herself, much as she had assured me — and it was undoubtedly true — that she and her mother had understood each other. It was as if everyone else she had known had failed her, and now she saw by how much.

'I know he was company for you.'

'Company? Oh, yes, he was company. But he was more than that. I'm talking about something you wouldn't understand, Jane: love, attraction, sex, if that's what you want to call it.' She blushed slightly as she uttered the word, but once it was out in the open went on to make herself clear. 'Sometimes he stayed on after the others had left. Oh, I made him comfortable, all right. He liked a game of cards; my little parties amused him. And when I saw him looking at me and knew what he was thinking . . . My heart, Jane!' Here she put her hand to her heart. 'He made me feel what I'd never felt before, not even when I was married. I knew he didn't love me. I knew I was making a fool of myself. But it's not easy for a woman of my age, for a woman of any age. And living the way I did, with all those other women . . . He understood me,' she repeated. 'Oh, you've all been kind enough, I dare say, but I felt more at home with Harry. More than I ever did with Hugo. Harry was my type; do you understand? I don't suppose you do, really.'

'You loved him,' I said, making the statement she was still too awkward to make herself.

'I really loved him,' she said, bending her head and fishing a handkerchief out of the sleeve which slipped loosely down her arm.

'And you gave him money,' I said, in order to

get the worst out of the way.

'I put money into the business, yes. Why not? There was nothing wrong with it; it was a going concern. And then one day, out of the blue, he said he was going abroad. I knew that was an excuse. I saw him in the Edgware Road the following day and taxed him with it.' (After having waited for him, I thought, but said nothing.) ' "When shall I be seeing you?" I asked him. "Oh, I'll see you around. I'll see you at the girls', perhaps." Because he knew I still went to Phyllis and Rose. "I've got a lot on my plate at the moment," he said. "Business is picking up. I'm putting in extra time. Buck up, darling. No need to look like that, is there?" He called me darling,' she said, with some return of pride. 'It makes a woman feel special, somehow.'

I could see him, the monster, bluffing it out, jovial to the end. And he would no doubt wave a modest hand, when teased by Phyllis or Rose, thereby adding further to his lustre as a man loved by women. I could see him now, in their ever more welcoming drawing-rooms, his foot wagging in time to his own invisible orchestra.

'So I stopped going to the girls,' Dolly went on. 'Then, a few months back I went to Rose's, just for a chance of seeing him. Just casually, you know.'

But he would have made quite sure that she did not see him, I thought.

'I still go occasionally. I'm sure we'll get together again one of these days. But it won't be the same.

Something died in me, Jane. Not that you would understand — you were always so cold. Funny little thing,' she said, putting away her handkerchief. The reproach was familiar, but her heart was not in it. That was the only time during the whole of the afternoon that I was mentioned. Of my own concerns not a word was broached, for which I was grateful.

'There's a quiche in the fridge, if you fancy a little supper,' I said.

'Oh, I couldn't eat anything after all those cakes. Are you going? I'll change my shoes and walk down to the corner with you. Come into the bedroom with me.'

She seemed unwilling for me to leave her alone. The bedroom was if anything dustier, the coverlet on the narrow bed faded. Where had Harry slept, I wondered? Or had he just left and gone home to his own comfortable house? Adjusting his clothing, was the thought that entered my mind, and once there would not be dislodged. The wardrobe opened with a creak onto a smell of faded scent. Dolly bent down and eased her feet out of her tight shoes, replacing them with a black flat-heeled pair that suddenly made her seem much shorter. She tidied her navy blue hair in the tarnished mirror of her dressing-table. By her bed, just as I had pictured it, was a small pile of novels by Delly and Gyp, their covers faded, one or two loose pages testifying to long use.

In the street she took my arm, as if she had not been out for a long while. She may even have been exaggerating her weakness, but I think not. I intended to walk to the main road to get the tube, but she led me down a quiet side street, and then stopped outside a small block of flats, where lights blazed cheerfully in most of the windows.

'Doesn't it look nice there?' she said. 'I wish I lived there.'

Her voice was so wistful that I asked her if she knew anyone who did live there.

'One or two ladies,' she answered. 'Just to say good-morning to. Oh, I know what you're thinking. Harry lives in Belsize Park, or did when I knew him. I don't know where he is now. I hate my flat, Jane. I hate going back to it, when it's empty. And it's always empty now. If I could live there,' she added, with none of her original slyness, 'I think I could be more settled, more comfortable.' She gazed up at the cheerful windows, as if willing herself inside those lighted rooms. Then of course I knew what I had to do.

I left her on the corner, looking oddly diminished in her flat shoes. I waited until I saw her turn and wander back. The sight was painful to me. When I got home I rang John Pickering and invited him for a drink.

'I'm thinking of buying a flat,' I said. 'As an investment.'

His expression changed from alarm to cautious approval.

'Always a good way to place extra funds. If you like I will look around for you.'

'Oh, I've found something,' I told him. 'Here's the address. If you could just make enquiries?' For I had seen a set of unlighted windows on the first floor and had an idea that that flat would be empty.

My manner must have been rather dismissive, for he left shortly afterwards. He was always remarkably intuitive to atmosphere.

My charity felt cold to me, as it was perhaps supposed to feel, as it had felt to my mother, to my grandmother. The saving grace was that the beneficiary would have no such misgivings. And yet even though I thought I knew all about Dolly's conscience, given that it existed, it was impossible for me not to feel her pathos, which I perceived for the first time. Her words had been banal, certainly not chosen to excite my sympathy. She had spoken of her lover in terms so devoid of interest that I might have been forgiven for thinking that she was a woman of no distinction, who could not put her passion into words, and who was perhaps as little skilled emotionally as she was in any other way. She had referred to her nights of love, such as they were, as if I would grasp all her meaning, yet a few moments later had denied me even that faculty, saying that I was cold, though she had no way of verifying this. No doubt what she felt was a generalised contempt for my kind, in which she included my parents, my grandmother, certainly her husband, with our correct manners and impassive faces. Again she lacked the skill to discern the temperament underneath, lacked the curiosity to enquire into our lives, lacked the fellow feeling to appreciate that we ourselves might have difficulties, might be frustrated, might feel loss or doubt, or even need.

The appeal of Harry had been his obviousness: his signals could not be mistaken. He was lazy, greedy, a sexual speculator, and a self-made man, comfortably off but a vulgarian, not burdened with too many refinements, a lover of rich food, fast cars, dance music, and the sort of luxury which could be paid for in ready cash. The appeal of such blatant accessibility had been profound. No need, here, to give one's usual performance, or if one did one could at least relax and enjoy it. Thus the bridge parties had taken on a new meaning, since the presence of her women friends, so tolerated, so detested, would be offset by the presence of Harry, and the meaningful glance with which he occasionally favoured her would repay her for numerous social humiliations suffered over the years.

His lovemaking would no doubt be expert, but he would enjoy the spectacle of a woman losing her dignity in bed. His instincts were perhaps very slightly criminal, for he would have seen that he was dealing with a woman who was, despite appearances to the contrary, unsophisticated. And the part of Harry that was itself unsophisticated would appreciate the comforting inconsequential feminine atmosphere of those gambling afternoons, would enjoy being spoilt, being cajoled, being tempted with plates of delicious food. It was when Dolly was at her worldliest that he would be tempted to stay behind, to linger in her company; it was then that it would amuse him to cut her down to size. And the more he did so, the more successfully he made her plead and beg, the less he thought of her.

If she had remained true to type, and exploited him as she exploited everyone else, he might have shaken his head in admiration; he might even have married her, thinking it better by far to have her as an ally than as an enemy. Instead she had grown tearful, lamenting his more and more frequent absences, and had finally been forced to track him down in the Edgware Road, perhaps peering through the glass window of his office, and waiting until he had finally consented to emerge, although with an excuse that he was short of time, that he was 'going for a quick coffee' (in which he did not invite her to join him), and had seen him, dapper as ever, cross the road on his glossy feet, and had known that she would only see him again if she engaged in the same humiliating stratagems, perhaps to the delight of former friends to whom she had considered herself superior, thinking them too stupid to notice her contempt.

Thus had Dolly's final education been inaugurated. Always needy, always greedy, she had at last to conclude that her methods had failed, that this time gratification was to be withheld, and withheld for ever. And this realisation had effected a profound change in her, one which manifested itself in a complete alteration of her physical appearance. I could not rid myself of the sight of her in her flat shoes, which made her walk seem awkward, quite different from her normal dancer's step. When she had accompanied me to the tube — holding my arm, as if made cautious by the bustle of evening — she had worn an ordinary cloth coat in a rather sour ginger colour, in any event unbecoming, and a world removed from the fur coat scented with Joy which dated from my childhood and which had been remodelled at great expense several times since then. The wardrobe door had creaked open on to the ghost of that scent, and on to the familiar collection of impractical silk dresses *('C'est fait à la main, tout ça')* now crammed indifferently together. She had worn one of those dresses, and it no longer fitted her. She had lost weight; her figure had fallen and flattened, so that the dress, designed for a plumper woman, looked merely clumsy. And the high-heeled patent shoes were far from new, as could be judged by the height and slenderness of those heels, which had once flattered her strikingly arched foot but now merely caused discomfort.

In her face, that face newly devoid of colour, could be read the first intimation that Dolly had been overtaken by that long resignation which marks the true onset of old age. That she was not technically old — a bare sixty-eight — made her new patience seem all the more shocking. I could see that she had been beautiful, could see traces of beauty still in the wide dreaming eyes which strayed continually to the window, in the finely arched brows, now sparse, in the tilt of the head, but that was only because I had known her before. Anyone meeting her now for the first time would simply register her as an elderly person, for this was her new card of identity, the one she proffered when she went to afternoon performances at the cinema or ate her lonely lunch at the Italian restaurant round the corner. The completeness of the change in her could be read in the wistful way she had referred to the 'ladies' from the small block of flats in which she longed to live, and to whom she occasionally said good-morning. What she wanted now, and wanted with all the ardour of her lost youth, was to be one of those ladies, in whose company she might revive, and whom she might eventually entertain, modestly and discreetly, with none of her former flourish, in her flat, which she would strive to make as close in style as possible to theirs.

Dolly was not domesticated; she could not cook. But she could learn. 'I'll never be a proud housewife', I remember her saying — and not without some complacency — to my mother. She had never become an ordinary woman, had never intended to; her eagerness had persisted throughout her life, as if she were eternally in search of the next pleasure, the next diversion. But some evil genius, from one of my fairy stories, perhaps, had seen to it that pleasure would be her downfall, that it would be pleasure, to use another fairy-tale locution, that would eventually stab her to the heart. The barb thus released, Harry's barb, would turn her overnight into an old woman. He had taught her a truth so unbearable that many women cannot face it, simply that a man does not care to be friends with a woman after their affair is over, that he will in future treat her to a vague smile of reminiscence, or a hasty wave of the hand if they meet, but that he will never, at the onset of a lonely evening, telephone to see whether she is all right, whether she needs anything, whether he might drop by. This callousness, which is in fact a complete emotional ineptitude, brings curious results: shame is felt not by the man but by the woman, who feels newly conspicuous, becomes fearful of public occasions, and avoids even the company of her friends. 'Harry left me,' Dolly had said, and the pain of separation was multiplied a thousandfold by the fact that she knew it, and that therefore everyone else must know it.

I had been brooding over this at my desk, and got up feeling physically cramped and mentally troubled. What troubled me most of all was the fact that I felt myself to be in some way inferior to Dolly. This was obscure, but uncomfortable. It seemed to me that for all her humiliation she had acquired a dimension that I still lacked. What I had hastily and no doubt superficially dismissed as a tragedy was not that at all, or rather to accept it as such would be to miss the point. What Dolly had lost was all too obvious: what she had gained was dignity. If Harry were to encounter her now he would be appalled at her appearance, but he would also instinctively mind his manners. It might even occur to him that her opinion of him had changed: it might even be that this was the case, though I doubted it. I suspected that she would love him for ever, or else consign the loving heart she had so lately discovered herself to possess, to a metaphorical grave. She would thus learn to live with a death that would come daily nearer, and in that way fulfill her earthly span.

I knew all this: somehow I knew it. What I had not learned before I learned now. I looked at the clock and saw with a start that it was half-past eleven. I had spent the entire evening brooding, but perhaps to some purpose. I bestirred myself to answer a few letters and to write others. With what I could arrange on paper Dolly's affair was cut and dried: the bank would raise no objections. I sent a birthday card to Miss Lawlor, whose present I would take round to her on an evening later in the week. I turned down an invitation to read a paper on Sleeping Beauty to a feminist seminar at a college for further education. I was not ready, perhaps for reasons which had to do with myself as much as with Dolly, to bring light to bear on this subject. Perhaps I never would be. Perhaps I would choose to remain asleep rather than be woken like Beauty. (And yet, I told myself, Beauty had only awoken because her prince had tried so hard to reach her; difficult to ignore the evidence of this. And she had been wounded in the first place by a spindle, the symbolism of which was easy to discern. Were we dealing here with a highly moral tale, which was in more ways than one an allegory of true love and a warning against mere physical curiosity? I promised myself that I would examine this matter further, when I was not so fearful of its implications.) Then I took another pen and began what was to be my second book, my second success. It was much harsher than the first, but I did not think that this mattered. Children need harsh lessons sometimes, if they are learned in an atmosphere of affection. What they learn then may save them from being duped in later life.

9

On my last visit to America, where I gave my talk on Sleeping Beauty and other related topics to two women's colleges, I was interested to note the variety of female responses. The older members of the faculty regarded it politely as a feminist entertainment, while the younger ones debated it fervently. I found to my surprise that I was more impressed by the former than by the latter. These placid dignified women, mostly in their fifties, mostly long divorced or else widowed, pursued a life of study in an all female atmosphere as if they were nuns in a mediaeval abbey. All had children or stepchildren, all taught a full syllabus, all had made their homes in the charming small towns and suburbs of Massachusetts and New Hampshire. They were all extremely gracious, in the American fashion, and manifested none of the recklessness, the combative vivacity of their younger counterparts.

Walking with one of these older women through the idyllic streets surrounding the campus I was not questioned on whether I had endured much sexual harassment in England but was shown the garden, invited to admire the dogwood, or indeed 'Janet's copper beech. I confess to a little envy: I haven't one of my own. But I can always look at hers. We have tea together at her house, when it's at its best, in October. Have you noticed that when the leaves fall they turn a dark ox-blood red? I dare say you have a fine garden at home.'

In the face of such magnificence I hardly care to tell her that I live in a small flat and that when I look out of the window all I see is the dirty river and the distant dull green of the park, no longer familiar to me. These days my walks no longer take me to the park, but only along streets increasingly choked with traffic. For this reason I am always glad, when I am on campus, to accept an invitation to walk round the lake from one of the younger women, perhaps a full professor at the age of thirty-two. They are so convivial that it would be churlish to refuse. But I find them exhausting, these women of goodwill, with their agenda of wrongs to be righted, of injustices to be eliminated. I want to stand still in the dusk and contemplate the lake, seeing only mist, hearing only a brief ripple where the wing of a bird disturbs the surface of the water, but I must respond intelligently, employ a certain kind of feminised argument, feel myself to be the victim of a monstrous wrong which has been passed down to me from generation to generation.

I am invited to share my experience in the workplace, and, remembering ABC Enterprises, reply truthfully that I was never happier. This seems to disappoint them, until I tell them that my colleagues were all women, when their faces clear. Then in all conscience I describe to them the later months, when the business was run by James Hemmings and his friends, and they become alert again. Any discrimination? I am demanded. Only being taken out to dinner by the boss, I reply, by which time I am regarded with the purest suspicion.

I am then questioned much more closely, and almost as a hostile witness, on my views on the position of women today. This is a key question, the answer to which will furnish material for seminar after seminar of feminist studies. These young women are painfully preoccupied with questions of gender. Yet most of them are married or in a relationship with some man. I have been introduced to one or two of the husbands and partners. They seemed nice enough, perhaps a little too conscious of sharing, as they put it. And yet their small children, where they exist, seem oddly anxious, as if this sharing were an alien concept, fit only for emancipated adults, who could discuss the matter until late into the night.

What the children want is not clear: perhaps they want a formal or even a traditional childhood, the kind they no longer read about in their politically correct story-books or encounter at their politically correct playgroups. Their parents reason with them, and the children know instinctively that they have not yet reached the age of reason. Besides, the reason they are being offered exists somewhere in the region of exasperation, and this they reject absolutely. And are right to do so.

As I stand on the edge of the lake, in the evening

mist, urgent words are being poured into my ears to which I must respond. Although I am still young I want to assure my interlocutor that she will not be sexually harassed in perpetuity, that when her hair becomes less abundant and her skin loses its colour and its firmness she will be able to pursue a peaceful career studying something non-sexist like physics, or better still agronomy. I do not do this because I want to remain a polite guest, and also because I do not want to fall into my old position of class enemy. 'What is that bird?' I ask, in an effort to divert this so well-meaning young woman. 'Look! The new moon!' These observations are regarded as frivolous, for there is work to be done, there are categories to be redefined, laws to be changed. And underneath it all I sense a bewilderment which I in fact share. Will we be loved, will we be saved? And if so, by what or by whom?

Self-sufficient as I am I too feel a longing which I am reluctant to ascribe to the feminine condition alone. I try to steer the conversation towards love and marriage, the substance of my talk. Is it, should it be a quest, I ask, as it is in the story? Or is that a trap, I wonder, designed to keep women passive and expectant? If they take matters into their own hands and emancipate themselves from their ancestral longings will they be disappointed? 'They will be living in the real world, assuming personhood,' declares my friend. 'I consider myself a person, not a wife or mother. Those things are important to me, but I keep them in perspective. Bob and I share everything.' But her voice is flat, as if she has made this statement many times. A critic might say that it has an obstinate sound, as if in keeping with the agenda. But I am not a critic, although it is becoming extremely difficult to convince these feminists that I am any kind of a woman.

I do not know what credentials I am supposed to present. I earn my own living: that is a point in my favour. I travel, I do creative work, I occasionally teach: good marks for all of these things. But do I have a relationship? This apparently is the one sign of personhood I have so singularly failed to come up with. In the renewed interest they are prepared to show in my unpartnered state, in the faintest hint of commiseration in their voices, they reveal themselves to be women of the most unreconstructed variety. It is not that they would necessarily want me to find love and marriage, in the sense of a happy ending. But if I were sharing household chores with some cheerful fellow in jeans and a shirt ironed by himself they could understand me better. How then to disappoint them by telling them that I prefer the fairy-tale version, and will prefer it until I die, even though I may be destined to die alone? To do so would be to ignore the laws of hospitality, of ordinary courtesy. They are intrigued by me, by my appearance: I am in danger of becoming — for the space of two weeks — a cult figure. And so I have been designated, entirely against my will. It is enough to make me turn my back on the lake, now fitfully gleaming under the new moon, and long for home.

When it is time for me to journey on I pack my bag with a sigh, for I have enjoyed the company of these women and am now not as anxious as I was to regain my solitude. I do not tell them that my views have perhaps been influenced by the most unreconstructed woman I have ever known, for although this is true I now see that Dolly belongs to another epoch, another world, a world in which the support of women could not be taken for granted. Her solitude and mine are totally opposed; that is perhaps why she is so uninterested in my life, which is, at any rate, uninteresting to her. As far as Dolly is concerned I am protected, as she herself has never been protected; she has even leapt to the conclusion that I am protected by John Pickering, whom she regards as a sort of godfather, not only to myself, but to herself as well, for he continues to manage her affairs, and as she is indifferent to him she has decided that he might do very well for me, might even be seen as an advantageous match, and indeed the only reason why his continued presence might be justified. For in her heart she thinks of him as a servant, and therefore doubly appropriate.

A woman of Dolly's type might marry a man like Pickering for security, but would never deceive herself into thinking that he might be loved. Whereas I try my utmost to love John Pickering as he should be loved, because I see him as lonely and often sad, remembering his absconding wife, and looking wistfully at my relative youth as if it were something forbidden to him to share. Sometimes I succeed in loving him, when I see him at the barrier at Heathrow and he lifts his hand in a contained gesture to greet me, or when he assures me that he has booked a table in my favourite restaurant for my first night at home.

One of these days I shall have to bring him down to my level, if we are to have any sort of life together. Dolly, of course, would have done this long ago, and perhaps rewarded him more than I could ever do. For I mind my manners with John; he is not a person I would ever wish to offend. And perhaps he longs for something more, as I do. The image he has of me suits him, but above all suits his conscience. I would not wish to hustle him into what I must call a relationship, for that, although gratifying, would obscurely disappoint him. Although his presence in my life is important I know that one day I may journey on, yet again: the thought occurs to me as I pack my bag, in this pretty room, with its white coverlet on the bed and the prints of Redouté roses on the walls. And I can see, as if it had already happened, that he will accept this, will approve of it, and might almost prefer it to a situation in which he would be obliged to lose his dignity.

It is a little hard for me to sustain my life without recognising the pull of old dependencies, old passivities. More than once it has occurred to me that it might be pleasant simply to watch the world from my window, the book fallen from my lap, and to note the slow movement of the hours until the darkness falls and the evening begins. This condition is linked in my mind with the idea of service, for at some point in this reverie I rouse myself to welcome others into my house and into my life, children of my own, and eventually their father. But either history or destiny or perhaps biology has forced me in the opposite direction, and I spend my days not at a window but at a desk, reviewing publications which occasionally strike me as exorbitant, but exorbitant in the sense of over-stimulated, suspicious, combative, characteristics sometimes notable in psychological profiles of the insane. Who really benefits from studies in re-reading gender in 1950s melodrama, or women's revolutionary fiction in Depression America? Is there any chance that a feminist theory of the state will ever be taken seriously? Must we campaign for surrogate motherhood? Or review the legal representation of lesbians in cases of discrimination by employers?

These works pour out from university presses, and are produced by the most excellent of women, many of whom have welcomed me with great cordiality. I appreciate them for their fervour and their courage. And yet a doubt creeps in. I do not want to fight. I want, rather, to explore the world without prejudice, and to be allowed a measure of lenity in my dealings with that world. Sometimes I even long to take the coward's way out and to live my life without benefit of any sort of agenda, relying simply on the kindness of others, whom I would reward, equally simply, with a more convivial version of myself.

It is at times like these, when I am particularly engrossed in this fantasy, that I hear a voice, somewhere off-stage, encouraging me in my shameful, perhaps even wistful broodings. This voice directs me to the real business of life, and offers advice on how to obtain success in that business. And the advice is the same that I have been hearing for as long as I can remember, and would be anathema to my so gallant American friends. What would they say, what would they think, if I proposed another model to them, one which I myself have rejected, but which in these enlightened times has all the attractions of archaism and futility, perhaps of something else? That so persistent voice opens doors on to older simpler longings, regrettable, no doubt, even deplorable. The voice is misguided, and yet it never falters, so that one is obliged to take note. Its lesson is deeply subversive, and serves to rally me once more to the side of my American correspondents, but not without a sigh. The burden of progress is taken up once again, with all its necessary paraphernalia, until the ghostly voice dwindles, and all that is left is a simple echo, fervent, but now almost disembodied, gaining in strength when I am at my weakest. Charm, Jane, charm!

When John has collected me from the airport, has taken me back to the flat, and has left me there with the unread letters and the unpacked bags, the telephone will ring, and it will be Dolly. This will not surprise me: she rings all the time now, and has probably continued to do so while I have been away. The details of my life are hazy to her: she claims not to remember why I have been away, but sees my absences as an interruption to the dialogue which we now sustain. 'Jane, Jane,' she will say. 'Are you coming over?' And when I say that I am rather tired she will not be very disappointed, for she will explain, not without a certain pride, that she is expecting a few of her friends, although she is very anxious for me to meet them.

Her tone will be buoyant, for these days Dolly is almost happy. She loves her new flat, which is warm and light, and she has furnished it with a few well-chosen modern pieces. Like a girl, or like a young bride, she delights in showing it off, and has made herself known to her neighbours, Mrs Foster, Mrs Williamson, and Miss Salter, the ladies whom she once greeted in the no-man's-land of the street. In due course she will ask them if they play bridge; so far they have only been invited to tea. In due course she will go to the *pâtisserie* in Swiss Cottage and buy delicacies for a more elaborate entertainment, after which, before leaving, her friends will be offered a thimbleful of the sweet liqueurs she prefers, cherry or apricot brandy. They will think this daringly foreign of her, for she will have given them an appealing version of her life story, her early years in Paris, her life in Brussels, her marriage into a satisfyingly stolid family (here *'chère Mère'* will be transformed yet again into 'dear Toni'). A discreet tear might be shed over the tragic disappearance from the scene of Hugo, and the ladies will sympathise, for two of them are widows, and the unmarried Miss Salter is known to approve of worthy sentiments. Of her later years and its stratagems there will be not a word. She will be accepted for what she has become, a blameless woman, perhaps a little eager, perhaps a little given to flattery, but really so touching and interesting, a real addition to their little circle.

She may get tired of this; perhaps she will. Perhaps she will at last be ready for stronger sensations than these so English friends can provide; perhaps she will long for an evening visitor. That visitor will be missing, and his absence will be her one source of pain, and the one element connecting her to the person she once was. But for the time being she is contented, perhaps more contented than it is in her nature to be. She will, if she feels a slight tremor of restlessness or of disappointment, get on the telephone to me, and ask me to come over, or rather not ask but expect, whether it is early in the day or rather late. Sometimes, when I sense that she is on the verge of distress or frustration, I tell her to expect me in half an hour. When she opens the door to me her old look of wistful anticipation — 'Love me! Save me!' — is directed at myself, and I feel unworthy of it.

These days she dresses discreetly, in the sort of garment from John Lewis once worn by my erstwhile colleagues Margaret and Wendy. She takes an odd delight in surveying the viscose racks, and selecting the brightest colours, the boldest patterns. When she greets me wearing one of these dresses I get a slight shock, for they are so out of character. And they seem to change her into something she should not really be, a suburban housewife. But she is genuinely pleased to see me, and does not seem to notice her changed appearance. Sometimes the belt of her dress hangs loose: she does not notice this either.

My feminist friends would not recognise the woman I become in Dolly's presence, nor could I explain to them the great revelation to which she made me a party, and for which I am indebted. My recent visit to her, just before I left for America, was banal, neither more nor less significant than other visits. But I realised then that love was unpredictable, that it could not be relied upon to find a worthy object, that it might attach itself to someone for whom one has felt distaste, even detestation, that it is possible to experience an ache in the heart because the face that responds to one's own circumspect smile is eager, trusting. When I turned to go, on that particular evening, the evening of my revelation, Dolly stood at the window and waved to me, continuing to wave until I was nearly out of sight. I knew that she would turn away from the window into an empty room, an empty evening, an empty life. Yet I think she was unaware of the implications of this emptiness. She would simply look forward to the next human contact, perhaps to my next visit. 'My niece', she calls me. 'My niece is coming today', I heard her tell a neighbour. There is no betraying such innocent assumptions. She will grow old: already she has a look of age, or rather of elderly girlhood. She will grow old, and I will make my way more frequently to her little flat, looking in the cupboards to see whether she has enough food, finally bringing the food myself. I shall not move in with her; I am too selfish for that. But I shall follow the adventure through to the end, I hope with honour, and even after she is gone I shall continue to see her at the window, waving to me ardently, as if I were her best beloved.